Good Guys Love Dogs

GOOD GUYS LOVE DOGS

Inglath Cooper

Fence Free Entertainment, LLC

CONTENTS

DEDICATION

To Mac, for the pink Jeep dream and
To Michele, sister, best friend

BOOKS BY INGLATH COOPER

A Gift of Grace
RITA® Award Winner John Riley's Girl
A Woman With Secrets
Unfinished Business
A Woman Like Annie
The Lost Daughter of Pigeon Hollow
A Year and a Day

COPYRIGHT

REVIEWS

Readers who have enjoyed the romantic, emotional stories of authors like Nora Roberts and Debbie Macomber will almost certainly enjoy this second chance story for small town veterinarian Colby Williams and big city investor Ian McKinley. "A great story about getting over the past and grabbing joy when it comes your way."

"If you like your romance in New Adult flavor, with plenty of ups and downs, oh-my, oh-yes, oh-no, love at first sight, trouble, happiness, difficulty, and follow-your-dreams, look no further than extraordinary prolific author Inglath Cooper. Ms. Cooper understands that the romance genre deserves good writing, great characterization, and true-to-life settings and situations, no matter the setting. I recommend you turn off the phone and ignore the doorbell, as you're not going to want to miss a moment of this saga of the girl who headed for Nashville with only a guitar, a hound, and a Dream in her heart." – **Mallory Heart Reviews**

"Truths and Roses . . . so sweet and adorable, I didn't want to stop reading it. I could have put it down and picked it up again in the morning, but I didn't want to." – **Kirkusreviews.com**

On Truths and Roses: "I adored this book...what romance should be, entwined with real feelings, real life and roses blooming. Hats off to the author, best book I have read in a while." – **Rachel Dove, FrustratedYukkyMommyBlog**

"I am a sucker for sweet love stories! This is definitely one of those! It was a very easy, well written, book. It was easy to follow, detailed, and didn't leave me hanging without answers." – **www.layfieldbaby.blogspot.com**

"I don't give it often, but I am giving it here – the sacred 10. Why? Inglath Cooper's A GIFT OF GRACE mesmerized me; I consumed it in one sitting. When I turned the last page, it was three in the morning." – **MaryGrace Meloche, Contemporary Romance Writers**

5 Blue Ribbon Rating! "...More a work of art than a story...Tragedies affect entire families as well as close loved ones, and this story portrays that beautifully as well as giving the reader hope that somewhere out there is A GIFT OF GRACE for all of us." — **Chrissy Dionne, Romance Junkies 5 Stars**

"A warm contemporary family drama, starring likable people coping with tragedy and triumph." 4 1/2 Stars. — **Harriet Klausner**

"A GIFT OF GRACE is a beautiful, intense, and superbly written novel about grief and letting go, second chances and coming alive again after devastating adversity. Warning!! A GIFT OF GRACE is a three-hanky read...better make that a BIG box of tissues read! Wowsers, I haven't cried so much while reading a book in a long long time...Ms. Cooper's skill makes A GIFT OF GRACE totally believable, totally absorbing...and makes Laney Tucker vibrantly alive. This book will get into your heart and it will NOT let go. A GIFT OF GRACE is simply stunning in every way—brava, Ms. Cooper! Highly, highly recommended!" – **4 1/2 Hearts — Romance Readers Connection**

"...A WOMAN WITH SECRETS...a powerful love story laced with treachery, deceit and old wounds that will not heal...enchanting tale...weaved with passion, humor, broken hearts and a commanding love that will have your heart soaring and cheering for a happily-ever-after love. Kate is strong-willed, passionate and suffers a bruised heart. Cole is sexy, stubborn and also suffers a bruised heart...gripping plot. I look forward to reading more of Ms. Cooper's work!" – **www.freshfiction.com**

PROLOGUE

Ian McKinley had finally made it. Reached the pinnacle. The top rung of the ladder. Tonight represented the crown jewel in the career he'd spent seventeen years of his life building. Thirty-nine, and by most definitions, he had everything. Money. Success. A teenage son. A beautiful fiancée.

Not to mention, having just brought on board the biggest client ever for CCI Investments of Manhattan, he was a hero to his partners. This party at the Waldorf Astoria had been thrown for him, the invitation list a who's who of New York City high rollers.

Standing here now among trays of champagne and tables loaded with exotic-looking foods, he should have been nothing but exhilarated. Somehow, he merely felt tired. Bone weary with the routine of his life, the predictability of it.

Every morning he bought his breakfast at the same bagel shop on Sixtieth Street, ate it at his desk with exactly two cups of coffee, no cream, no sugar. Every day he ran six miles at noon. He couldn't remember when he'd done anything remotely spontaneous.

But this was the life he had wanted. This was what he'd worked so hard for—to prove a poor boy from the wrong side of Manhattan could make it to Park and Sixty-First. He only regretted that neither Sherry nor his mother had lived to see his success. He'd promised them both he would make something of himself one day. He wondered if they would have been proud of him. But then, if Sherry had lived, maybe he wouldn't have been quite so driven. Wouldn't have buried himself in his work. Life would have been more about family. More normal for him and for Luke.

Did he even know what normal was anymore?

For the past three weeks, he'd gotten no more than five hours of sleep a night. That might explain his fatigue, except that part of him felt as if he'd been tired for years. He needed a vacation. Away from the city. When was the last time he'd taken one? The last time he'd spent more than an hour alone with his son? Guilt gnawed at him. He would plan something for them to do together. Soon. And he would make sure he kept his word.

"Why is it you look like a man headed for the gas chamber instead of the man of the hour?"

Ian swung around to find Rachel looking up at him with inquisitive eyes and a smile on her lips. "Hey," he said, putting a hand on her shoulder and giving it a soft squeeze. "A pillow and a bed sound pretty good about now."

"I could go for that. Especially since I've been getting just a little jealous of the stares half the women in the room have been sending you all night." She leaned in to kiss the corner of his mouth, her right breast pressing into his chest. He waited for the surge of attraction that should have followed her deliberate provocation and decided, when it did not come, that he was more tired than he'd realized.

"Hey, we can't have any of that." Curtis Morgan clapped a hand on Ian's shoulder. A short man with a receding hairline and an expanding waistline, Curtis was one of Ian's partners at CCI. "Not until after the wedding, at least. Ms. Montgomery, you'll have our guest of honor ducking out before I've had a chance to make my toast to him."

"I suggest you hurry up and do it," Rachel said with a raised brow. "I'm afraid he's nearly dead on his feet."

"No wonder. You really gave this one everything, Ian," Curtis said. "Our firm will see the benefit of it. We're all very appreciative."

"Yes. I'm so proud of him," Rachel said. "Now, if I could just get him to agree on a wedding date...."

She looked up at Ian with wide eyes that attempted to convey innocence, but Ian suspected Rachel knew exactly what she was doing.

As methodical about her personal life as she was about attaining senior partnership status at the law firm of Brown, Brown and Fitzgerald, Rachel made no secret of the fact that she thought a marriage between them would be mutually beneficial. She'd continued pressing her case for the past couple of years until she'd finally convinced him she was right.

Two weeks ago, when Ian asked her to marry him, it had been with the understanding that there was no rush. Both their lives were full, and a piece of paper wouldn't change things drastically. Or so he had told himself.

When Sherry died right after Luke was born, he said he would never marry again. Unexpectedly losing his wife at the age of twenty-three was the most painful, life-altering thing he'd ever known. Something inside him simply shut down. For the first five years after her death, he didn't date at all. When he did start seeing someone, he made sure it never lasted for any length of time, never long enough to let things get serious.

With Luke almost grown now, he didn't relish the idea of spending the rest of his life alone. His relationship with Rachel was a comfortable one. It made no demands or even hinted at happily-ever-after and white picket fences. At one point, he'd believed in destiny and people who were meant for each other. A young man's dreams. He no longer believed in any of that. If what he had with Rachel met the definition of compatibility more than love, he still appreciated her. Smart and beautiful, he personally knew of a dozen men who envied him.

"So what's the holdup, Ian?" Curtis asked with a punch to his left shoulder. "You need a reason to leave the office before midnight."

A waiter approached them and handed Ian a cordless phone. "There's a call for you, Mr. McKinley."

"Now, who could that be?" Curtis joked. "We're the only ones who ever bother you at this hour, and we're all here."

Ian shrugged and moved to the window, away from the noise of the party. "Hello."

"Mr. McKinley?"

"Yes?"

"This is Detective O'Neill with the New York City Police Department. Is Luke McKinley your son?"

Alarm shot through Ian. "Yes, he is."

"He was arrested tonight for possession of marijuana, Mr. McKinley."

It took a moment for the words to sink in. One by one, they finally did, even as disbelief washed over him. "Is he all right?"

"Yes."

"There must be some mistake. Luke has never—"

"No mistake, Mr. McKinley."

The detective gave him the address of the station and told him where to find Luke. Ian hung up, feeling as if someone had just punched him in the gut. He found Rachel and told her everything he knew. When she offered to go with him, he asked her to stay and explain to the others that he'd had an emergency.

He caught a cab outside the building, imagining, during the drive, a hundred different scenarios involving Luke and jail.

When the driver pulled over at the police station, Ian handed him a fifty and sprinted for the door, his stomach churning. Inside, he took the elevator to the third floor. Even at this hour, the place vibrated with purpose. Still dressed in his tuxedo, he got his fair share of stares as he wound his way through a maze of desks littered with coffee cups and mounds of paper.

From the far corner of the room, a thin man with

graying hair and skin that could use a little sunshine waved at him and called out, "You Mr. McKinley?"

"Yes."

"Your son is in the room across the hall. Go on in. I'll be right with you."

"Thank you," Ian said, while the detective went back to his call.

At the door, Ian stopped and drew in a deep breath before quickly turning the knob. Relief flooded him at the sight of Luke standing by the window with his hands jammed in his pockets.

His hair, long in front and short at the sides, halfway covered his eyes. His stance screamed defensive, his mouth set in a straight line. "Guess I messed up your party, huh?" he asked, his tone belligerent.

If Luke felt any fear, he wasn't showing it.

"Is that what you meant to do?" Ian asked quietly, not at all sure where to go with this.

"I didn't mean to do anything." Luke shrugged, clearly a rebel with a cause, the origins of which Ian couldn't begin to guess.

"They said you were arrested for drug possession."

Another shrug. "Big deal."

"Big deal?" Ian repeated. "Do you have any idea how serious this is?"

"It must be if you left your party to come down here."

The verbal slap achieved its intended sting. "I know things have been busy lately, but–"

"Lately?" Luke interrupted with a short laugh.

"You've been saying 'lately' since I was six years old. Probably before then, I just can't remember so far back. You only have time for work. And Rachel, of course, now that she's going to be your wife."

Bitterness layered the declaration. The vehemence behind it shocked Ian. Luke wasn't a big talker. For the past few years, getting information out of him took the finesse of a secret service agent. Ian chalked it up to teenage rebellion. The boy had been even less communicative since he'd told him about his engagement to Rachel. He looked at his son now and felt as though he were seeing him for the first time in a very long while. "I think we need to talk."

"So pencil me in before your nine-thirty, and I'll tell you all about how I know you wish I'd never been born."

The anger in the boy's voice hit Ian like a brick in the face. "Why would you say a thing like that, Luke?"

"Because it's the truth."

"No. It's not. Son—"

"If it hadn't been for me, she wouldn't have died," Luke yelled. "Don't you think I know that?"

Ian grappled for composure. "Nobody could have prevented what happened to your mother. She had a stroke. How could you possibly think I would—"

"I don't know," he interrupted. "Maybe because you work all the time just so you don't have to be around me."

"Luke!" Ian stopped, at a complete loss for a response. Somehow, when he hadn't been looking, something had gone terribly wrong between the two of them. Staring across at his son, part boy, part man, Ian wondered how Luke had felt this way without his knowing. How long had Luke been trying to get his attention? "Does this have something to do with my marrying Rachel?"

"I don't care who you marry. I'm sure you'll make all the time in the world for her."

Ian felt as if someone had just held a mirror in front of him. He didn't like what he saw. He thought about the party given in his honor tonight and realized the price. He'd spent the past seventeen years trying to make sure Luke had the things he himself never had as a kid. He'd sent the boy off to a camp in Wyoming every summer and to Austria in the winter with his ski team. In fact, he'd given him everything possible except one thing.

Time.

Maybe if he had, none of this would be happening.

Maybe if he had, he wouldn't have needed this kind of wake-up call to see what a mess he'd made of things.

Ian sank down on the chair behind him. He raked a hand through his hair and wondered how he'd gone from such heights to such depths in the span of one night. Luke was in trouble. Ian could blame no one but himself.

1

Monday morning started like every other Monday morning of this past month. Heaven help her, Colby Williams did not understand the adolescent mindset.

She shot a glance at her watch. "Baby, why can't you just wear the first outfit you put on? We're late. I've got to get to the clinic."

"Don't call me that, Mom." Lena frowned. "I'm not a baby. And the first outfit looked like dogsh—"

"Lena!" Surprised, Colby stared at her daughter. Lena didn't talk that way. At least not until recently.

Lena rolled her eyes and stomped up the steps to change for the third time. "Dog poop," she called out. "The first outfit looked like dog poop."

Critter, Lena's one-eared cat, pounced up the stairs behind her. From the Oriental rug on the living room floor, Petey and Lulu, reigning house dogs, eyed Lena's ascent as if they knew it wouldn't be her last.

"You're probably right," Colby said to the pedigree-free duo, then dropped onto the oversize sage green chair next to the fireplace. She surveyed the small but cozy room with some measure of satisfaction. At least order prevailed in this part of her life. Bookcases lined the wall to the right of the couch, shelves filled with hardbacks collected since her childhood, everything from *Beezus and Ramona,* which she'd read in the fourth grade, to *Gone with the Wind,* which she still pulled out on rainy days.

The home she and Lena furnished and decorated together with casual, country touches could be called more than comfortable, but someday, Colby hoped to buy them a house big enough to have a room for her books and a bigger bedroom for Lena. She'd hoped that house would be Oak Hill, an old farm outside of town. But it had sold recently, and that hope was no longer a realistic one.

From the radio on the kitchen counter, a singer twanged an appropriate tune about not dwelling on stuff you couldn't change. Following her advice, Colby got up and began putting things away, her thoughts turning to Lena. She didn't know whether to laugh or cry these days where her daughter was concerned. She was a thirty-four-year-old woman. A mother. A veterinarian with a thriving practice. And she was losing control of her fifteen year old.

The worst part? She had no idea why.

In the past several weeks, Lena's grades dropped from almost straight *A*'s to nearly all *C*'s. Lena was smart. Colby knew that wasn't the problem. Lena had always been a good child. Maybe too good. Colby had been spoiled by that. Her relationship with her daughter had been the most fulfilling aspect of her life for so long that she couldn't imagine it any other way.

The difference in Lena seemingly happened overnight, as if aliens had swooped down and stolen her beautiful, fun-loving daughter, replacing her with a surlier version of herself. The kid who lived with her looked just like Lena, sounded like Lena. But she wasn't Lena.

More than once, Colby started to drive over to her parents' house and plead for their advice on how to deal with this new side to her. She'd stopped herself each time. Samuel and Emma Williams had always been there for Lena and her. They'd helped put Colby through college and then vet school, lending a hand when Lena was a baby and Colby had been determined to stay in school. They'd been the best of parents, and she'd called on them far too often. She'd find a way to work this out on her own.

The phone rang. Tucking her shoulder-length hair behind one ear, she picked it up with a distracted, "Hello."

"I know you're headed out the door, but I've got a proposition for you."

"Does it involve convincing whoever stole my daughter to bring her back?"

Phoebe Walker laughed. "Hormones raging, huh?"

"I don't know what it is. Isn't there some kind of pill I can give her until it goes away?" Colby stretched the cord across the kitchen and picked up Lena's plate of uneaten French toast.

"You're the doctor," Phoebe said. "You ought to know."

Colby dumped the toast in the disposal and stuck the plate under the faucet, watching the syrup slide down the sink. "My expertise is in cows. They don't turn on their mothers."

Phoebe chuckled. "If it's any consolation, I think this is normal."

"It's not," Colby muttered, swiping at a water spot on her blue cotton shirt, and then wanting to change the subject, "So what's the proposition?"

"An invitation, actually. To dinner."

Colby tucked the phone under her chin and grabbed a paper towel to dab at her shirt. "What kind of dinner?"

"The kind where you put on a dress, add a spritz or two of perfume and leave your calf-birthing clothes at home in the closet."

"You want me to do all that just for you and Frank?" she asked, deliberately misunderstanding.

"Well—"

"That's what I thought. Thanks, but no thanks."

"*Colby*—"

"Don't *Colby* me." She slipped the plate into the dishwasher. "Have you forgotten what I told you the last time you tried to fix me up?"

"Are you going to hold that against me forever?" Phoebe asked, a whine in her voice.

"I should. You certainly deserve it."

"He wasn't that bad."

"Yeah, if your idea of a hot date is an octopus pickled in Brut."

"Oh, for Pete's sake, Colby, you're too picky!"

"And you've got too much time on your hands." As Colby's best friend, Phoebe refused to stay out of her love life, saying she'd known her since the beginning of the world and therefore had a vested interest in her happiness. Personally, Colby thought she should join the garden club or take up knitting, anything to relieve Phoebe's self-appointed burden of finding Colby a husband.

No matter how often they went over it, Phoebe just didn't get it. She refused to believe a woman could be happy living her life without a man—maybe because she happened to be married to one of the last good men on earth. But Colby qualified as walking proof she was wrong. She'd tried the dating scene off and on over the years, thinking Lena needed a father figure. Once in a while, she'd even dated out of a true desire for companionship. But at some point, it stopped seeming worth the trouble. The only men she ever met were either newly divorced and neurotic or looking for a housekeeper instead of a wife.

She'd long ago decided love rarely turned out to be the way Hollywood depicted it. But then, she'd learned that when she'd been eighteen and too green to know better than to fall for a great-looking guy with a great-looking car who came from a different world than the one she knew.

"Exactly who are you going to meet," Phoebe

continued, "tromping around in dairy barns in waist-high rubber boots?"

"The bulls I run into are a lot more interesting than most of the men I know."

Phoebe let out an inelegant snort.

Just then, Lena tromped down the stairs in black military boots, her purple bombshell replaced by a tie-dyed explosion of orange, red, and green that made the first outfit look tame by comparison. The streaks of purple hair, in tribute to the discarded ensemble, remained. "It looks as if Lena's finally decided on the look of the day," Colby said, lowering her voice. "I've got to get going. We're already late."

"Wait! You didn't answer my question. Dinner this Friday. My house. Be here."

"Phoebe—"

"I promise you won't regret it." Phoebe added a hasty goodbye and hung up before Colby could argue further. If she'd had the time, she would have called her back and given her a definite no on the spot, but Lena would be late for school and Colby had an early appointment. Turning down Phoebe's invitation would have to wait.

2

Ten minutes later, Colby parked in front of Jefferson County High School. It sat on a small rise, and, built of brick with classic lines, it was the kind of building that would never look outdated. A football stadium—impressive for a town the size of Keeling Creek—sat to the right of it.

The engine of her old Ford truck shook a bit as she put it into park. Out of habit, she leaned across to give Lena a goodbye kiss on the forehead.

"Mom!" Lena strained against her door as if Colby had just come after her with a hot branding iron.

Colby sat back in her seat, her hands resting on the steering wheel. The kiss had been a reflex action, one of those things that seemed impossible to stop when she'd been doing it for so many years. It had only been in the past several weeks that Lena started rebuffing her affection. A lump of emotion lodged in Colby's throat. She hated to see Lena grow up. If this was how the young made themselves independent from their parents, then she only wished the process over. Watching her daughter pull away from her day by day hurt too much. "Are you coming by the clinic after school?" she asked, keeping her voice light.

"No. A bunch of us are going to the Dairy Queen."

Lena hadn't come by the office in weeks. Ever since she'd started kindergarten, she hightailed it to the practice as soon as the bell rang, helping out with dog baths and feedings, anything to be around the animals. Now, she seemed to have lost interest. Colby forced herself not to respond, but it hurt, nonetheless. "What time will you be home, then?"

"The usual."

Colby refrained from mentioning that "the usual" recently stretched its boundaries to anywhere between four and six o'clock. "Just be back by dinner."

A black Mercedes sedan rolled into the spot in front of them, its bumper barely missing the hood of Colby's truck.

"Oh, no!" Lena slid down in her seat.

"What is it?" Colby asked, startled.

"The new guy. Luke McKinley. Oh, my gosh, he's so awesome!"

Not once in fifteen-plus years had Colby ever heard such words from Lena. She'd always been a tomboy. As a child, she'd have chosen playing in the dirt over playing with dolls any day of the week. Not so long ago, boys rated the same level as fish bait.

Colby wished they'd stayed there. Nonetheless, she strained her neck for a glimpse of the boy.

"I gotta go, Mom," Lena said, reserve creeping into her voice as she slid out of the truck.

From the back seat, Petey and Lulu barked in protest when Lena forgot to say goodbye.

Colby glanced at the wounded-looking pair. "So you've noticed too, huh?" She put the truck in gear, stretching for another glimpse of the vehicle in front of her. The boy hadn't gotten out yet, and she could hardly sit here all day. She wheeled around the Mercedes, watching Lena linger at the door, no doubt waiting for Awesome Luke.

3

Colby headed up Main Street toward the clinic, frustrated by the twenty-five-mile-per-hour speed limit. Joe Dooley tooled along in front of her in his farm-use pickup, an old Chevy that had seen its fortieth birthday and then some. A firm believer that laws were laws, Joe kept the needle of his speedometer safely on twenty-four.

Telling herself to stop fretting and enjoy the early September morning, Colby waved at Ruby Lynch who was sweeping the sidewalk at Thurman's Hardware. Keeling Creek had become known as one of the few towns that, so far, had been bypassed by the fast-food chains and super shopping stores. Small family-run businesses still flourished, and Colby liked it that way.

Just past Thurman's sat Tinker's Drug and Soda Fountain. Then came the First Bank of Jefferson

County. Across the street, Kirk's Department Store had occupied the same spot for four decades. Next to Cutter's Grocery sat the Dippety-Do Hair Salon, where she went for a monthly trim and the current dose of gossip that came free of charge with it.

Ahead, the county courthouse loomed whitewashed and noble. Euell Clemens and Oat Henley, local farmers, stood talking at the door, waving at her as she drove by. In two more blocks she reached the Dairy Queen, where Joe Dooley turned off, no doubt making a pit stop for his morning egg biscuit. Colby waved and sped up a little, only to spot the town maintenance crew up ahead, doing some kind of repair work that brought the traffic to a halt. She glanced at her watch and sighed. Late. About to be later.

She rolled down her window and waved at Ellis Holbrook, now holding the Stop sign at the front of the line of cars. He stepped back to her truck. "Mornin', doc."

"Good morning, Ellis. Think this is going to take long?"

Ellis shook his head and adjusted his Jefferson County High Eagles cap, wiping the sweat from his forehead. "Shouldn't be but a few more minutes. I'd tell you to back up, but you've got too many cars behind you now."

"I understand," she said. "How's Toby?"

Ellis reached through the window to pet Petey, then turned his attention to Lulu, impatiently waiting her turn. "He's fine. Nasty cut on his leg, but it seems to be healin' up real nice."

"He's lucky he didn't lose it, getting tangled up in that barbed wire."

"I wager he'll steer clear of it from now on. I'd better get back up there. We'll have you movin' shortly, doc."

"Thanks, Ellis." Colby rolled up her window, thumped her thumbs on the steering wheel and flicked on the radio. WKKI announced the First Baptist Church's plans for a bake sale on Court Street this Saturday and then promised to be right back after a few messages from its sponsors.

This was Colby's favorite season, when summer wound down and took the heat with it, leaving cool mornings and warm days in its place. Traditionally, a time of year that she and Lena always enjoyed together, shopping for school clothes and supplies, registering for school and buying textbooks. But this year had been different. Lena merely endured each of those outings, as if she couldn't wait for them to be over.

A song came on, as promised, and Colby's fingers followed the rhythm on the center of the steering wheel while she wondered if she'd somehow taken a wrong turn in her efforts to make up for Lena's never having had a father. Being a good parent was the most important thing in her life.

In most ways that counted, she hadn't let Doug be the stumbling block that he could have been. She'd done exactly what she'd always planned to do. Gotten her college degree and gone to vet school. Opened the first female-owned practice in Keeling Creek. In fact, since Dr. Granger retired two years ago, she had become the only veterinarian in town. All of that in spite of being a single mother at nineteen. All of that despite Doug Jamison's refusal to take any responsibility for the daughter they created together.

Doug left singe marks on her soul where relationships were concerned. Phoebe didn't understand that. And Colby gave up trying to make her see that even if she ever met someone worth the effort, she couldn't put her heart on the chopping block again. She'd had it pulverized once in her life, and once had been quite enough for her.

4

Some twenty minutes later, Colby pulled up to the Jefferson County Animal Clinic. She parked the truck in her usual spot and hopped out. Petey and Lulu, used to the routine, waited for her to raise the seat so they could get out. She'd found them three years ago at a gas station in Grayson County where someone apparently dropped them off. Viewing her as their savior, they wanted to go everywhere she went and hated to be left at home.

She hurried across the full parking lot toward the brick building enclosed by a white rail fence with red-and-white impatiens circling each post. She rushed through the door with Petey and Lulu at her heels, all three of them nearly tripping over Don Juan, who lay stretched out like a welcome mat at the clinic entrance. Don Juan lived there, along with several other pets with problems that made people decide they no longer wanted them. Colby refused to take them to the animal shelter, so they ended up making the clinic their home. She and Lena christened him Don Juan because all the female dogs loved him and trailed him like lovesick señoritas. Even the cats adored him.

For the past two years, Colby had been trying to raise enough private funds to build a no-kill shelter where pets stayed until someone adopted them. Unfortunately, she still had a long way to go to meet her goal, and, meanwhile, her collection of animal dependents continued to grow. She gave Don Juan a quick rub behind the ears. "We're going to have to find you another snoozing spot, lover boy."

The waiting room overflowed with pets and their people, several of whom offered Colby and her entourage welcoming smiles. The others simply looked annoyed at her tardiness. She didn't blame them. "Sorry, everybody. I'll try to make up for lost time here."

Luckily, her two assistants, Laura and Ruth-Ann, already had the examining rooms ready, a petrified-looking dachshund in one, a bored-looking Saint Bernard in the other. "We took it as far as we could without you, Dr. Williams," Laura said, smiling. "I did the fecal for little Slim Jim and Ruth-Ann is in the back cleaning up. George there decided not to go to the bathroom this morning, but when she pressed on his bladder, he changed his mind."

"Just another day at the office," Colby said, shaking her head and smiling. Laura chuckled and handed her the white jacket hanging on the coat rack behind the door.

One o'clock came and went before she finally got a breather. Her last patient had just left when Stacey Renick walked in with a can of Coke held out in front of her. At twenty, Stacey started working at the clinic after graduating from high school. Customers counted on her smiling face. Colby often wished for the ability to clone her. Stacey's only character flaw was that, she too had the matchmaking bug and constantly reported in on recent "hunk sightings."

"A receptionist's job is never done," Stacey said. "Here. You look like you could use this."

Colby took the Coke. "Thanks."

Petey padded in and plopped down on the floor beside Stacey. Laura and Ruth-Ann had gone to lunch, the place empty except for the two of them and a couple of part-time girls who did grooming.

"You've barely looked up since you got here." Stacey leaned against the doorjamb, taking a sip of her own Coke.

"I can't seem to get Lena out the door these days."

"I take it you two are still at odds?"

Colby ran her thumb across the condensation on the side of the can. "She's like a different child or something."

Stacey shrugged. "Maybe that's just it. She's not a child anymore. Is there a guy in the picture?"

"She did mention someone this morning. Some new boy at school. But that's the first time she's said anything. I don't know what to do."

"Kids go through a stage a week at that age," Stacey said, waving a hand.

Colby grinned. "I'm surprised you can remember that far back."

The doorbell dinged outside the examining room. Stacey stuck her head around the corner and said, "Be right with you." She turned to Colby then and mouthed a whistle along with a silent "Wow!"

"What is it?"

"*Major* hunk sighting!" Stacey stage-whispered before heading to the front desk. Petey followed, tail wagging. Colby heard her greeting someone in a far more welcoming tone than even good-natured Stacey usually managed.

Colby put the Coke on the counter behind her and began cleaning up the instruments she'd used earlier.

"Dr. Williams?"

She swung around, finding herself face-to-face with the hunk in question. The man nearly filled the doorway in both height and breadth. Dressed in faded jeans and a crisp-looking cotton shirt, he had dark, thick hair with a few flecks of gray at the sides. His eyes, in startling contrast, were blue. And his face—

He had the kind of striking good looks that turned women's voices to squeaks.

"May I help you?" she asked, a little shaken by how much he reminded her of Doug.

"Your sign said you don't begin appointments again until three o'clock, but she's got a briar in her paw," the man said in an accent so neutral she knew he wasn't from around here. "Could you take a look?"

Only then did Colby notice the yellow Lab standing by his side, her right paw suspended in midair. Uncharacteristically rattled, Colby knelt down in front of the dog, smoothing a hand across her back. "What's her name?"

"Smidge."

She looked up at him, trying not to smile. "Smidge?"

"She's my son's dog. He named her that because she was such a little puppy. You can see that didn't last."

"No, it didn't." Colby gently picked up the dog's paw. She carefully turned it over and pulled the pads back to see where the briar had lodged. It was stuck in the middle, fairly deep. Smidge whimpered.

"Sorry, girl. Let's get that out for you." She stood up and added in a calming voice, "I'm going to put you up here where I can see you now. Easy, girl."

She bent over to pick up the dog just as the man leaned forward and said, "I'll get her." Their heads collided with a *thwunk.* Colby saw a few stars. They both stood up and began to apologize at the same time.

"It's all right." Colby held up one hand and rubbed her forehead with the other, amused. "I'll get her. I'm used to it. Really."

The man stepped back, nodding in surrender. She picked up the dog and placed her on the table.

"Sit, Smidge," he said in a kind but authoritative voice.

Smidge sat, still dangling her right paw in front of her and keeping her sorrowful gaze on the man.

"She's a little wary of being here," he said. "She got into a box of hot chocolate once and had to stay at the hospital for a few nights."

"It's okay, Smidge. I'll fix you up and send you right home."

Smidge's pink tongue lolled to one side.

"She thanks you," the man said.

"I think you're right." Colby had a habit of judging people by how they treated their animals. So far, he made the A-list.

He really didn't seem anything like Doug. It was just the confidence with which he carried himself, the way his clothes proclaimed him comfortable with status, the fact that he obviously came from a very different place than Keeling Creek. Or maybe the situation with Lena had her making comparisons.

Focusing on the task, she went to the cabinet behind the table and took out a pair of tweezers and an antibiotic dressing. Holding Smidge's paw with one hand, she extracted the briar while the man rubbed the dog's head and kept her calm.

Colby doused the wound with peroxide. "There," she said. "I'll wrap it up and give you an antibiotic for her. We don't want to let an infection set in. She'll need to take the entire course."

"You're very good with animals," the man said. "But then, why wouldn't you be?" he added, looking embarrassed. "You're a vet."

She smiled and put the tweezers in a jar of

disinfectant, saying over her shoulder, "Comes with the territory. She seems to like you pretty well."

"I can't do any wrong with Smidge."

"That's the great thing about dogs." Colby unrolled a package of gauze and snipped off a strip. She began wrapping it around the still-tender paw, her touch light.

"Wish the same were true of kids," the man said.

"You and me both." She looked up. "You must have a teenager in your house too."

"As a matter of fact, I do. Don't tell me you're old enough to have one yourself."

She made sure the gauze was secure and that Smidge couldn't work it loose too easily. "I've been told she's probably just in a stage, but if it doesn't pass soon, I'll look plenty old enough."

"I know what you mean."

"There." Colby stepped back. "That should take care of it. Keep an eye on it. Change the gauze daily. If you notice any redness, swelling, or heat in the paw, bring her in immediately."

"I'll do that." He lifted the dog down from the table, setting her gently on the floor and patting her head. "Good girl."

Smidge looked up, her tail thumping.

"She should be fine." Colby wiped her hands on her jacket, annoyed with herself for not letting her gaze quite meet his. She'd been off-kilter since the moment he'd walked in the door.

"I'm Ian McKinley, by the way." He stuck out his

right hand. "We've only been in town for a couple of weeks."

"Welcome to Keeling Creek, Mr. McKinley," she said, gripping his hand with her own and wondering why that name sounded familiar. "I hope you and your family will like it here."

"I hope so." He let go of her hand, though his gaze stayed fixed on her for a second longer. He glanced away, then backed toward the door. "Come on, Smidge. Let's get you home so you can put your paw up for a while."

Colby smiled and followed them through the doorway. "Don't forget to make sure she takes the full seven days' worth of medicine."

"I won't." He raised his hand in a wave before stopping at the front desk to pay Stacey, who beamed a thousand-watt smile his way. He took out his wallet and smiled at her, apparently oblivious to the admiration in the young woman's eyes.

Colby went into the examining room, wondering about the man and what he was doing in Keeling Creek, the familiarity of his name still nagging at her.

The door dinged. She waited another second or two to make sure he'd left before she went back out.

"Incredible or what?" Stacey asked from behind the computer.

Colby ignored her dreamy-eyed receptionist and went to the door. She watched Ian McKinley get into the same black Mercedes she'd seen at the high school that morning.

Ah. Ian McKinley was Awesome Luke's father.

5

Colby Williams was the first person Ian McKinley met in Keeling Creek who didn't look at him as if he'd just stepped out of a flying saucer. She'd been polite but asked none of the questions he'd been getting from almost everyone he met. People were curious. He got that. He was the outsider, after all, in a small town. Very small. He still hadn't gotten used to that, or to the quietness. Police sirens were background noise in New York City. He couldn't remember hearing one since he and Luke moved here two weeks ago.

Flicking on his blinker, Ian turned off Main Street onto 152 and headed out of town.

So far, Smidge was the only one who had happily adjusted to the move. She loved it here. Her tail had barely stopped wagging since they'd first let her out of the car.

Luke? Another matter altogether. He hated it here and made no secret of the fact.

There were times when Ian still couldn't believe he'd actually packed up everything and left the city. But the night Luke was arrested opened his eyes in a big way. Luke had always been an exemplary student, never got into any trouble. Seeing him in the police station shook Ian to the core, Luke's accusations of his deliberately not spending time with him the biggest curve of all. It sickened him to think his son had been suffering those kinds of feelings and he hadn't realized it. After that night, Ian knew only that he wanted to be the father he'd always intended to be.

Judge Watley Townsend took Luke's case under advisement, putting him on one year's probation with the admonition that if he got into similar trouble again, the incident would go on his record. After the hearing, Ian met with the judge in his chambers. Not sure how his request would be received, he said, "Your Honor, with your permission, I'd like to move Luke out of the city for his senior year in high school. I've bought a home in a small town in Virginia where he'll be exposed to a different way of life."

The judge peered at him over the rims of his tortoiseshell glasses and said, "With all due respect, sir, what makes you think Luke's surroundings will have any effect on his behavior?"

"I grew up in one of the roughest parts of this city, but when I was about Luke's age, I spent some time in Virginia at a football camp. Needless to say, things were a little different in that part of the country. It made an impression on me I've never forgotten. I realize that temptation exists everywhere, but I believe a change of scenery would be good for my son. And I've realized recently that I've let my work get in the way of spending as much time with Luke as I should have. I've decided to take a one-year leave of absence so I can do that."

The judge's eyebrows rose above his glasses. "You're a single parent, Mr. McKinley?"

"Yes, I am."

The judge sat for several long moments, thrumming his fingers on the top of his desk. "If you think your time and attention can make a difference in your son's life and where he goes from here, then I'm not going to stand in your way. I'll grant permission for him to leave the state under the terms of his probation. But I'll want him to report to an officer there on a regular basis."

If Ian had been pleased by the judge's response, no one else had been. His partners at CCI were less than thrilled at the prospect of his taking a leave of absence. Rachel even less so. Since they'd been engaged only for a few weeks, she couldn't believe he wanted to put things on hold for a year. He'd explained to her how important it was to him to try to get his relationship with Luke back on track, but she'd accused him of overreacting, telling him that the situation wasn't as dire as he perceived it to be. Nevertheless, Ian saw it as a turning point—and he believed it had happened for a reason. Luke was almost a grown man, and Ian felt as if this might be his only chance to right some of his wrongs before the boy moved out on his own.

When Rachel realized she wouldn't change his mind, she reluctantly agreed to postpone their wedding plans. He reassured her that nothing would be different between them. Once school ended, he would return to New York and pick up his life where he'd left off. And maybe by then he could mend the rift between him and his son.

6

Mabel Atkins waited at the door while Ian parked his car at the rear of the house a few minutes later. "Did they get you all fixed up, Miss Smidge?" she asked, wiping her hands on her apron.

"She'll be fine." Ian followed his plump, flour-dusted housekeeper into the kitchen.

"Well, that's certainly good news," she said, giving the dog an affectionate pat on the head.

Ian had known Mabel little more than a week, but he already felt as if he'd known her forever. She made no attempt to hide herself from the world. Blunt and to the point, she took great pride in her work. Although she claimed to have once been more than five feet tall, she now stood an inch or two under that height and frequently complained that she would soon need a step stool to reach the sink. She wore her hair in a kinky perm and had a penchant for chocolate malt balls, which she kept in the cabinet above the stove, high enough to make her think twice about pulling them out.

Ian spent his first few days in Keeling Creek thinking he'd do everything on his own. He and Luke could manage. But when the laundry started to pile up and the dirty dishes multiplied exponentially, he'd given up and gone in search of a housekeeper.

They'd been in town less than a week when he'd asked Maude Cutter at Cutter's Grocery if she knew of anyone who would be interested in the job. She'd said Mabel was just the woman he was looking for. And she'd been right. Mabel fit in as if she'd always been here. She'd taken a firm hand with Luke too, informing him of kitchen rules on her first day in the house. Luke needed that kind of structure, something Ian hadn't been around enough to give him.

Smidge managed an exaggerated limp over to her bowl where Mabel had a dish full of leftover chicken waiting for her. No dog was a bigger ham when a little sympathy could be conjured up.

"Now if she'll just stay out of the blackberry bushes," Ian said.

"She's lived in the city all her life," Mabel replied in the dog's defense. "Been running around like a wild thing set free since you got here. She'll learn soon enough."

"Let's hope so," Ian said doubtfully. Only a few days before, they'd found her in the creek behind the house, hip deep in mud and howling.

"Did you get to meet Colby?" Mabel asked.

"Dr. Williams?"

"Funny as that sounds to me, yes." The older woman chuckled, stirring the contents of the pot simmering on top of the stove. "Known her since she stood knee-high to a grasshopper. Still can't believe she's old enough to be called doctor."

"She seemed very good." Ian opened the refrigerator and took out the pitcher of lemonade Mabel just made that morning.

Colby Williams didn't fit his stereotype of a small-town veterinarian. She was attractive. Very attractive, if different from the women he knew in New York. Her style said casual, a blue cotton shirt tucked into slim-fitting Levi's, her straight blonde hair in a ponytail, emphasizing a face with nice cheekbones and expressive green eyes.

"Even as a little girl, she wanted to be the first female vet in town," Mabel said. "And she was. We're lucky to have her."

Intrigued, Ian said, "She mentioned having a daughter. How old is she?"

Mabel ladled out a bowl of soup from the pot on the stove and set it in front of him. "A little younger than Luke, I believe. Colby raised her by herself. Nice kid, so she must have done a good job."

"She's not married?" The question popped out before he even realized he wanted to ask it.

Mabel turned to look at him, both eyebrows disappearing beneath gray bangs. "As a matter of fact, she's not."

Ian swallowed a spoonful of soup and burned his mouth in the process.

"Careful there." Mabel eyed him with a thoughtful look on her face. "It's hot."

"You're right, it is." He washed away the sting with the lemonade and wondered at the glint in his housekeeper's eye. "Good, though."

"Glad you like it. After my Thomas was gone, there was just me, and food doesn't taste nearly as good if you're not cooking it with someone other than yourself in mind. It's a real pleasure to have you and Luke to cook for."

"Thomas was a lucky man. You'll spoil us if we're not careful," Ian said with a smile. He knew what she meant about eating alone. When Sherry had died, he thought he too would die of loneliness. Knowing that the small, helpless infant who was his son needed him had been the one thing that kept him going. Despite what Luke thought, Ian didn't know what he would have done without him.

Mabel dropped the soup ladle into the sink and turned to give him an assessing look. "That's all right by me. I know you said you and Luke would only be here until he finished high school, but if you and Colby happened to hit it off, you might not want to return to the big city."

He nearly choked on his soup. Mabel scurried across the kitchen floor, whacking him on the back. "You okay, Mr. McKinley?"

Once he'd gotten his coughing under control, he nodded and wiped his eyes with his napkin. Not wanting her to get any ideas, he said, "If you remember, Mabel, I mentioned that I recently got engaged."

"Oh, yes, you did, didn't you?" the older woman said with a deadpan expression.

"She's coming down this weekend. On Saturday."

"I didn't mean to be making any untoward suggestions, Mr. McKinley," Mabel said hastily. "And if your intended is planning a visit, then I'd better quit yakking and get this place in tip-top order, hadn't I?" She left him in the kitchen to finish his soup alone.

Ian put his bowl in the sink and went out on the front porch of the two-story brick house. Smidge followed him, sprawling on the floor beside him. With his glass of lemonade in one hand, Ian leaned against a porch column noticeably in need of paint and stared out at the oak trees lining the driveway. Oak Hill was a beautiful place. No denying that. A lot like Tara must have looked to Scarlett after the war.

Built in the late 1800s, the farm had been used to raise both cattle and horses until a few years ago when it went up for sale and had since become run-down.

Ian had asked his Manhattan real estate agent to find Luke and him a place in need of some work. The thought of that appealed to him, even though he didn't own a toolbox and had next to zero experience in carpentry work. Coming here had been his decision, but going from a sixteen-hour workday to a one-year leave of absence felt like being forced to a halt halfway through a marathon. He'd consoled himself with the thought that he might spend part of his time making improvements to the house. He'd also hoped that might be something he and Luke could do together. A common ground.

The agent found him what he'd been looking for. But photographs of the place didn't reveal just how much work the farm would require. The barn was in dire need of paint, and a good number of boards needed replacing, as well as the roof. The fields beside and behind the house looked as if they hadn't been mowed in years. But the house itself was the most daunting of all, with peeling wallpaper, floors in need of refinishing and bathtubs that needed resealing. There wasn't a room that didn't need something done to it. He definitely had his work cut out for him.

He heard the school bus in the distance roll to a stop and then move on down the road. A few minutes later, Luke appeared at the top of the driveway, his book bag slung over one shoulder, his baseball cap and loose, baggy clothes marking him as the city kid he was. His expression remained set and unsmiling until he spotted Smidge wobbling across the yard toward him, limping on her bandaged leg.

Luke looked up at Ian, a worried frown on his face. "What happened to her?"

"She had a briar in her paw. I took her to see the vet. She got it out and gave her something for infection."

Luke plopped down on the ground and wrestled with the ecstatic dog for a couple of minutes while Ian watched them, a catch in his heart. The boy loved the dog, and he had to admit he wished Luke showed as much affection for him.

Luke had been even less communicative than usual since they'd arrived here at the end of August, and Ian hoped patience would eventually pay off. He knew the changes weren't easy for him. A new school. New kids. But schoolwork had always come easily to him. He was smart and, if anything, often bored by his classes. He'd been one of the top soccer players at his school in the city, but Jefferson County High didn't have a team, and so far, he'd shown no interest in any other sports.

Luke got up and bounded up the porch steps past Ian without saying a word.

"How was school today?" Ian asked.

Luke turned around at the screen door, his gaze on Smidge. "Great," he said, his tone less than convincing.

"It can't be that bad. Surely you like some of the kids."

"They're all too wild for me."

Ian ignored his sarcasm. Despite his intelligence and athletic ability, Luke had a shy side that made it difficult for him to make new friends. "I started chipping away the old paint on the porch this morning," Ian said. "I thought maybe you'd like to help this weekend."

Luke kicked at a twig on the wood floor. "You're the one who wanted to come out here and play farmer. I didn't want any part of this. Believe me, if I'd known you were going to bring me to this no-action town, I'd have asked that judge for jail time instead. There wouldn't have been much difference anyway." He disappeared inside the house, the screen door slamming closed behind him.

"Luke!" Ian called, starting after him, then deciding against it. He dropped down on the top step of the porch. He'd known that nothing about this would be easy. So far, he'd been right. His relationship with Luke didn't fall apart overnight and it would certainly take longer than that to fix it.

7

At five minutes past five that afternoon, Colby stepped through the front door of the Dippety-Do Hair Salon for her monthly trim. Her basic, shoulder-length cut required little more effort than a nip off the ends.

A bell dinged, announcing her arrival. A waiting area held several chairs and a couple of couches. Magazines littered the coffee table, *GQ* and *International Male* among them. Louise Mason, the owner of the salon, theorized that her customers didn't come here to read about the latest tuna casserole recipe or how to paint their kitchen in less than five hours. Here, women were free to gossip, ogle men's magazines and generally let their hair down, so to speak. Judging from the fact that the place rarely had an empty chair, Louise apparently had the right idea.

"Hey, Colby. You're on time, as usual," Louise said, approaching the desk. At five feet, ten inches tall, Louise often joked that the only thing that kept her from being a professional model was her looks.

"Hi, Louise. You keeping busy?"

The woman threw a glance at the shop behind her, where hair dryers buzzed and the smell of permanent solution hung in the air. "If it weren't for vanity, I'd be in the poorhouse."

Colby smiled and followed the heavyset woman to the back. Louise shampooed her hair and applied an apple-scented conditioner. When she finished, she wrapped a towel around Colby's head and led her to her station up front.

"So what are we gonna do today, honey?" Louise asked after Colby settled in the chair.

Colby met her hopeful gaze in the mirror. "Just the usual."

"How'd I know you were gonna say that?"

Louise had been trying to talk her into going the way of big hair for years. "Men like a lotta hair," she'd said more times than Colby could count. "You walk into a nightclub, and you gotta compete with all those Dolly Parton types. You can't just let yourself blend into the woodwork."

Like Phoebe, Louise ranked Colby's lack of interest in the dating scene right up there with self-administered haircuts and chipped nail polish. It simply didn't do.

Smiling, Colby said, "I have to give you credit for trying, Louise."

"Now, Colby, you know I think you're one of the prettiest gals around. I'd just like to pizzazz you up a bit, that's all."

Pizzazz, as Louise defined it, meant frosting and a perm. "Thank you, Louise, but—"

"I know. I know. You like it how it is. I just thought with that new man in town, you might have changed your mind. Let's see, what's his name? McKlellan, Mc—" Louise snapped her fingers, searching for the name.

"McKinley," Ellen Ann Edwards offered up from the next station. "Ian McKinley."

That name again.

"I shoulda known you'd have it down pat," Louise said to the other woman with a chuckle.

"Well, why not? It's not as if someone like that moves to Keeling Creek every day of the week," Ellen Ann declared.

"You're right about that," Louise agreed. "I saw him at the DMV when I was gettin' my county sticker, and he was in front of me. Didn't even mind spendin' my lunch hour standing in line. That is one fine-looking man."

Ellen Ann's nod of agreement carried with it a look of wistfulness. She added another permanent rod to her customer's hair. "I saw him out jogging on the way to work yesterday. All I could do to keep my eyes on the road."

"Oh, that's good, Ellen Ann. All we need is for you to run over him."

Ellen Ann rolled her eyes at Louise. "Somebody said he's from New York."

"City?" Louise asked.

Ellen Ann nodded again.

"So what's he doin' here, you think?"

"Beats me, but I'm not complaining."

"Me, neither. If I didn't already have me a fella, I'd go knock on his door and introduce myself. He's got a boy at the high school, but nobody's seen hide nor hair of a wife."

"Now what would you do with an uptowner like him, Louise?" the customer in Ellen Ann's chair asked with a giggle.

"I could think of one or two things," Louise replied with a wink and a nod.

The remark brought on a fit of giggles from the women around them, all of whom had been listening to the conversation.

The woman in Ellen Ann's chair waved a copy of the *National Tattler*. "He might find himself a wife here. I just read a story about a prince from some small country on the other side of the world. He came over here on a visit and met some little gal from Kentucky. Married her and took her back to his kingdom."

"Sounds like paradise," Colby said, deciding that the women of Keeling Creek had been seriously deprived for too long. All this fuss over one man moving to town. Okay, so he was good-looking. He'd seemed nice enough earlier, but from all appearances, he'd fit in here like the proverbial square peg in a round hole.

"What I want to know," Louise went on, "is what Colby here thinks of him. After all, she's the one who's free and single."

"And not likely to forget it," Colby chimed in.

"I can see why you're choosy, hon," Louise sympathized. "The bachelor pickin's are pretty slim around here. You better get in on this one. Cindy Stoneway came in this morning trying to figure out a way to meet him. Last I heard, she'd decided on a flat tire in front of his house."

"Tell her good luck for me next time she's in," Colby said.

Louise brushed the loose hair off Colby's plastic cape. "Just don't hold your breath waitin' for another one like this to land in Keeling Creek. Might as well be holdin' out for aliens."

"I won't, Louise." Colby shook her head and smiled. "I won't."

8

By the time Friday arrived, Colby felt shopworn. The last thing she wanted to do was go to Phoebe and Frank's for dinner. But Phoebe called that afternoon for a confirmation. The clinic had been swamped and Colby, having no time to argue, gave her a hasty, "I guess so." She would have looked forward to dinner alone with the two of them. It would have given her a chance to talk with them about Lena. But she knew Phoebe, and she'd bet her last dollar there would be another man sitting across the dinner table from her. A new lawyer from Frank's firm, or someone Frank met playing golf, or the brother of someone Phoebe did aerobics with. Going to Phoebe's house had become a lot like facing a firing squad. The only bright spot in the evening was that once she'd given the man the thumbs-down, she'd have a couple of months' reprieve before Phoebe got brave enough to try it again.

With two children and a farm she practically ran herself, Phoebe should have better things to do anyway.

Colby filled the bathtub, then sank into the bubbles with a sigh, rationalizing that if her first love had been a man like Frank, she wouldn't be such a cynic on the subject. But Doug was nothing like Frank.

They met on her second day at the University of Virginia. He'd been the complete opposite of the boys she'd dated in high school and competed with at local 4-H fairs. He'd grown up in Philadelphia, where his family name was written in blue ink on the social register.

He nearly ran over her in his red Porsche at a crosswalk in front of her dorm. He'd been speeding and barely able to avoid plowing right into her. Angered by his carelessness, she'd been prepared to give him an earful. But he'd gotten out of the car, apologizing profusely. His dark good looks and polished manners caught her off guard, and she had reluctantly forgiven him.

The obvious differences between the two of them made her both wary of him and attracted to him at the same time. He'd asked her out to dinner to prove that he was really sorry, but she turned him down, telling herself she'd be better off staying away from him. He was persistent, though, and one night when he nearly knocked a hole in her dorm window trying to get her attention, she pushed aside her doubts and went downstairs to meet him.

From then on, they spent all their time together. He treated her well, took her to dinner at fancy places, and met her at the library every afternoon. When they ended up making love in his room one night after a party where they both had a little too much to drink, it seemed a natural, if unplanned, extension of where they were headed.

She attributed her first missed period to stress. She took her studies seriously, and she'd been agonizing over a couple of classes in which she aimed to make A's in spite of the teachers' tough reputations. Doug had been moody with her lately, accusing her of caring more about school than she did him. He didn't look at college the same way she did, but then, regardless of what kind of grades he made, he would still have a whopper of a trust fund waiting for him when he turned twenty-five. Flattered to have one of the most sought-after guys on campus wanting to spend all his time with her, she still determined to make the grades she needed to keep her scholarship and get her into the vet school at Virginia Tech.

When the second month went by with still no sign of her period, Colby panicked. Feeling sick inside, she made a doctor's appointment without telling Doug. Maybe she'd known deep down what his reaction would be.

The test result was positive. She spent three days agonizing over what to do, still keeping the secret to herself. She finally told Doug one night in her room.

He'd gotten up from the bed and gone to the window, staring out at the campus for several long minutes before turning to her and saying, "There's only one thing to do. It's not too late."

She'd already thought about that, but it wasn't a solution she would even consider. "I can't do that."

"We don't have a choice," he said, his voice rising. "My parents would cut me off flat if they found out."

She'd asked him to leave then, needing to be by herself. He hadn't said the things she had hoped he would say. The decision tore at her for days. In the end, she decided that Doug was right. She would be only nineteen when the baby was born. How would she possibly finish school? What would her parents say? She could only imagine their disappointment.

She got as far as the examining-room table before the reality of what she was about to do hit her. Although she hadn't yet felt the baby's physical presence, something changed within her the moment she'd learned of its existence. How could she do away with something so precious and fragile? Her reasons suddenly felt selfish and shallow.

Doug sat outside in the waiting room when she ran from the office. He sprinted after her, calling out for her to wait. She stopped at the corner of the street, her breath coming fast and uneven.

"What happened?" he asked, taking her by the shoulders.

"I won't do it."

"You can't back out now," he said, looking incredulous.

"I was only thinking about myself. About my life. Not about the baby. Lots of people have children and still get through school."

Doug stepped back, his expression closed. "We agreed."

"No. I won't do it, Doug. I'm sorry. I just can't."

They drove to the dorm in silence. He dropped her off without saying goodbye. She didn't hear from him for the rest of the week. When she went to her room on Friday after class, a note from him hung on the door.

From then on, she'd been on her own. Looking back, she supposed she'd thought he would come around, own up to his share of the responsibility. But he hadn't. She'd eventually realized that it would have been a mistake for the two of them to try to make a go of it for the baby's sake. After the initial shock, her parents had been anxious to help. She got an apartment off campus, determined to be independent. She ran into Doug a few times during her pregnancy. Their meetings were awkward, and he clearly couldn't wait to get away. Colby wondered what she'd ever seen in him. She hoped he would be very happy with his Porsche and his trust fund.

The following year, he transferred to another college, closer to Philadelphia, without once trying to see Lena. For the first few years of her daughter's life, Colby agonized over what to tell her about her father when she asked, as she inevitably would. And she had. Colby never intended to lie to her, but when Lena took her initial answers of "Your daddy went away" to mean he had gone to heaven, she never corrected that impression. Somehow, it seemed a lot more palatable than the truth.

She hoped Lena would never have to know.

Glancing at the watch she'd left on the side of the tub, Colby got out and dried off. She'd lingered in the bath too long, and now she would have to rush to be on time. But then, that was what she got for dwelling on things better left in the past.

9

After fixing Lena a hurried dinner and leaving it on the kitchen table, Colby went to the bottom of the stairs and called her name.

No answer. The bass from her stereo beat a tattoo on the floor beneath Colby's feet. She ran up the steps and stopped in her daughter's doorway. "Lena, honey, I'm late. Are you sure you have a ride to the game?"

Lena leaned over and turned down the volume. "Yeah. Millie Mitchell's mom is taking us," she said in the same sullen tone that had been there for the past month.

"You'll be home by eleven-thirty?"

Lena nodded without raising her gaze from the magazine in front of her.

Lena spent more time at her friend's house than she did at home. Trying to ignore her own bruised feelings, Colby said, "I'll see you tonight, then."

A few minutes later, she backed out of the driveway and headed toward Phoebe's place, some five miles outside of town. How long would this go on? She'd asked Lena over and over what was wrong, only to be given a hostile-sounding, "Nothing, Mom."

Colby missed the child she loved. She felt as though someone had stolen her best friend. And she didn't know how to get her back.

At the Walkers' turnoff, she put on her blinker and swung onto the road that led to their farm. She loved it out here. Most of Jefferson County lay in a bowl of land beneath a ring of the Blue Ridge Mountains. Now, just before sunset, they really did look blue. Colby eventually planned to buy a place outside of town with plenty of land. She'd been interested in Oak Hill, the farm that bordered the Walkers' place, for years. When she'd learned that it had been sold a few weeks ago, she'd been more than a little disappointed.

Pulling up in front of the house, Colby got out and knocked at the door. A few seconds later, Phoebe opened it and greeted her with a hug.

"You're here," she said. "And on time too. No last-minute calls to make?"

"I even left my calf-birthing clothes in the trunk."

"So you do own a dress." Phoebe gave her a long look and a whistle. "Is that new?"

"No."

"That shade of blue has always been your color. You look great."

"So do you," Colby said, nodding at Phoebe's coral-colored blouse and chunky gold jewelry. Layered around the bottom, her dark hair always seemed to be moving, and her dark brown eyes rarely hid her thoughts.

"Thanks," she said. "Come on into the kitchen and help me check on things."

"Where's Frank?"

"He's getting ready. He'll be down in a few minutes."

"And where's Mr. Right?"

Phoebe shot her a look of innocent surprise. "What makes you think there is one?"

"I'm fairly certain there isn't. But when was the last time you invited me to dinner without trying to convince me otherwise?"

"You're entirely too cynical for your age, Colby Williams."

"Hey, I earned my stripes in the trenches."

"So you've been out with a few duds. Big deal."

"A few?" Colby folded her arms across her chest and rolled her eyes. "Let's run through some of your more memorable setups. Harvey Matthison, who brought his mother on our first date. And then Tip LaPrade, who slipped a prenuptial agreement under my dessert plate while I went to the ladies' room. Oh yes, there was Dr. Payne, who washed his hands nineteen times between the time he picked me up and dropped me off—"

"All right, all right," Phoebe grumbled. "Several. But that doesn't mean they're all like that."

"I wish you would just accept the fact that I'm not

going to kiss a thousand toads on the minute chance that I might eventually find a prince."

"If you call this one a toad, I will officially resign from all matchmaking duties."

"Is that a promise?" Colby asked hopefully.

"Only if you give him a real chance. The problem is, you're looking for faults from the first moment you meet a man."

"I hate to disillusion you, but when they're as obvious as the San Andreas, they're not that hard to spot."

The doorbell sounded from the hallway. Colby heard Frank's voice and then another male voice that sounded somehow familiar.

"Oh good, he's here," Phoebe said, wiping her hands on a kitchen towel.

Biting back a resigned sigh, Colby leaned against the counter and yearned for the evening to be over.

Frank appeared in the doorway. "Hello, ladies," he said, stepping aside while the man behind him moved into the kitchen. Surprise and a tidal wave of embarrassment washed over Colby. Ian McKinley. What was he doing here? She glanced at Phoebe who looked extraordinarily pleased with herself.

"Colby?"

She realized that Frank was speaking to her. "I—yes. I'm sorry," she said.

"This is our new neighbor, Ian McKinley. Ian, this is Colby Williams, our local veterinarian and Phoebe's best friend."

"Former best friend," Colby said in a voice only Phoebe could hear.

The new neighbor moved across the floor and shook Colby's hand. He smiled down at her, something in his expression indicating that he had been caught off guard by this as much as she had. "Hello again, Dr. Williams. We've already met," he said to Phoebe and Frank. "She fixed up my son's dog for me."

"Please, call me Colby."

"Only if you call me Ian," he said.

"Ian it is. How is Smidge?" she asked, forcing her gaze to remain level with his and trying not to look as thrown by this as she felt.

"Playing it up for all it's worth."

She smiled despite her discomfort. "Good. She deserves a little extra pampering."

"How about a drink?" Frank suggested. "We can go into the den."

A few minutes later, Colby sat in a chair with a glass of red wine in her hand, plotting an appropriate payback for Phoebe. Nothing horrible enough came to mind. Of all people for her friend to have fixed her up with. To think she'd met him earlier today and hadn't known—

Of course, he probably thought she *had* known. This was getting more amusing by the moment.

"Isn't that right, Colby?" Phoebe asked.

"I'm sorry?" Colby had no idea where the conversation had gone.

"I was just telling Ian that you'd been interested in Oak Hill for years."

"Oh. So you're the one who bought it? It's a beautiful farm, Ian."

"It is. Needs some work, but I hope to get it in shape. Virginia's a beautiful state. It's a full one-eighty from New York City."

"I'm sure. What are you planning to do with Oak Hill?"

"Right now my main objective is to get the place in presentable condition. I'm afraid I don't know very much about farming."

"Oh, that's too bad," she said, thinking it an injustice for some New York City tycoon who wouldn't know an alfalfa field from a turnip patch to get the farm she'd dreamed about buying herself someday.

"I need to check on dinner," Phoebe said, getting up and heading for the kitchen. "You stay put and enjoy your wine, Colby. I'll be right back."

Colby got up from her chair and forced a smile at the two men. "I'll go give her a hand. She's far too thoughtful to ask for help."

In the kitchen, Colby thumped her glass down on the counter. "Phoebe, this may be grounds for breaking up."

Phoebe looked up from the vegetable lasagna she was removing from the oven. "Don't tell me he's not drop-dead gorgeous."

"I was too embarrassed to notice."

"Why on earth are you embarrassed?"

"Because!" she said, throwing up her hands in

exasperation. "He was in my office with his dog earlier this week. He probably thinks I knew about this then."

Phoebe lit up with delight. "Haven't you always said good guys love their dogs? What more perfect way for you two to meet."

"I don't want to meet anyone!"

"Well, I know you think you don't. . . ."

"This is the last time, Phoebe Walker! I'm not ever coming to your house for dinner again unless you sign a legally binding statement that there will be no potential husbands sitting on the other side of the table."

Phoebe placed the lasagna on the stovetop with a frustrated look on her face. "Once the single women in this county get wind of this man, they'll be knocking the door down. I was just trying to get you in the starting gate a little ahead of the others."

"Do I look that desperate?" Colby said, thinking of Cindy Stoneway's flat tire.

"No," Phoebe protested. "I hate to see you alone."

"I'm not alone. I have my daughter."

"That's not the same."

Frank appeared in the doorway, interrupting them. "Dinner ready?"

"We were just about to bring the food out," Phoebe said with a bright smile.

Colby grabbed a couple of bowls and followed Frank out of the kitchen, feeling every bit like an old racehorse.

10

Colby ended up seated beside Ian at dinner, with Phoebe and Frank directly across from them. Once they all filled their plates, Phoebe dimmed the chandelier above the dining room table. Although the ambience hinted a little too strongly at romance, Colby was grateful that she didn't have to look directly at Ian for the entire night.

By this point, she accepted the humor in the situation. It was kind of funny that she'd met the man on Monday without any idea that he would be the main ingredient in Phoebe's matchmaker soup.

Their seats were close enough that they kept bumping shoulders. Every time his jacket sleeve brushed her bare arm, she felt as though she'd encountered a force field of electricity. She ended up sitting poker straight in her chair, keeping her elbows tucked tightly at her side.

Phoebe smiled at her every now and then, imploring her with her eyes to loosen up.

If it had been anyone else beside her, maybe she would have after a few sips of wine. But there had been something about meeting Ian McKinley the first time that stayed with her, brought up thoughts of Doug and the past. Handsome in the same too-good-to-be-true way, he drove an expensive car and obviously had enough money to buy the farm she hoped eventually to buy. He simply wasn't her type. Why didn't Phoebe realize that?

To his credit, he made every attempt to make the meal as painless as possible, asking about her practice, mentioning that Mabel Atkins told him she was the first female vet the town ever had.

"From kindergarten on," Phoebe chimed in, "Colby had the career aspirations. I never understood what was so wrong with Betty Crocker."

They all laughed.

"Frank told me that you're the one who keeps this place running while he practices law. With two children, I would think that takes quite a bit of effort," Ian said graciously.

"Well, I don't have much time for bonbons," Phoebe admitted, obviously pleased by the compliment.

"How do you know Mabel?" Colby asked Ian, taking a sip of her wine.

"She came to my rescue when I mistakenly thought I could do my own housekeeping. Luke and I were nearly drowning in laundry when she agreed to take over."

Colby smiled, doubting that a man like him would be able to locate the on button of a washing machine, much less wash his own clothes. "You're in good hands with Mabel."

"I've already gained five pounds since we moved here," he said, patting his stomach. "She claims the two of us need fattening up. I'm trying to outsmart her by adding a couple miles to my run every day, but I think she's on to me."

"Mabel's known for her fried chicken at church dinners, so you're right. You are in trouble," Colby said.

Again, they all laughed, and Colby found herself reluctantly wanting to know more about him. "Are you a big runner?"

"I try to do six miles a day."

"You must be in good shape," she said.

"Not sure I could run six yards right now," Frank said with a chagrined smile.

"I'm not that fast," Ian said modestly. "But I enjoy it. I started running as a stress reliever during the day. It was a good way to clear my head."

"What kind of work do you do?" Colby asked.

"I'm a stockbroker for a company called CCI in Manhattan."

Phoebe looked impressed. "From Wall Street to Keeling Creek. That's quite a leap. So how did you end up—"

Colby's beeper went off, interrupting Phoebe's question.

"Oops. Sorry about that. I'd better call and see

what's up." Colby stood up. Ian stood too. She headed for the kitchen phone, telling herself that just because a man had the good manners to stand when a woman left the room in an age when most men had forgotten how didn't mean he was without character flaws.

She called her answering service, then came back into the dining room and said, "There's a problem with one of the cows at Pasley's Dairy. I have to go."

"What!" Phoebe looked positively stricken by the assertion.

"I'm sorry to leave so early," Colby said. "It was nice to see you again, Ian. Say hello to Smidge and Mabel for me."

"I'll do that," he said.

"If you don't mind, I'll change clothes in the bath off your garage, Phoebe."

"Sure," Phoebe said, clearly miffed.

"Thanks for the dinner." Colby let herself out the front door, feeling strangely regretful that she had to go.

11

The horrible noise coming from the driveway told Ian that as glad as she must have been to leave, Dr. Colby Williams wasn't going anywhere anytime soon. They'd heard her engine grind for the third time when he stood up from the table and said, "I'll go see if I can give her a hand."

Frank started to get up as well. "I'll go with—"

"That's all right, Frank," Phoebe said. "Ian probably knows all about cars. You can help me with the dishes."

Frank sat down, while Ian tried to appear oblivious to Phoebe's not-so-subtle matchmaking tactics.

It had been apparent to him from the moment he arrived tonight what was going on. When the Walkers called a few days ago and invited him for dinner, he'd accepted, thinking he should make an effort to get to know his neighbors. If he'd known what they had in mind, he'd have saved both Dr. Williams and himself the discomfort of the attempted fix-up. Once he'd arrived, he hadn't wanted to embarrass them or their friend by telling them that he was engaged. He knew Phoebe talked to Mabel earlier in the week about inviting him to dinner, and he had a feeling his not-so-innocent housekeeper conveniently neglected to mention that he had a fiancée.

He stepped out into the Indian summer night, the air warm and fresh smelling. He still hadn't tired of the simple pleasure to be found in breathing it in.

From the driveway came the sound of the engine grinding again. He crossed the driveway, and at the truck door, bent down and tapped on the window.

Colby's head shot up, sheer frustration etched on her face.

The window lowered with a slight squeak. "I know that was awkward, but was I that bad?" he said.

She sat back in her seat, failing in her attempt to look surprised by the question. "No. I just—" she began, then stopped, looking chagrined.

"Their intentions were good. They obviously think the world of you."

She shook her head. "What's that old saying? With friends like that, who needs enemies?"

He laughed then. She did too, and he found he liked the sound of it. The awkwardness hanging between them eased, and he realized how good laughter felt. He didn't laugh that often. "If you'll pop the hood, I'll take a look. I don't know much about engines, but it sounds like your starter's bad. Got a flashlight?"

She rummaged through the glove compartment, then handed him the light. She popped the latch, and he said, "Give it another try."

She did, and he spotted the problem. "Yeah, that's it. You're going to need a new one," he called out.

"Great," he heard her say. She got out of the truck and came around to the front.

He straightened and lowered the hood, pressing it closed. He noticed then that a pair of blue coveralls had replaced her dress. "I'll be glad to give you a ride."

"I can't ask that of you," she said, not quite meeting his eyes.

"I don't mind. Let me just go thank the Walkers. Be right back."

Ian went inside and explained what happened to Phoebe and Frank. Phoebe was anything but disappointed by his departure. She looked so happy that he wondered if she'd ruined the starter herself. He said good night and headed back outside, where the other victim of Phoebe's matchmaking stood unloading some things from her truck.

"Would you like to put that stuff in the trunk?"

"Yes, please." He stuck the key in the lock and opened it. She dropped her bag inside. He started to close it just as she reached in again. He grabbed her arm and jerked it back, barely in time to prevent the lid from slamming on it.

They both stood in shock for a second or two while his hand still gripped her arm. She took a hasty step backwards. "Thanks. I forgot to put my keys in the bag."

"No problem. But I'd hate to be the person responsible for putting the town's only vet out of commission."

She smiled, rubbing her skin where his fingers had just been.

He opened her door, and she slid inside the car. To his surprise, he found himself noticing that she had a very nice shape beneath the faded coveralls. Wondering if it had been a mistake to offer his taxi services, he went around and got in on his side. "You'll have to tell me where to go."

"Take a right out of the driveway. It's about ten miles from here."

Ian backed up and headed away from the house. They'd just reached the main road when she said, "I'm really sorry for Phoebe's lack of tact."

"It's all right." From the sound of it, Phoebe Walker was in a lot of trouble with her friend. Strangely enough, he hadn't minded the evening, setup or not. The Walkers were nice people. "If it makes you feel any better, I won't be pestering you. I knew as soon as I saw your face tonight that you had nothing to do with it."

"I didn't mean to be rude," she said quickly. "Now I'm embarrassed."

"There's no reason to be," he said, glancing at her with another unexpected jolt of appreciation. She was undeniably pretty. He started to tell her about his engagement. The moment felt right, but the words somehow wouldn't come, and he couldn't say why. Except that he didn't remember ever meeting a woman quite like Colby Williams. And he was intrigued. "It was a nice dinner. And I'm glad to have the chance to get to know my neighbors better."

Silence lingered between them for a few moments, and then she said, "What made you move here from New York?"

"My son needed a change of pace. We'll just be here for his senior year," he said, not wanting to elaborate further. The last thing he wanted to do was put a black mark on the boy in the eyes of the community before he'd had a chance to prove himself.

"Oh," she said. "My daughter mentioned him. He's made quite an impression on the girls at Jefferson High."

Glad to hear that maybe things weren't as awful as Luke wanted him to believe, Ian said, "How old is your daughter?"

"Fifteen going on thirty."

Ian smiled.

"She's a sophomore, but young for her class. It seems like yesterday that she just learned how to walk and—" She stopped, her expression troubled.

Wondering if her relationship with her daughter might have problems of its own, he said, "It's a tough age. They grow up before we know it."

"Yes, they do," she said, sounding resigned. "I'm just not ready to admit it."

He drove for a few minutes, then flipped on his turn signal when she directed him to take the next left-hand turnoff. "Go on down to the barn. The lights should be on."

He stopped just outside the open door. A man in overalls and a red-checkered flannel shirt trotted out to greet them. "Hurry, doc. She's having a lot of trouble."

Colby got out of the car, grabbed her bag and ran after the man who had disappeared inside the barn. Ian sat there for a minute, thinking about her. He found her easy to talk to, intelligent. And apparently able to handle with grace and good humor what turned out to be an uncomfortable situation for both of them.

He'd nearly slammed her arm in the trunk. That would have topped the evening off nicely. He thought about those few moments when his fingers encircled her wrist. The contact shocked him every bit as much as it apparently had her. He recalled now that she had very small wrists and hands. She was petite, probably not more than five-three. But somehow he hadn't noticed it initially. Something about her exuded strength and self-sufficiency.

He got out of the Mercedes and made his way toward the barn. A single light hung above the door, making it hard to see where he stepped. Farm smells permeated the air, a combination of hay and manure and a fresh country breeze. Cows mooed in the fields. A stretch of mud lay between the gravel-covered driveway and the entrance to the barn. With no way to go around it, he waded through, his leather shoes squishing in the mire. He knew then how the city mouse must have felt visiting the country mouse.

Inside, he stopped outside the stall. A black-and-white cow lay stretched out on the straw-covered floor, straining heavily. Her eyes looked wild and pained. Sympathy for her plight stabbed through him.

Colby looked up at him, pulling supplies from her bag. "Ian, this is Harry Pasley. Harry, Ian McKinley. He's new in town. My truck broke down, so he gave me a ride out here."

"Nice to meet you," Harry said, his hands tucked inside bib overalls, his weathered face concerned.

"It's nice to meet you too," Ian said.

"Would you like a pair of coveralls to put on over those clothes?"

Ian looked down at his pants, the bottoms of which were now rimmed in mud. "Oh, no, that's all right. It'll come out in the wash."

Ian watched while Colby pulled on two plastic gloves that reached all the way to her shoulder.

The cow's straining ceased, and she lay still. "Is she okay?" he asked.

"She's taking a breather. Let's see what we have here," she said, reaching her right arm inside the cow. A few seconds passed before she said, "There's the tail. Definitely a breech, Harry."

Ian watched as a frown crossed her face. "Uh-oh. There's a nose," she said. "We've got a second one on board."

Just then, the cow began straining again. Colby went still. She looked up at him and said, "When she's working, I rest. When I'm working, she rests."

"Oh. I see."

"Have you ever seen a delivery?" she asked.

He'd never even been around a cow, and certainly not one in this condition. The closest he'd gotten was a city petting zoo, and that had been years ago, when Luke was five or six. "Ah, no, I haven't. Is there something I can do?"

"If she tries to get up," Harry said, "I might need your help getting her back down."

"Sure," Ian said, tempted to ask how they could possibly get what looked like an eight-hundred-pound cow to lie down if she decided to get up. But he didn't, not wanting to sound like any more of a greenhorn than he felt.

When the cow stopped straining again, Colby said, "Okay, my turn."

She wedged her left hand inside the cow and began to push forward. Without looking up, she said, "What I'll try to do is push this little guy up enough that I can straighten his hind legs out. In a normal birth he would have come out front hooves first."

Ian watched in amazement as she slowly pushed the calf forward. As the cow began to strain again, she stopped and held the position. It was a long, slow process. He couldn't take his eyes off the scene. He'd never witnessed anything like it in his life. Colby, up to her shoulders in work a lot of men wouldn't have the fortitude to do.

She approached the effort matter-of-factly, when she spoke, her voice low and soothing. He saw that she too sympathized with the cow's pain.

Her coveralls had been splattered with blood, and a strand of her hair clung to the side of her face. He subdued an unexpected urge to smooth it back for her.

After what seemed like forever, she said, "Okay. I've got the back hooves out. We're on the right track now."

Ian stood to the side of the cow, his arms folded across his chest, the drama of the situation making him tense. The process went on for a good while longer, with the cow pushing and Colby helping to pull the calf forward until it finally slid onto the straw in a heap.

"There you go," Colby said, smiling. "You were doing your best not to join us out here, weren't you?"

Harry picked up the calf and moved it close to its mother, placing it back on the straw. Wonder assaulted Ian. He thought about his own son's birth and how incredible it had been to hold the tiny body in his arms. He recalled the instantaneous love he'd felt for him, and his chest ached with the memory of it and a yearning for things to be right with Luke again.

"Let's get the other one," Colby said, reaching back inside the cow.

When the second calf emerged onto the straw with Colby's help, the same sense of wonder washed over him. This one was noticeably smaller, its eyes round and startled. Ian's heart contracted.

"Okay, girl. We're almost there," Colby said to the mother cow, looking up at Ian and adding, "I just need to make sure there's not a third."

"She could have another one?" he asked, incredulous.

"Oh, yes. I've had it happen."

Amazed, Ian hoped for the cow's sake that it didn't happen now.

A minute or so later, Colby said, "Looks like that's it." She sat back on her heels and patted the cow's side, her face alight with satisfaction and what looked like the same kind of relief he felt for the animal. "You're all finished."

Ian bent down and stroked the cow's head. He'd never really thought about it, but he would have imagined this sort of thing became routine for a veterinarian. But the look on Colby's face suggested it was just as gratifying to her now as it would have been the first time she'd helped with a delivery.

The second calf raised its head and let out a halfhearted bleat. Colby laughed. "Looks like she arrived with an appetite."

Harry Pasley bent over to give the cow a pat on the side. "You did good, girl. You too doc. But then you always do."

The cow weakly reached around to swipe the closest calf with her tongue. If the birth of the first one amazed Ian, the second seemed like a miracle.

"These three have some bonding to do." Colby wiped her damp forehead on her shoulder, then looked up at Ian and smiled. "Thanks for being so patient."

Ian didn't remember a smile ever affecting him quite the way hers did in that moment. He'd witnessed something incredibly special. He thought of the business he'd put his life into over the past seventeen years and couldn't remember one incident during that time that made him feel this way.

Crazy but true.

And he had no idea what to make of that.

12

Colby finished cleaning Tilly up and gave her a shot to fight off infection. "Let me know if they have any problems, Harry."

"I'll do that, doc. Thank you for coming out so late. I really appreciate it."

"No problem." She pulled a fresh pair of coveralls from her bag and said, "May I use your office to get into these?"

"Sure thing," Harry said.

Alone, Colby wondered what Ian thought of being here. It couldn't have been his cup of tea, but throughout the past few hours, she'd been surprised by the range of emotions she'd seen on his face: sympathy, interest, amazement. After she'd changed, she left the office and returned to the stall, where Harry still stood. "Good night," she said. "Call me if you need me."

"Night, Doc Williams," Harry said. "Thanks again."

Outside, Colby found Ian staring up at the night sky. "Sorry to keep you waiting," she said, coming up behind him and glancing at her watch. "It's after midnight. I didn't realize it was that late."

He turned around, his gaze finding hers. "I'm in no hurry. How did you do that?" he asked, pointing at the coveralls.

"I keep an extra pair in my bag. You don't want me riding in your car with the other ones on," she said.

"It wouldn't have mattered," he said, shrugging.

"Are you sure you don't mind taking me home? I could ask Harry—"

"Of course not," Ian said. "Come on, get in. You're probably tired after all that work."

Giving in, she got inside the car and gave him directions to her house.

He put the car in reverse and backed up, cutting the wheel to the right.

"I wouldn't turn around in the driveway if I were—" Before she could finish, the two back tires dropped off the gravel. "Uh-oh. I should have mentioned the mud back there. You can't see it in the dark."

"Shouldn't be any problem." He pushed the gas. The back wheels made a whirr-hissing sound, spinning uselessly.

"I'll go get Harry," Colby offered. "He'll give us a pull with his tractor."

"That's okay," Ian said, opening the car door.

"Watch out!" she warned just as he slid out and mired up to his shins in mud.

Silhouetted in the light shining from the car's interior, he looked at the ground where his two feet were currently held prisoner. He pulled one free, then the other. They made a loud, sucking noise.

Laughter bubbled up in Colby's throat. She clapped her hand over her mouth to stop it, but failed miserably.

Ian ducked his head back inside, chagrined. "Guess I should have taken Mr. Pasley up on those coveralls, huh?"

She did her best to keep a straight face, but the tears leaking from the corners of her eyes gave her away.

"Can you slip across and get behind the wheel? I don't recommend getting out."

"Sure." Colby's cheeks hurt with the effort of trying not to laugh.

He made his way to the back of the car, mud slurping at his shoes with each step. "I'll let you know when I start to push," he called out. "Give it the gas when I say go."

"Okay."

She adjusted the seat so her feet reached the pedals. A few seconds later, he said, "All right. Hit it."

She pushed the pedal. The car groaned and protested, the back tires whirring again.

She stopped, and he called out, "One more time."

They repeated the process, only this time the tires spun once, then the car shot out of the mud like a launched rocket.

Back on the gravel, Colby parked and got out.

Harry came out. "What happened?"

"We got stuck," she said.

"I'd have pulled you out."

"It only took two pushes," she began, and then stopped when Ian stepped back into the light shining from the barn.

She stared at him in disbelief. "Oh, no!"

"It kind of splattered," he said, wiping a hand across the side of his mud-covered face.

Harry chuckled. "I'll say."

Colby couldn't hold back her laughter any longer. The sophisticated New Yorker beside whom she'd sat at dinner earlier that evening now stood covered in mud, head to toe. "I'm sorry," she said, trying to stop. "It's not funny. Really. It isn't."

"No, actually, it kind of is," he said, his smile broader now.

"How about those coveralls?" Harry offered. "I've got a hose inside if you'd like to rinse off."

"I think I'll take you up on them this time," Ian said, disappearing inside the barn with a grinning Harry.

Colby waited outside, drying her eyes with the back of her hand. At least the man had a sense of humor. She thought about Doug and the comparisons she had made between the two. When she and Doug started dating, she brought him home one weekend to meet her parents. She'd taken him out to the Bowers farm, where she'd worked part-time in high school, doing odd jobs. She tried to teach Doug how to milk one of the cows, and when he'd been less than gentle at the task, the cow planted a hind hoof beneath his chin. From then on, Doug did a poor job of hiding his eagerness to leave Keeling Creek. She'd often thought that was the point at which she should have seen they had no future. The Doug she had known would not have laughed about what happened here tonight.

Harry and Ian reappeared. Ian wore a pair of old blue coveralls that would have sold *Today's Farmer* a record number of copies had he been wearing them on one of their covers.

He had apparently taken Harry up on the use of his hose. His hair was wet, the mud no longer evident on his face and hands.

"Sure you trust me to drive you home?" he asked with a sheepish grin.

"Of course," she said.

Shaking his head, Harry waved good night and went back inside.

Ian threw his discarded clothes in the trunk, and they both got into the car. Their gazes caught and held for a second before they started laughing again.

When she finally stopped, Colby wiped her eyes and said, "I'm really sorry about all this."

"Hey, it's not your fault. I'm the one who backed into the mud and then insisted on playing Superman."

She chuckled again. "Yeah, but I should have warned you."

"I'm a little bit like Smidge. I might have to bumble my way through a few mishaps before I get the hang of country life."

"That could have happened to anyone."

"Right," he said, looking skeptical. "Thanks for trying to save my pride, but I already left it in tatters back there in the barnyard."

Colby smiled. "You've been a good sport tonight."

"You're the one who did all the work," he said as they headed down the driveway. "That was pretty amazing in there. Are twins uncommon?"

"Not really. With the hormones they're giving the cows these days, the odds are increased. Unfortunately, the little girl will probably be sterile. She won't be of much use to Harry."

Ian frowned. "Meaning?"

"He'll sell her to the stockyard."

"Oh. That's too bad," he said, sounding more than a little bothered by the thought.

"That's one part of my job I don't think I'll ever get used to. Farming is a business. Feed costs money."

He stayed quiet for a moment and then said, "You were great in there."

The offhand compliment pleased her. "Thanks. So, you'd never seen anything like that?"

He shot her a sideways smile. "City born and bred. We don't have too many cows in Manhattan."

"How did you end up in Keeling Creek?"

"I had a realtor looking in this part of the state."

"It's a long way from New York. In more ways than one."

"I think I pretty much found that out tonight."

Colby turned her gaze back to the road. It had been a strange night, yet she felt more relaxed than she had in ages. She couldn't remember the last time she laughed so much. Even if it had been at Ian's expense, she had the impression he really hadn't minded. Although she wouldn't admit it to Phoebe in a million years, she actually enjoyed his company.

Ian swung the vehicle into her driveway, braking to a stop just short of the light from the porch. Colby reached into the back seat for her bag, then said, "Well, thank you for the ride. And for waiting around for me. I'm really sorry about the mud."

"No problem. I actually learned a few things tonight. If you need any help getting your truck—"

"Oh, no. Thanks. I'll get a tow truck out there tomorrow. You've already gone way beyond the call of duty for someone duped by the local matchmakers."

Ian smiled, and Colby noticed that he had a memorable one. The kind that reaches the eyes and transforms them.

They studied each other for a second too long, saying nothing in a moment of unexpected awareness. Colby looked away first, climbing out of the car and ducking back to say, "Well, thanks again. Good night."

"Good night," he said, then waved and drove away.

Colby watched his taillights disappear down the street, surprised to find herself sorry that the evening had ended.

13

Ian had been on the phone with Curtis Morgan for a full two hours on Saturday morning when the other man finally said, "Well, that should bring you up to date on the past few days, anyway."

"Thanks, Curtis. Sounds like things are pretty crazy around there."

"Are they ever any other way?" Curtis asked, a smile in his voice. "I still can't believe you walked away from all this. Aren't you missing this place?"

"It's only until the end of the school year," Ian said, strangely unable to say that he missed it. So far, he didn't at all. But then he'd been overdue for a vacation. He'd be missing it before long.

"A year must seem like forever in a place like that. Not a whole lot going on, I'll bet. Not when you're used to the life you led here."

"It's different, that's for sure."

"You deserve a father-of-the-year award for what you're doing."

Ian disagreed with his friend. Judging from his success with Luke so far, that was the last thing he would qualify for. The two of them talked on for a while longer before Ian hung up.

Even though he'd taken official leave, he felt obligated to keep himself apprised of what was going on. He turned his attention to the computer screen, checking stock prices.

He glanced out the window to the side of his desk. The huge old maple tree had begun to absorb the tint of fall. The view here won hands down. A lot more peaceful. For now, at least, he would let himself enjoy that. Soon enough, he'd be back in the city where the trees were rare and the noise omnipresent.

He glanced at his watch as the sun stretched full tilt across the room. Nearly noon. Rachel would arrive any minute. The trip had been planned since before he'd moved here, but he almost wished she weren't coming now. Why was that when he hadn't seen her in three weeks?

Ian turned his chair toward the window again and thought about Colby Williams. No doubt she'd considered him a first-class buffoon last night. He couldn't have looked any more convincing as an outsider had he been trying for an Academy Award.

After he'd dropped her off, he'd driven home, wondering why he never got around to telling her about his engagement. Some part of him had been intrigued by her. And he had enjoyed himself more than he had in a long time.

The doorbell rang, interrupting his thoughts. Ian left his study and went out into the front hall. Rachel stood on the porch, dressed in black pants and a red silk blouse, looking as out of place in the countryside as a polar bear in Arizona.

"Ian." She stepped forward and put her arms around his neck. "I've missed you."

She pressed her lips against his and kissed him with intent. He placed his hands on her waist and pulled her to him, seeking a connection that would put him back on track. Her perfume smelled familiar, as did the feel of her, and he told himself he had done the right thing in asking her to marry him. Rachel was part of his real life, the life he'd created here just temporary. Rachel represented all the things he would go back to when the year ended. And go back, he would.

14

Colby spent Saturday morning at the clinic. Things were busy, and she didn't see her last patient until after two o'clock that afternoon. She'd called Granger's Tow Service and asked them to pick up her truck and take it to the shop to have the starter repaired. They'd done so, and someone dropped it back off shortly after noon.

On Sunday, she and Lena went to church, a weekly ritual. Growing up, Colby had been part of the youth group of Keeling Creek First Baptist, going on retreats to other churches and summer bus trips to Busch Gardens in Williamsburg. Now, Lena did those same things in the kind of small, close-knit church where everyone knew everyone else, and a sense of family existed among the members.

They sat in the second row with Colby's parents, both of whom were actively involved in the church's social life, organizing such events as summer Bible school and monthly breakfasts in the fellowship hall where the men cooked for the women. They were good people with strong roots in the community, well-liked and respected. The only rough points in her relationship with them had come when she'd tried to get through school with Lena. They wanted to help, and, out of guilt or pride, she had been determined to do as much as she could on her own. They had let her flounder even though, as a parent herself, she knew it hurt them to do so.

After the services, she lingered at the door with her mother while her father and Lena chatted with the preacher. The sight of her purple-haired daughter nestled in the crook of her grandfather's arm warmed Colby inside, and at the same time, brought forth a surge of regret for the closeness with Lena she seemed to have lost.

"Things aren't any better with you two, I take it?" Emma Williams asked, placing a sympathetic hand on Colby's arm.

She turned her gaze back to her mother. "I've tried to talk to her, but she won't open up. I keep telling myself it will blow over."

"More than likely it will. You had a rebellious streak of your own, you know," Emma said with a smile.

"I remember," Colby confessed. "I don't think it ever really affected my relationship with you or Daddy."

"No. Thankfully, it didn't," she admitted. "But all children are different."

Colby shook her head. "I'm beginning to wonder if I'm doing something wrong, if maybe I'm just not a very good mom."

"Now you stop that, dear," her mother admonished her. "You're a wonderful mom. You know how proud your father and I are of you for the way you've handled things."

"Thank you, Mama," Colby said, somehow needing to hear the words today.

She squeezed Colby's shoulder. "You had to become responsible at a very young age," she said, her voice softening. "And you didn't take the easy way out. You made a life for yourself and that child. I know there were times when you must have wondered what it would be like not to have all that responsibility. To be free to do as you wanted."

Colby gave her mother a grateful smile. "You know I'd never have done it without you and Dad."

"Oh, yes, you would have. I know you well enough to be sure of that," she said with pride in her voice. "Maybe Lena could spend the afternoon with us. You go be good to yourself."

Colby sent a glance at her daughter, laughing now at something the pastor had said. "I'm sure she'd like that."

Her father and Lena waved goodbye to the preacher and joined them across the lawn. "What do you say I treat my three favorite ladies at Libbie's for lunch?" her father said.

Lena's relaxed demeanor disappeared behind the sullen facade she'd been wearing for the past few weeks. As much as Colby would have liked to go, it would be good for Lena to spend some time alone with her grandparents. "You three go on. I've got some things to do at home, Daddy."

"You sure, honey?"

She nodded and smiled her most convincing smile.

"All right, then. We'll bring the punkin' home later," he said, ruffling Lena's hair.

"We'll have her there by dinner," her mother promised.

"Have a good time, honey." Colby waved as the three of them headed to her parents' car. But Lena didn't answer. She merely tucked herself closer in the curve of her grandfather's arm while Colby watched them drive away, a dull ache deep inside her.

BACK AT THE HOUSE, Colby straightened up, then put in a load of laundry. She rarely went to the clinic on Sunday unless there were dogs or cats in the hospital, since the part-time help came in to feed the animals on the weekend.

After turning on the washing machine, she made her way into the kitchen and stared at the items lining the pantry shelves. Macaroni. Tomato soup. Black olives. Fat-free cookies.

Critter sidled against the back of her legs, letting out a soft meow.

Colby looked down at her and sighed. "I know. Kind of lonely around here, isn't it?"

Critter answered with another meow.

She reached down and picked her up, tucking the

kitty under her chin. The cat purred like a lawn mower. Petey and Lulu lay under the kitchen table, looking across at her with sleepy eyes. "I guess in a few years, it'll be just the four of us, huh?"

Petey groaned in protest and rolled over on his back, his paws in the air.

"I know how you feel." She considered her own question for a moment. In the past, she hadn't allowed herself to dwell on what things would be like after Lena grew up and left home. She'd meant it when she'd told Phoebe that she was happy with the way things were. She had a full life. She didn't need a man to make it complete.

But would the house always be this quiet once Lena moved away?

She thought about Ian McKinley and wondered if he felt the same way about his son leaving home. But then, a man like that probably had enough female companionship to ensure that he never got lonely.

She was being silly. Lena wouldn't be going to college for another two years. A very long time away.

The phone rang, mercifully diverting Colby's thoughts. She picked up the receiver with her free hand and managed a hello as the cat swatted it with her paw.

"I want all the details. Every single one," Phoebe demanded, not bothering with a greeting.

"You're just now getting around to it?" Colby asked in mock surprise.

"Frank's mother's been here. I've barely had time to go to the bathroom! Well?"

"Well, nothing. If I were smart, I'd disown you as a friend."

"You're not still mad at me, are you?" Phoebe cajoled.

"I should be."

"I'll admit that, but can't you just give me the down-low anyway?"

"You're impossible." Colby never stayed upset at Phoebe for long. Not even in the fifth grade, when she told Ricky Peters that Colby stuffed her bra. "Besides, he's only going to be here for a year. You forgot to figure that into your perfect-for-Colby equation."

"A year!" Phoebe said, disbelieving. "Maybe you could change his mind," she added, rallying. "So, what happened after you left here?"

"He watched me deliver twin calves and then took me home," she said, leaving out the part about the mud bath. Even now, the thought of it made her smile.

"That's all?" Phoebe asked, her disappointment evident.

"That's all," she said, unwilling to give her friend more bait than that.

"You've been out of commission for too long—" Phoebe broke off and shouted her son's name. "Oh, shoot, Colby. I'll have to call you back. Jacob's hanging by his knees on top of the swing set. Gotta run."

Colby hung up, glad to be spared Phoebe's inquisition. Throughout the church service that morning, her thoughts kept returning to Friday night.

Despite still being miffed by Phoebe's meddling, she had to admit the night had been full of surprises. Ian had certainly been more than gracious about the whole thing, considering that he'd been set up and all but forced into driving her out to Pasley's when her truck broke down. On top of that, he'd ended up ruining what must been some very expensive clothes. She could bake him a pie as a thank-you. She enjoyed baking when she had the time, derived a certain pleasure in creating something from scratch. Over the years, she'd gotten pretty good at it.

Imagining the gleeful look on Phoebe's face if she found out, she almost nixed the idea. But deciding she would go crazy without occupying her mind and hands with something, she went to the pantry and began pulling flour and sugar from the shelves. From the back porch, she retrieved some of the Red Delicious apples she'd bought yesterday afternoon, and, for the next hour, she got busy putting together two homemade pies. While they baked, she sat at the table and leafed through the newspaper, asking herself what was wrong with doing a little something for someone who'd done her a favor. Didn't good neighbors do that?

15

Colby took the left-hand turnoff onto the road that led to Oak Hill. The driveway stretched ahead for a mile or more, lined with enormous oak trees, most of which were nearly a hundred years old.

Oak Hill had always been one of her favorite places. Once one of Virginia's most prosperous farms—tobacco and wheat its mainstays—it became a well-known horse farm in the mid-1950s. In the past twenty years, the place went downhill, since the house sat empty for so long. She could hardly resent Ian for beating her to it, but nevertheless, she wished he hadn't.

She stopped in the circular driveway behind a car with New York license plates. He had company. Maybe she should forget delivering the pie. She didn't want to interrupt. But it would be silly not to leave it now that she was already here. She and Lena wouldn't be able to eat two pies, even if they were Lena's favorite.

She knocked, then stepped back, holding the dish in front of her.

The large oak door opened, and a tall, very beautiful woman stood in the entryway. Dressed in navy pants and a white silk blouse that somehow managed to look elegant and casual all at the same time, she smiled, her expression expectant. "May I help you with something?"

Colby glanced down at the pie, suddenly too conscious of her own khakis and UVA sweatshirt "I just wanted to leave this for the McKinleys."

The woman stared at her for a moment, before smiling again and extending her right hand. "How nice. I'm Rachel Montgomery. Ian's fiancée."

"Oh!" Colby shifted the pie to her left hand, returning the woman's firm handshake, noticing that the proffered hand felt smooth and manicured against her own work-roughened skin and short, unpolished nails. She took another step back. "I'm Colby Williams."

"Ian says the people here are very nice. It seems he was right."

"My truck broke down the other night, and he helped me out. This is just a little thank-you. I hope you all enjoy it."

"Would you like to speak to Ian?" Rachel asked. "He's in the shower, but he should be out anytime."

Colby backed down the steps, raising a hand and wishing she could grab the darn pie and run without

Ian ever knowing she'd been here. "No. Really. That's all right. Nice to meet you, Miss Montgomery."

A mile or so down the road, Colby pulled over and glanced in the rearview mirror, her face flushed and hot with embarrassment. *Way to go, Williams.* Why had she ever given in to the impulse to do such a stupid thing?

She sat back in the seat, feeling more than a little foolish. It wasn't at all like her to have gone to Ian's home. She, the same woman who told Phoebe she wouldn't do the song and dance that came with the dating scene.

And yet, she'd baked the man a pie.

A pie, of all things! A pie she had ended up presenting to the man's fiancée.

Anger with Ian edged its way past her own embarrassment. He'd sat through dinner at Phoebe's and never bothered to say he was engaged. And what about the rest of the evening? He'd had more than ample opportunity to do so. But he hadn't.

And Phoebe. Her own best friend, who supposedly had her best interests at heart. Phoebe, who neglected to mention that one small but critical detail about Ian McKinley.

16

"I didn't know. I swear."

"How could you not have known?" Colby asked in disbelief.

"Mabel never mentioned it when I called her to ask if she thought he would like to come to dinner. I even told her that you would be there and that I wanted to introduce you two."

"Don't tell me she's in on this too!"

"She said she'd been hoping you two would get a chance to meet. How could I know he was engaged?" Phoebe wailed. "What was I supposed to do? Ask for a full personal history before inviting him to dinner?"

"Yes."

"Next time, I will."

"There won't be a next time."

They were sitting in the wooden swing attached to two old maples in Phoebe's backyard, the day Indian-summer warm. The shade surrounding them did little to cool the heat in Colby's cheeks.

"I can't believe he's engaged," Phoebe said, still looking shell-shocked.

"Believe it. I met her. What more proof do you want?"

"Well, he never said anything about—"

"No, he didn't. He probably thought it was some grand joke. And no doubt still laughing about it."

"Oh, Colby, I don't think so. He seems like a nice guy—"

"Then how do you explain his not bothering to mention having a fiancée?"

"I don't know."

Colby dropped her head back against the swing and stared up at the cloudless sky. "I can't believe I actually made him a pie. What is it about attractive men that turns normally intelligent women into noodle brains?"

"Now, Colby, that was a perfectly nice gesture. If I'd thought of it, I would have suggested it myself."

Colby sent Phoebe a look out of the corner of her eye. "And that's supposed to make it intelligent?"

"Legitimate. It makes it legitimate."

"Right. I'm giving you fair warning, Phoebs. No more setups. That's the last one. My life is complicated enough now."

Phoebe let out a long-suffering sigh and gave the swing a push. They swung in silence for a few minutes before she said, "Everybody has complications, Colby. Including me. I think Frank's having a midlife crisis."

Colby looked up, surprised. "He's not old enough to have a midlife crisis."

"How old do you have to be? I've known the man since I was fifteen. He's never had an ounce of interest in clothes. All of a sudden, he goes out and buys two new suits. *Armani* suits. Do you know how many mortgage payments you can make on two *Armani* suits?"

Colby had to admit it didn't sound like Frank. She'd known him almost as long as Phoebe, and he'd never shown a penchant for high fashion. "Maybe he's trying to impress you."

"Impress me? He came downstairs wearing one of the darn things Friday morning and was almost . . . I don't know, embarrassed, when I questioned him about it."

"I wouldn't make too much of it, Phoebe. It's probably just a phase."

Phoebe chewed her lower lip. "A phase is what teenagers go through. Adult men don't have phases."

"Says who?"

"Dr. Green. That lady psychologist who's on the radio every morning."

"You called her?" Colby asked, staring at her friend in disbelief.

"After Frank left Friday. I call her a lot," she said a little defensively. "She's very smart. She said there's always a reason for the things people do. A change in behavior means something is different."

"Oh, Phoebe, for heaven's sake. The man bought a couple of new suits. You'll let this woman convince you he's having an affair. Frank, of all people."

"Why not Frank, of all people?" Phoebe asked, sounding offended.

"Because you've been together since Adam and Eve. And besides that, he's nuts about you."

Phoebe slumped back in the swing. *"Used* to be nuts about me. He's been so distracted lately, we've done nothing but sleep in the same bed."

Getting the point, Colby said, "The two of you need to talk."

"I've tried. He thinks I'm being silly."

Colby didn't know what to say. For as long as she could remember, Phoebe had been the one with the rock-solid relationship. The thought that it might not be as stable as she'd assumed was unthinkable. But then, maybe lasting relationships really weren't possible for people of her generation.

Colby stopped the swing with her foot and got up, shoving her hands into her jeans pockets. "I'm going home, Phoebs. Go inside and seduce your husband. You probably just need some time alone together. Since the kids are at your mom's house, you have the perfect opportunity." She headed across the yard, waving over her shoulder.

"Hey, Colby."

She turned around just short of the truck. "Yeah?"

"He'll come along."

"Who?"

"The good guy you've been waiting for."

Colby rolled her eyes. "I'm not waiting for anyone."

"I'm still not convinced it isn't Ian McKinley," Phoebe said, ignoring her. "Engaged isn't married, after all."

Deceit was deceit, though, Colby told herself as she drove away.

It was really none of her business whether he was engaged or not. So why did she feel angry with him for not mentioning it? And why, beneath the anger, did she feel this ridiculous sense of hurt?

Maybe because she actually let her guard down for a little while Friday night. Something she didn't do very often.

Back on the main road, she told herself to forget about it. She certainly had better things to do with her time than stew over an unavailable guy who had trouble with the truth.

COLBY'S FATHER dropped Lena off just before six that night. Colby met them outside. Lena gave her grandfather a hug and then went inside the house without so much as a hello. Trying to keep the hurt from her expression, Colby said, "How about some dinner, Dad?"

"I should get home." His gaze followed Lena and then rested on Colby, his dismay evident. "Emma'll have dinner ready. Don't want to make her wait."

"She's a better cook, anyway."

Samuel put his arm around her shoulders, then pulled her close. "Don't be too hard on yourself over this thing with Lena."

An unexpected surge of emotion swelled in Colby's chest. "Oh, Dad, I wish I could just wave a magic wand and make everything like it used to be."

"That's both the beauty and the sorrow of life, honey. Nothing ever stays the same. But she'll come around with whatever's bothering her soon enough. Take my word for it."

Colby hugged her father, grateful for his steady reassurance. She wanted to believe him. More than anything, she wanted to believe him.

17

Upstairs, Lena turned on her stereo, putting on the heavy metal group she knew her mother liked least. She cranked the volume and flopped down on the bed, telling herself that she *did* like it. Staring up at the ceiling, she forced herself not to think about the hurt look on her mother's face when she'd ignored her. She didn't want to be so mean to her, but she just couldn't help it. It felt like some ugly person had gotten inside her, and she no longer had any control over herself.

Flipping over on her side, she reached in her nightstand drawer and lifted out the wrinkled envelope she'd found in the top of her mom's old closet at Grandma's house. The letter had been written on notebook paper, the kind with blue lines and read so many times that it had gone thin and lifeless.

Lena unfolded it and let her eyes scan the page, even though she'd long since memorized the words.

Dear Colby,
I wish I didn't have to say this, but things aren't working out. There are too many differences between us for it ever to last. As for the baby, the decision was yours. I can't be a part of it.

Doug

Unwanted tears stung Lena's eyes. She refolded the letter and carefully tucked it back inside the envelope. All these years, she'd believed her mother when she said her father died. She remembered asking her mom why they had the same last name as Grandma and Grandpa Williams. Her mom explained that she'd just decided to keep her own when she and Lena's father married. And after he had "gone away," as she always put it, she'd wanted them both to have the same surname. At the time, she'd been too young to question the story. Looking back on it, she remembered the guilty look on her mom's face and knew now that the lie had been behind it.

Lena's father never married her mother. Lena had been born out of wedlock. Given her mother's maiden name.

A knock sounded at the door, followed by her mom's voice. Lena shoved the envelope back in her nightstand drawer and sat up on the bed, clutching a pillow to her chest. "Yeah?"

The door opened. "I've got dinner ready," her

mother said, sticking her head around the corner. "Why don't you come on down?"

"I'm not hungry." Lena studied the bedspread, hearing the sullen note in her own voice. "I have homework to do."

"I made your favorite. Macaroni and cheese."

The desire to hurt, as she hurt, felt too strong to resist. She glanced up at her and said, "No, thanks."

"You're sure?"

Ignoring the look of surprise in her mother's eyes, Lena reached for the book on the nightstand and turned to the marked page. "Yeah, I'm sure."

After a second or two, her mother stepped out and closed the door behind her. Lena almost called her back but squashed the desire before the words were out.

She lay there for a few moments, regretting her actions, but then pushed away her remorse and let her thoughts wander to Luke McKinley instead.

She thought about him all the time now. The problem? He didn't know she existed.

She'd been trying to find a way to introduce herself to him since the first day of school. But what did a girl say to a guy like that? He was gorgeous. No, more than gorgeous. He had coal black hair and moody blue eyes that looked as if he'd seen things most of the kids here hadn't even thought of yet.

She'd had her chance one afternoon after school when she and Millie went to the Dairy Queen. Lena had just placed her order at the register when she turned around to find him standing behind her in line. At first, she completely blanked, but realizing this might be her only chance, she smiled and said, "Hi. I'm Lena Williams. You're new here, aren't you?"

"Yeah," he said, looking surprised. "I'm Luke McKinley."

"I know. I mean, someone mentioned your name."

He didn't say anything for several seconds. He just stared down at her with those incredible eyes of his while her cheeks caught fire, and she longed for enough sophistication to throw out something cute and flirty, but nothing came to mind. He finally said, "I'd better place my order."

She stepped back and lifted a hand. "Okay. See you around."

"Yeah. See you around."

Lena went back to her table, where Millie demanded all the details.

At home that night, Lena longed to talk to her mom about Luke. Ask her how to get him to notice her. She and her mom had been best friends for as long as she could remember. She'd always asked her advice on everything. But all that changed when she found the letter. Her mother had lied to her. Now that Lena knew that, how would she ever believe another word she said?

18

Monday morning turned out to be a busy one at the clinic. After things finally slowed down a bit, Colby told Stacey to go to lunch with Laura and Ruth-Ann. Cecil Maynard had just brought in his German Shepherd, Wally, for his yearly shots, but she'd manage that on her own.

"The old lady was supposed to bring him in during her lunch hour," Cecil said when Colby lifted the dog up on the table. "She had to work though, so I just brought him in myself."

Colby opened the cabinet beside her and took out the supplies she needed. She'd never considered herself a bra-burning feminist, but there were times when she understood why the whole movement got started. "Exactly how old is Myrna, Cecil?"

His eyebrows rose in surprise. "She's forty-something."

"I see her car at the Exercise Hut on Tuesdays and Thursdays. I'd say she's a pretty well-maintained forty-something."

"Reckon she is."

"Then why do you call her your 'old lady'?"

A few seconds of puzzled silence followed the question. "Heck, I don't know, doc. It's just a figure of speech. What difference does it make?"

"Let's put it this way, Cecil," Colby said, aware that some of her outrage for Myrna stemmed from her own recent experience with the lack of sensitivity on the part of the male gender. "She doesn't go to the Exercise Hut twice a week to keep herself looking good just so her husband can call her his old lady."

Another pause and then a chagrined, "I expect you're right."

"Hello."

Colby looked up to find Ian standing in the doorway of the examining room. The sight of him caught her by surprise. She struggled for a professional smile and said, "I'm with someone at the moment. If you'll have a seat in the waiting room, I'll be with you when I'm finished."

"Sure," he said, looking a little taken aback by her tone.

So much for tact today. First, she'd attacked Cecil on behalf of womankind, and now she was giving Ian the deep freeze. After giving Wally his shot, she put the dog back on the floor and said, "Stacey's at lunch, so we'll send you a bill."

"Sure thing, doc. I'll be sure and tell *Myrna* you said hello," he said with a grin.

She smiled and shook her head. "You do that."

Once Cecil left, Colby took a moment to gather her composure. Cool, calm, poised. That was the picture she would present. She didn't want to provide Ian with another reason to think she'd given a second thought to his surprise fiancée. Tucking her hair behind her ears, she stepped into the room and found Ian sitting on one of the benches with Don Juan stretched out beside him, the dog's head in his lap. He stood up and smiled at her. "Very diplomatic. I'm surprised Myrna didn't hit him over the head with the frying pan a long time ago."

Colby shrugged and met his gaze head-on. "I guess some men don't realize how their words or actions might be perceived by others."

Ian shoved his hands in the pockets of his jeans and looked more than uncomfortable. "Including me, right? Look, Colby, I should have said something about being engaged Friday night. I started to, but once I figured out what Phoebe and Frank had in mind, I didn't want to embarrass them or you. As it turns out, Mabel played a little part in all this. I threatened to hide her kitchen step stool if she ever did it again."

As hard as she tried not to, Colby smiled. He made it difficult to stay angry with him. After all, he'd been under no obligation to tell her anything about himself.

"I never meant to deceive you, Colby," he said.

"Everything about that night caught me off guard. I guess I was just enjoying myself and. . . ."

They stood for a moment looking at each other, and she found herself wishing he would finish the sentence.

But he didn't. "Well," he said, running a hand around the back of his neck. "I'd better be going. I just wanted to stop and thank you for the pie. It was all gone by last night. I couldn't keep Luke out of the refrigerator."

"You're welcome. The least I could do to repay you for carting me around. Not to mention getting your car stuck in the mud."

"That was my fault," he said, smiling suddenly. He stood there for a few moments, watching her, before saying, "Okay. I should go."

"Yeah. I've got things to do."

Still, neither of them moved. They just stared at each other until he finally backed away, then turned and pushed through the door. Colby heard him pull off and told herself that it made no difference that he semi-redeemed himself by apologizing as if he really meant it. The man was engaged. And even if he hadn't been, she wouldn't be fooled by some too-handsome, too well-off, out-of-towner who was nothing if not a surefire prescription for heartbreak.

19

On the way home, Ian stopped by Thurman's Hardware to pick up some paint. In the back, leafing through sample chips, he overheard a conversation with his name in it. He stretched his head around the corner and saw two older men in bib overalls standing by the cash register. He recognized them as the Nolen twins, Dillard and Willard. The other times he'd been in the store, he'd noticed them sitting on the wooden bench where locals gathered to talk. Willard had just reached into his pocket for a pack of tobacco when Dillard said, "It's a shame to see the place go to weeds like that. I'd hoped whoever bought it would get it back in shape."

"Yeah, that's some of the best farmland around," Willard agreed.

"That McKinley seems a nice enough fella, but I

doubt if he'd know the front end of a tractor from the back. City slicker if I ever saw one."

They both chuckled. Ian stayed put, feeling inadequate in ways he'd never imagined would bother him. He'd gone to college on scholarship and built a career that earned him more money than he would ever likely spend, and yet he felt like less than a man because two old geezers labeled him as the city boy he was.

When he got home, he put the paint inside the storage building behind the house and looked out at the farm. As much as he hated to admit it, the Nolen brothers were right. The weeds were taking over. And it was up to him to do something about it.

The tractor sat parked at the back of the barn, full of gas, the mowing blade attached. If he drove a car, he could certainly drive this thing. Not like it could be that hard. He'd show those two old-timers city slicker.

Luke was in school, and Mabel had taken the day to visit her brother two towns up the Interstate. Rachel had returned to New York. At least if he messed up, there would be no one here to witness it.

He found the ignition and turned the key. The tractor sputtered and lurched forward, coming dangerously close to rolling through the wall in front of him. He slammed his foot on the brake, realizing he'd forgotten to press in the clutch.

Honest-enough mistake. Might have happened to anyone.

He tried again. The old tractor labored to life, black

smoke billowing out the back. He fumbled with the gears until he hit reverse. The tractor torpedoed backward out of the barn at a speed that would have flattened anyone unlucky enough to be standing in its path. Ian sent a frantic glance over his shoulder to make sure it hadn't done exactly that.

Saying a quick prayer of thanks, he finagled the transmission into first with a grinding of metal against metal, then lurched toward the south pasture. He arrived there in a frenzy of jerks and starts that suggested the engine might be on its last leg. He stopped at the gate, got out and opened it, then rolled through, the sputtering tractor bouncing him around like a basketball at center court.

Inside the field, he worked with a few levers until he figured out how to raise and lower the mean-looking blade attached to the back. That took no time at all, and with a ridiculous sense of pride, he set off across the pasture, the tall grass falling in his wake.

Despite feeling as if he were in the middle of a *Green Acres* episode, he decided this wasn't too bad after all. No problem. Over the years, he'd grown so used to financial success that it simply became a part of what he did. As a reward, it had lost some of its gratification. But this, crazy as it sounded, made him feel as if he'd accomplished something. He considered driving into town just to roll past Thurman's Hardware and see the look of shock on the faces of Dillard and Willard Nolen.

He had too much time on his hands. Clearly. Either that or he was losing his mind.

He worked on for an hour or more, feeling something almost peaceful about jostling along on the old tractor with the warm September breeze tugging at the collar of his shirt. He rolled across a slope now, the tractor at what all at once seemed too steep an angle. He probably shouldn't go any higher. . . .

Suddenly, the machine tilted. For a moment, it held there, suspended, then tipped and teetered drunkenly. He tried to hold on, thinking it would right itself.

In the next instant, he went airborne, projecting himself as far from the machine as he could manage. He landed on his back with a crack that ripped the air from his lungs. The blade hung over him, swaying like a guillotine about to drop.

Ian rolled, tumbling down the hill, his head slamming against the ground. And before he figured out whether he'd outrun the blade or not, the blue sky above him went black.

20

He would have come back for them sooner or later.

Colby eyed the set of keys bouncing on her dashboard. She wouldn't have bothered to drop them off if she hadn't needed to deliver some medicine to the Carter farm anyway. When she'd gotten back from lunch, Stacey found them on the bench where Ian had been sitting next to Don Juan. Realizing they must have been for something other than his car, Colby told Stacey she would take care of them, not mentioning that she thought they were Ian's. That way there would be no probing questions.

She could have mailed them to him. Asked Stacey to run them by his house. Left them outside the clinic for him to pick up. But here she was. Delivering them in person when common sense told her she shouldn't be.

Pulling up to the house, she cut the engine and sat

for a moment. The front yard looked newly mown. The pasture gate hung open. She went to the back door of the house and knocked, but no answer. Ian's car sat in the driveway though.

She peered out across the yard, then toward the field behind the barn, hearing a noise she didn't recognize.

It sounded like an engine running. Faint, but a definite *chug, chug, chug.* A tractor engine.

She stepped down from the porch and called out, "Ian?"

Silence except for the still idling machine.

She ventured to the open gate. He wouldn't be out on the tractor. Would he? She'd walk out a bit and see.

She'd gone no more than fifty yards past the gate when she spotted the tractor sitting at a crazy angle on the hill. And then she saw Ian. She took off at a run for the ravine at the bottom of the incline.

He lay flat on his back, his face turned to one side. Her first thought? He was dead.

Her heart pounded against the wall of her chest, and sweat beaded across her forehead.

Dropping down beside him, she checked his pulse, relieved to find it steady.

"Ian?" She put her hand to his cheek and repeated his name several times.

His eyes opened finally, slowly, his pupils dilated and unfocused. "What happened?"

"You must have had an accident. Can you move? Where do you hurt?"

"I'm not sure." He tried to struggle up on one elbow,

then sank back onto the ground, one hand going to his neck. "Ouch. That answers that."

"Don't move," she said. "You might have a concussion. Wait here and I'll go call the rescue squad."

"No. Don't. No need for that."

"We won't know until we get you checked out. I'll be right back, okay?"

He nodded, wincing again as if the action made his head hurt.

"I'm going to turn off the tractor first," she said, heading up the hill at a run.

Part of the blade lay on the slope, as if it had been broken off. A few yards from the machine, she thought she noticed one tire roll back slightly. She kept her gaze on the tires. The right one slipped a notch. It was moving! She sent a frantic look over her left shoulder. Ian lay in the direct path of the now-rolling tractor.

She had no time to try to stop it. Without thinking, Colby sprinted toward Ian, reacting on pure adrenaline. A glance back told her the machine was gaining on her. She tackled him, and rolled, pulling him with her. Over and over they went. She groaned with each turn.

They came to a stop at the edge of the creek, Ian lying on top of her. Neither of them moved.

"Do you want to tell me what that was—" he began, then glanced up the hill and spotted the tractor, which now sat where he had just been lying, the engine stalled. He looked down at her, a stunned expression on his face.

Colby tried to find her voice, too aware of the muscular length of the man whose body pressed into hers.

She scooted out from under him as if someone had just set a match to the seat of her pants. She tried to sit up, moaned and sank back down on the grass, feeling as if the tractor had actually run over her.

Ian slumped beside her. One palm braced his forehead. "You just saved my life," he said in a shaken voice.

She slipped a hand inside her jacket, pulled out his keys. "Now I remember why I charge extra for house calls."

He took them from her and dropped them in his shirt pocket. Despite his pained expression, a hint of a smile played about his lips. "Are you all right?"

"A little flatter than a few minutes ago, but I've been meaning to do some ab work," she said.

He stared at her for several seconds, shaking his head. A half smile spread across his face. "Just send me your bill. I'll expect it to be a big one."

Colby studied the blue sky above them. They could joke about it now, but she didn't want to think what might have happened if she hadn't found him in time.

Ian sobered, too, and she wondered if he was also weighing the close call he'd just had.

"I can't believe I did that," he said finally.

"Accidents happen."

"But I endangered your life too."

"Oh, hey, the life of a veterinarian is a risky one."

That prompted another smile.

"What happened?" she asked.

"It just started tipping, and over it went. Serves me right. The only reason I got on the blasted thing was because I overheard Dillard and Willard Nolen talking about how unfortunate it was that Oak Hill had been bought by a city slicker who would never do anything with it."

Chagrin laced his voice, and she realized that what they'd said mattered to him. He cared what they thought. He'd gotten on that tractor in an attempt to prove them wrong. The realization touched her somehow, made him more human to her, vulnerable in a way that only increased his appeal. She glanced out at the field where rows of fallen hay now lay. Despite resenting the fact that he'd been the one to buy Oak Hill, she had to admit he seemed determined to give new life to the place. She admired him for that. "It looks like you were doing a fine job."

"There's no reason for you to be so kind. I make a lousy farmer, but thanks for what you just did. I don't know too many people who would have done that," he said.

"If I'd taken the time to think about it, I doubt I'd have done it myself."

"Yes, you would have," he said quietly. "You're not the type to stand around waiting for someone else to do things for you, are you?"

Colby knew his comment was a compliment, and yet something inside her wanted him to say something altogether different. What, though? That she was feminine and beautiful? That she made Rachel look like last year's prom queen? Right.

Maybe *she* was the one with the concussion.

She tried to get up, pushing off with her left hand, and letting out a pained yelp.

"What's wrong?" Ian asked, sitting up and looking a little gray himself.

She rotated her left wrist and barely suppressed another moan of pain. "I think I've sprained it."

Ian felt sick with guilt. He got to his feet, swaying with the willow tree just behind him. "Come on. I'm taking you to the emergency room."

Before she'd realized his intent, he bent over and scooped her off the ground, delaying her protest for a few seconds because of the absolutely satisfying fit of his arms. His chest felt exactly as it should have. Broad and firm. Masculine in a way that made her feel protected, something she would have sworn she couldn't care less about.

His arms felt just right. Tight and secure around her. The only thing wrong with the picture? He was about as steady on his feet as a seasick sailor. "Ian, this is ridiculous. Put me down. I sprained my wrist, not my leg."

"Can you walk?" he asked, sounding as if he hoped she would say yes.

"I'm fine. You're the one with the possible concussion."

When he'd lowered her to her feet, she said, "You wait here and I'll call an ambulance."

He shook his head. "We tried that once and almost turned into pancakes."

She smiled. "Are you sure you can make it?"

He nodded, and with one hand at her elbow, set off up the hill, his expression determined. She suspected that he felt much worse than he let on.

At the house, a short altercation ensued over who would get behind the wheel. Colby came out the winner since she could manage to keep them on the road with one wrist incapacitated, Ian's ability to stay upright still in question.

She got them to the hospital's emergency room door without incident. She knew most of the doctors and nurses, and, of course, all ears perked up when she relayed the story of the near-fatal tractor incident. It would be all over town within an hour or two. And because she didn't have enough money to pay everyone for their silence, she would just have to live with it.

Two separate nurses wheeled them into individual examining rooms. Molly Cramer took charge of Ian. A sweet girl with big, blue eyes and a perky smile, she went to Colby's church. Unfortunately, Colby heard everything the young woman said to Ian. The conversation centered around Molly's awareness that Ian was the recently relocated bachelor the single women in town had been talking about since he'd arrived.

Colby tried not to wince when the nurse took an X-ray of her wrist. While she waited for the results, she had to endure Molly's all-too-audible giggles and admonishments to Ian. Little did Molly know that she'd be wasting her time with all the flirting.

The resident returned a few minutes later to tell Colby what she already knew. Her wrist hadn't been fractured, but she did have a sprain.

They wrapped it for her and advised light use for a few days. Once he'd finished with her, she was released and free to go. She went back to the emergency room to check on Ian and found him waiting by the door.

"How's the wrist?" he asked.

She held up her bandaged arm. "It'll live. How about you?"

"Just a knot the size of an egg. I'm a free man."

"Come on, then. I'll drive you home."

This time, he got into the truck without arguing.

21

Neither of them said much during the drive back to Oak Hill. Ian's head pounded, and he felt subdued by the reality of what had nearly happened that afternoon. Apparently, Colby felt the same, quiet too and concentrating on the road in front of her.

She stopped the truck in the driveway and left the engine idling. "Would you like some help getting inside?"

"No, I'll be fine. I think you've done quite enough for me today."

"It was nothing."

He cocked a brow at her and shook his head. "Right."

He opened the door but didn't move. "Sure that wrist is all right?"

She gave him a stiff wave. "Be good as new soon."

"You really did save my life, you know. I won't forget that."

"I'll be sure to send you the bill," she said, a smile on her lips.

After six now, the light had begun to fade, casting shadows across her face. He sat there in the twilight, knowing he should go and yet not wanting to. The wrongness of that did not escape him. "Would you like to come in?" he asked before he realized his own intention. "I could fix us some dinner."

She looked down at her wrist, toyed with the bandage and then shook her head. "I'd better not."

She was right to turn him down. Since the moment he'd found himself lying at the edge of the creek with her pinned beneath him, things somehow felt different between them. The urge to kiss her now nearly overpowered him. Just as he wondered where the devil that thought had come from, the screen door of the house wheezed open. Luke stepped out. Ian waved him over, glad for the diversion.

"What happened?" Luke asked, eyeing the scrapes on Ian's face.

"I kind of had a run-in with the tractor," Ian explained. "Dr. Williams came by and saved me from myself."

"Are you all right?"

Ian wondered if he'd imagined the note of worry in his son's voice. "I'm fine. Thanks to me, Dr. Williams has a sprained wrist, though. Luke, this is Colby Williams. Colby, my son, Luke."

"Hello, Luke," she said. "It's nice to meet you. You might know my daughter, Lena."

Luke scuffed a tennis shoe against the pavement. "Yeah, we've met."

Colby studied him for a moment, and then said, "Well, I've got to get going."

"I owe you one," Ian said.

"We're all good," Colby said.

He waved as he watched her drive off, telling himself what he felt just then was nothing more than gratitude.

22

Colby had been home for less than an hour when Phoebe called, wanting to know everything. A tennis buddy of hers who worked with a nurse at the hospital told her that Colby had saved Ian McKinley's life.

"The town grapevine is up to the speed of light now, I see," Colby said, shaking her head.

"And you didn't tell me?" Phoebe asked indignantly.

"Phoebe, I just got home. It was no big deal, anyway."

"No big deal? Did you really push him out of the way of a rolling tractor?"

"Sort of."

Phoebe's whoop of laughter sounded less than ladylike. "Incredible! How could a man resist a woman who saved his life?"

"Phoebe—"

"Well, really, Colby. I couldn't have planned it better myself."

"The man is engaged. What is it about that word you don't understand?" Colby asked, exasperated.

"Things change. You never know."

"My dinner's burning. I'll talk to you later." She hung up, feeling only slightly guilty for the exaggeration. The pot on the stove did need stirring. She removed the lid and checked the boiling potatoes.

It was way past time Phoebe gave up on this particular venture. Colby thought about those last few moments at Ian's before Luke appeared. The tension between Ian and her was easily explained. People who went through traumas together often felt a temporary sense of closeness.

That night, Lena joined Colby at the dinner table without being prodded to do so for the first time in weeks. Colby hid her surprise and sat down with her daughter as if her presence were nothing out of the ordinary.

"What happened to your wrist?" Lena asked, any concern that might have prompted the question adequately concealed.

With the way things had been going between them, Colby was surprised she'd asked at all. "I had a little accident at the McKinley farm. It's nothing major," she said, not wanting to elaborate.

Lena looked as if she wanted to know more, but didn't ask. Colby asked her about her day, how school was, all the things she would automatically have asked her not so long ago.

Lena answered each of her questions in monosyllables.

Colby had nearly given up hope of a two-sided conversation when Lena said, "There's a campout two weeks from this Friday. The Fellowship of Christian Athletes is sponsoring it. Is it all right if I go?"

She realized then what Lena's sudden appearance at the dinner table had been about. Disappointment stabbed at her, and she wished for the first time since Lena's birth that the child didn't have such power over her heart. "Sure."

Lena dropped her fork, obviously startled by the unexpected response. Judging from her defensive posture earlier, Lena expected an argument. Colby wouldn't give her one. She no longer had the energy. She got up and dumped the remains of her dinner into the garbage.

With her back to the table, she heard Lena get up and leave the room. Sighing, she began gathering up the bowls of vegetables they'd barely touched. For the first time in fifteen years, she disliked being a single parent. It had never been like this before. Always, she and Lena had been able to work out whatever minor difficulties they might have had. How small they seemed in comparison to this. Lena wanting her ears pierced. Lena wanting to meet Chuck Bailey at the ninth-grade dance. Lena wanting to learn how to drive out in her grandparents' pasture. Those issues seemed so simple now.

She put the frying pan in the sink. With her good hand, she scrubbed it hard. She resented this sudden yearning for a partner to share these decisions. She chose to be single. And she couldn't just pull a father for Lena out of a hat. She'd never wanted to marry anyone enough to give up her own independence.

Unbidden, Ian McKinley popped into her thoughts. Her hand stilled, and she stared out the kitchen window at the stars dotting the September sky. She remembered what it felt like to find herself stretched flat out on the ground with Ian on top of her, the unexpected surge of longing that swept through her.

She cut the memory off.

Engaged. Taken. Spoken for.

So stop thinking about him, Colby, she told herself. Just stop thinking about him.

23

She stuck to her own mental guns for the next week, keeping busy at work and spending her nights making one-sided conversation with Lena.

On Thursday morning she stopped at the bank before dropping Lena off at school. They were sitting in the drive-through line when she spotted Ian coming out of the post office across the street, her first uncensored thought that it should have been illegal for anybody to look that good in a pair of blue jeans. He wore a worn-looking leather jacket, a Nike T-shirt, and running shoes. Dark sunglasses hid his eyes, his black hair slicked back and wet, as if he'd just gotten out of the shower.

Warmth assaulted her midsection.

The car behind her tooted its horn. She pulled forward just as Ian looked up and caught sight of her.

He waved. She waved back. Casually. Smiling as if she'd just seen him too.

He crossed the street and stopped at the truck door. Colby lowered the window and said, "Hello."

"Hi. How's the wrist?"

"Fine. I already got rid of the sling. How's your head?"

"Hard as ever, I'm afraid." He smiled, and something inside Colby shifted. Despite what Dillard and Willard Nolen thought, there was nothing slick about this man. His crooked smile crinkled the corners of his eyes and hinted at possibilities. As weapons went, particularly deadly.

"Good," she said, hating the breathlessness in her voice.

He ducked down and peered across at Lena. "Hi. I'm Ian McKinley."

"Sorry," Colby said. "Ian, this is my daughter, Lena."

Lena looked at both of them curiously. "Hello."

"I can see beauty runs in the Williams family. Nice to meet you, Lena."

Lena actually blushed! But then, Colby's own face felt warm too.

The car in front of them eased away, and it was their turn to move forward.

Ian stepped back. "I'm holding things up. See you later," he said, his gaze lingering on hers a second too long.

She waved goodbye, and, pretending intense concentration on her banking business, ignored her daughter's scrutiny.

AT SEVEN-THIRTY the following Sunday, Colby and Lena arrived at church for the monthly women's breakfast prepared in the fellowship hall by the men of the congregation.

A big, open area in the basement, the hall was used for dinners and get-togethers of this sort. The aroma of buttered toast and fried apples greeted them as they entered the room already abuzz with conversation. Lena waved at her grandparents and went over to join them.

"I just want to make it clear that I'm not the one who invited him."

Colby turned around to find Phoebe standing in defense mode with one hand on her hip. "Who?" she asked, knowing full well her friend could only be talking about one person.

"It was all Frank's doing. He invited Ian to go fishing at our pond, and then he asked Luke and him to come to the breakfast."

"As a deacon of the church, that was a nice thing for Frank to do," Colby said, trying to sound unconcerned.

With a suspicious look on her face, Phoebe said, "You mean you don't mind?"

"Why would I mind?"

"I just figured you would accuse me of trying to fix you two up again."

"Now that you know he's engaged to someone else, I know you wouldn't do that," Colby said deliberately.

"Of course not," Phoebe said with angelic innocence.

"How are things with Frank and you?"

"I don't know." Phoebe sighed. "He's just so distracted all the time now. He barely hears what I'm saying to him. It's as if he's in another world or something."

"Maybe it's something at work."

Phoebe shook her head. "He says everything is fine."

Josephine Robertson approached them, saying, "There you are, Phoebe. The Reverend Thomas asked me to get together with you on the quarterly fund-raiser. Do you have a minute?"

"You two go right ahead. I'll talk to you later, Phoebe." Colby hung up her jacket and headed for the front of the room, stopping to chat with several people along the way.

Just as she headed over to speak to her parents, Davis Fralin stopped her with a tentative smile. "Morning, Colby."

"I see they've got you on table-setting duty."

"You know what they say about too many cooks in the kitchen," he said.

"Especially when they're all men," she said, smiling.

He laughed. "You might be right about that."

A dairy farmer, Davis was a nice man, tall and broad at the same time. He had dark brown hair and shy eyes. His wife left him a year or so ago, and from what Colby knew about the situation, he'd been badly hurt by it. He'd been asking her out for the past few months. She'd turned down his invitations because she herself had no intention of getting serious with anyone, and she sensed that he wanted someone to fill the hole left in his life by his divorce.

Just as Davis began telling her about a problem he'd been having with one of his heifers, Colby glanced behind him and caught sight of Ian in the kitchen with the other men, a smile on his face. He wore a white shirt and tie, apparently having taken off his suit jacket.

Lena and Luke were standing on the opposite side of the counter from him, Lena trying to explain something to him. Surprised, she watched as Lena went around to stand beside Ian. She picked up an egg and cracked it on the side of a measuring cup, showing him how to break it without getting any shells in the mixture, just as Colby had shown her years ago. Since Lena recently made a point of rejecting all advice or parental guidance from her, the sight did Colby's heart good.

Ian picked up one and tried it himself. Lena reached for a fork and fished a piece of shell out of the cup. Something about watching the two of them together touched Colby. The only real male role models Lena ever had were her grandfather and Frank. Seeing her with Ian brought on familiar feelings of guilt for the things her lifestyle had caused Lena to miss out on.

Ian looked up just then and caught her gaze. He nodded at something Lena said, but he didn't look away. Colby's pulse quickened. The look couldn't have lasted more than a moment or two, but it seemed like much longer. She forced her attention back to Davis, her voice a little unsteady when she said, "I'll come out Monday and take a look at her if you'd like."

"I'd appreciate that. Sometime after lunch?"

"Sure," she said. "I haven't said hello to my folks yet, so I'll see you later."

"Enjoy the breakfast, Colby," he said, a wistful look in his eyes.

She joined her parents on the other side of the room, where they were chatting with Mabel Atkins. She kissed her mother on the cheek and gave her father and Mabel a hug.

"You're looking awfully stylish today, Mabel." Colby tilted her head at the woman's green silk dress.

"When you get to be my age, you start hoping people notice the dress and not the way you look in it," Mabel said with a chuckle. "You're the one who gets prettier every time I see you."

"We'd have to agree with you there," Colby's father said with a smile.

"Aren't you supposed to be in the kitchen?" she chastised him.

"Just taking a little break for as long as I can get away with it."

She laughed. "That doesn't surprise me."

"Me either," her mother agreed.

"Mabel introduced us to Mr. McKinley a little earlier," Colby's father said. "And she told us how you saved his life the other day."

"It was no big deal," she said, certain that Mabel had stretched the story into Paul Bunyan proportions.

"If you call nearly getting run over by a tractor no big deal," Mabel objected. "If a person believed in fate and that kind of thing, I'd say the two of you—"

Not willing to let Mabel get started on that particular tangent, Colby said, "You know, it looks as if they're asking us to be seated. We'd better find us a place before they're all taken."

The Reverend Thomas called for the group's attention. Once everyone grew quiet, he said, "I'd like to thank you all for coming. Our turnouts for this event keep getting better and better. I'd have to say it probably has something to do with the cooking skills of our volunteers in the kitchen."

The men sent up a round of applause for themselves, and everybody laughed.

"I'd like to introduce two new faces to you this morning." The Reverend Thomas stepped back and summoned Ian and Luke forward. "Ian and Luke McKinley. They came today as guests of Frank and Phoebe Walker. We welcome both of you to Keeling Creek and to our church. We hope you'll feel at home here."

"Thank you," Ian said. Luke merely stood beside him looking uncomfortable.

All the women sat down while the men began serving the food. The women joked good-naturedly about whether or not it would be edible, even though the men had proved themselves in the past. The smells were mouthwatering—homemade biscuits with scrambled eggs and gravy and freshly brewed coffee.

Lena joined Colby and her mother at the far end of the table. Phoebe and her two boys sat across from them.

"Would you like to ask Luke to sit with us?" Colby asked Lena.

Lena shrugged, and, looking as if it didn't matter, said, "I already did. He said he'd just hang out in the kitchen."

Colby knew her daughter well enough to recognize rejection on her face when she saw it.

Frank filed past with the gravy, ladling some over the biscuits on their plates. "This will no doubt be the best item on the menu," he said with a wink. "I made it myself."

Phoebe shook her head. "I might have to argue with that, since he barely knows the location of the frying pan at home."

"Now, now, honey. We'll just let the ladies judge for themselves."

Behind Frank appeared Ian with a big blue bowl in his hands, the image somehow incongruous. He gave her a sheepish smile. "They put me in charge of the grits, and since I didn't even know what they were until twenty minutes ago, I'm not making any promises on how they turned out."

"I'll take my chances," Colby said with a half-smile, uncomfortable, because her mother and Phoebe were taking in every word of the conversation.

He put some on her plate. "If it hadn't been for

Lena, they probably would have thrown me out of the kitchen."

Lena smiled up at him, looking for the moment like her playful, lighthearted daughter of old, and Colby wondered if Ian had that effect on all the women who crossed paths with him.

24

The next day, Colby ran errands on her lunch hour, on her way out of Tinker's Drug when she looked up to find Ian coming in.

"Hi." He reached out to right a box of tissues threatening to slip out of one of her bags.

"Hi," she said, her heart suddenly beating too fast.

"Here, let me help you with that."

"Oh, no, that's okay. I've got them. Really."

He ignored her protests and took the bags from her. "Where are you parked?"

"Around the corner. But you don't have to—"

"That's the least I can do for someone who not only saved my life, but ate my grits without any obvious ill effects." Smiling, Colby followed him, running a hand across her hair and wishing she'd thought to put on some lipstick.

At the truck, she unlocked the door, and he stuck

the bags inside before turning to her and saying, "How about letting me treat you to some lunch? I still haven't paid you back for saving my life."

She should have said no. Any number of excuses would have been plausible enough to send her on her way. But she did have a little time before her next appointment. Reluctant as she was to admit it, lunch with Ian McKinley sounded appealing. "All right, I'll take you up on it."

Tinker's Drug and Soda Fountain had been around for fifty years or more, unchanged to speak of during that time. It was busy now at lunch hour. Inside the front door, they were greeted by the smell of grill food, French fries and onion rings. They made their way down an aisle of soaps and toothbrushes to the snack bar at the back of the store. A row of booths lined one wall. The seats were red vinyl and squeaky clean. A white Formica counter with red-topped bar stools offered a view of the grill.

This was one of Colby's favorite places in Keeling Creek. Growing up, she'd come here with her dad every Saturday morning for a Coke float and a little spot of time that had been their own.

"Booth or counter?" Ian asked.

"Counter," she said, thinking the booth sounded more intimate. Sitting there in full view would be less private, like they'd just run into each other. Which they had.

"Counter, it is." He waited for her to take a stool and then sat down beside her.

Thomas Tinker approached them with a smile and

a menu. He ran the place with the same pride his father had taught him to have in the family establishment. "Hey, Colby. How're things out at the clinic?"

"Busy," she said.

"I believe it. Your waiting room stays busier than Doc Smiley's office. Who's your friend?"

"This is Ian McKinley. Ian, Thomas Tinker."

The two men exchanged small talk, with Ian explaining that he'd recently moved to town. Thomas's welcome sounded sincere.

"I can't get used to the friendliness," Ian said when Thomas left them with their drinks. "I guess the city's made me a cynic, but I keep expecting to find out they're putting me on or something."

Colby smiled, fiddling with the edge of her menu. "Things are pretty different here."

Thomas came back for their order. Ian ordered a burger, the house specialty.

"I'll have my usual, Thomas."

The older man shook his head. "Lettuce, tomato, and cheese on a bun, coming right up."

"Vegetarian?" Ian asked when Thomas headed for the kitchen.

Colby nodded. "Yep."

"Never eaten meat?"

"When I was a kid, my mom didn't consider the table complete without a roast or a baked chicken. I made up my mind about all that after I left home."

Ian appeared to think about that for a moment, then said, "Mr. Tinker?"

Thomas turned from his stance at the grill. "It's Thomas. What can I get you?"

"Cancel that burger. I'd like to try one of those veggie things she's having."

Thomas shook his head again. "She's getting to you, huh?"

"My doctor has been after me to make a few changes in my diet. No time like the present to start."

Surprised, Colby said, "I hope you didn't do that because—"

"A veggie sandwich sounds good."

Casual and easy, the declaration pleased her. Too much so. Most of the men she knew thought vegetables were for sissies. "So, you're planning to fix up Oak Hill?"

Ian nodded. "I'd like to do most of the work myself, so it might take a while."

"I actually had a notebook of plans, things I wanted to do to the place if I ever bought it," she said on impulse, and then, feeling silly, added, "My dad and I used to drive by there about once a week when I was growing up. I always made him stop so I could look at it. It sat empty then. I thought it looked lonely. Like it needed a family. And it has one now."

"I feel bad for messing up your plans," Ian said.

She waved his apology away. "First come, first serve."

"If it helps any, I don't know how long I'll hold on to it. I can't say anything definite, but there's a good possibility I'll be willing to sell it at some point down the road."

"Really? I mean, I guess that would make sense. When you move back to New York, you'll hardly have any reason to keep a big house like that."

"No, probably not," he said. "I'll certainly give you first dibs on it."

It was a nice gesture. She should have been overjoyed. The house might still be hers, after all, but something about the thought of it fell flat now. "Thanks," she said. "I really appreciate that."

Ian took a sip of his iced tea. "At one time, it was a grand old place."

"It would be again with the right person giving it what it needs. Sometimes things just need a little love and attention."

"Yeah, I guess they do. That's something I've realized myself recently," Ian said.

She sensed the statement held more meaning than readily apparent. But Thomas brought their veggie burgers just then, and he didn't elaborate. They ate in silence for the first few bites while conversation hummed around them. She felt a few gazes on them and knew the gossip would start that afternoon. No sooner had the thought crossed her mind than she caught a glimpse of Louise Mason and her twelve-year old daughter waiting for a booth. Louise spotted her and all but sprinted over.

Colby managed a smile. "Hello, Louise. How are you?"

"Oh, I'm fine," she said, patting Colby's shoulder. "Aren't you going to introduce me to your friend?"

Grace won out over reluctance. "Ian, this is Louise

Mason. She owns the hair salon in town. Louise, Ian McKinley. But I don't have to tell you who he is."

Louise grasped Ian's hand in a handshake that Colby knew from personal experience rivaled any sumo wrestler's. "Well, I've just heard so much about you, Mr. McKinley. And I'm so glad to see you've managed to get our Colby out and about. We'd just about given up hope of her finding a good guy."

"Nice to meet you, Miss Mason," he said, looking more than a little amused.

"Oh, it's Louise," she said, all but preening. If the woman hadn't had a wedding ring on her finger, Colby thought Louise would have knocked her right off the stool and bowled Ian over with her charm. Colby said a prayer of thanks when Louise's daughter called out to her from their table. "I'd better be getting back. You two enjoy your lunch," she said, winking at Colby.

Colby lowered her forehead onto one hand and stared at the counter in mortification. "I can't believe she said that."

"She's harmless," he said, chuckling. "There's no reason to be embarrassed. Really."

"Easy for you to say." The humor in the situation hit her, and she smiled despite herself. "I wonder what it would be like to live in a place where people actually have a little privacy."

"Lonely, sometimes."

"It might be worth it once in a while," she said. "Being the eligible carrot on the end of the stick does get a little old. Fortunately, the positives of living in a place like this outweigh the negatives. The people who can't keep their nose out of your business are the same ones who would be there for you in a flash if you ever needed their help. Maybe this wasn't a good idea, though. There will be talk, you know."

"About what?"

"The two of us having lunch together. Louise will have everybody in the Dippety-Do informed within thirty seconds of getting back to the shop."

Ian toyed with a French fry. "I've never cared too much about what other people think."

Colby tilted her head and said in a low voice, "Since you're engaged, I didn't think you'd want anyone to get the wrong impression."

He held her gaze for a moment too long while something inside her flared to life, the feeling inappropriate, she knew. Nonetheless, there.

"To be honest, I could use a friend here," he said. "Does my engagement have to stand in the way of that?"

His question brought with it a surge of disappointment. From an adult standpoint, nothing wrong with the two of them being friends. They had two difficult teenagers in common. She found him easy to talk to, as, apparently, he did her. Friends. Nothing wrong with the two of them being friends.

"No, it doesn't." She pushed her half-eaten sandwich away. "As a matter of fact, I'm going to a meeting on Thursday night you might be interested in attending. The hospital hosts a lecture series each month. This month's topic is 'Understanding Your

Teenager.' I thought I'd go just to see if they can convince me there *is* any understanding them. You're welcome to come if you'd like."

"Fiction or nonfiction?" he asked with a half-grin.

"Non, supposedly," she said, smiling. "We'll see."

"Are you serious? About my going?"

"Sure, if you think it might help things with Luke."

"It certainly couldn't hurt."

She glanced at her watch, ignoring the voice inside her that questioned what she'd just done. "I'd better be getting back. I have a full afternoon ahead."

Ian reached for the ticket. "Yeah, I've got to go too." He looked up and caught her gaze. The increasingly familiar awareness resurfaced. She resisted its pull.

But sitting beside him, staring into those too blue, too appealing eyes, she wondered if she was kidding herself. Friends? Friends.

Colby twisted her stool around and slid to the floor. "Thanks for the lunch. The meeting is at the Kramer building on Sycamore Street. Room 212. It starts at six."

"I'll be there," he said, and her traitorous heart fluttered in gladness.

25

Maybe he wouldn't come.

Colby arrived a few minutes early for the lecture, but at almost six o'clock, still no sign of Ian.

Maybe he'd changed his mind.

Maybe it would be for the best if he had.

A hand touched her shoulder. She looked up to find the source of her thoughts looking down at her with an apologetic smile on his face.

"Sorry I'm late," he said.

"They're just getting ready to start." She turned to the side so he could take the chair next to hers. Before they had time to say anything more, the lecturer stepped to the podium and tapped the microphone to get the room's attention. "Good evening, everyone. Thank you so much for coming. I'm Dr. Betsy Watson, and I hope to say a few things this evening that will convince you there is light at the end of the tunnel for you and your teenager."

Laughter rippled across the room, indicating that everyone knew what she was talking about. For the next hour and a half, they listened while Dr. Watson discussed some of the ways in which they, as parents, might make the teenage years of their children's lives more bearable for all concerned. The most important thing, she stressed at the beginning of the talk, would be keeping the lines of communication open. Easier said than done.

Colby made an attempt to listen intently. As things were with Lena, she needed every morsel of intelligence she could garner. But awareness of the man seated beside her eroded her concentration until she barely heard the speaker's words, too disturbed by Ian and the knowledge that a fraction of an inch lay between them.

Minute details assaulted her senses. The fresh, clean smell of his cologne; the starched crispness of his white shirt; and the contrast it made with the sun-browned skin on his well-shaped hands.

At one point, he dropped his program and bent to pick it up. His left shoulder brushed her right thigh. Colby jumped.

Ian sat back up and whispered, "Sorry."

She shook her head and waved his apology away.

Feeling ridiculously self-conscious, she forced her attention back to the speaker. That lasted for all of thirty seconds, before her senses took over again, and she felt grateful when the meeting finally drew to a close. For the past hour and a half, she'd felt as if she were on sensory overload. Standing, she introduced Ian to some of the people she knew. After a few minutes, they moved about the room, separately, until a half hour or so later, they both ended up near the door.

"Ready to call it a night now that we've learned how to deal with our kids?" he asked.

"I'd stay until morning if I thought I could go home and make things like they were when she was ten."

"If I got anything out of what our speaker said, that's so much wishful thinking."

"Unfortunately, I think you're right," she said.

A few people called out good night as they left the room.

"Nice people," Ian said in the hallway.

"Yes, they are." They took the stairs to the first floor, then hung back in the hallway.

"How about a cup of coffee somewhere?" he suggested.

A tempting invitation, but something told her it would be better to end the evening here. He looked entirely too good in a smart-looking jacket and black wool pants, both of which had Italy written all over them. Definitely not the kind of clothes that inspired women to think about friendship. She glanced at her watch. "It's late. I should get home."

"Sure. I understand."

But she didn't think he understood at all. She didn't know if she did herself.

Despite her declaration, they made no move toward the door.

He leaned up against a locker, his arms folded across his chest. "She was a good speaker."

"Yes. I got the feeling she'd definitely been through it," Colby agreed, hoping he wouldn't ask her opinion on something that had been said when she'd been paying more attention to him than to the lecturer.

"I think that's the only way anyone could understand it. Firsthand experience."

"It's hard to know what being a soldier is all about until you've been on the battlefield."

"Some days I definitely feel that way." His expression grew solemn. "I just wish I had the chance to go back and do some things differently."

Regret threaded his voice, and she knew there was more to his situation than he'd let on. Sensing that he wanted to talk about it, she said, "Why did you move here, Ian?"

He looked down at the floor for a long while, his hands shoved deep in his pants pockets. "Luke got arrested on a drug charge," he finally said, his voice low. "I wanted to get him away from the city."

The revelation took her totally by surprise. She'd never imagined anything like that. She thought of her own problems with Lena and felt lucky. "Oh. I'm sorry, Ian. It's not easy being a parent these days."

"I wasn't doing a very good job of it, I'm afraid. I spent too much time working and not enough time knowing where my son was and what he was doing."

"You can't blame yourself for—"

"Oh, but I do," he interrupted firmly enough to indicate that he'd spent a great deal of time thinking about exactly that. "I do."

Again, Colby felt fortunate not to have had that kind of trouble with Lena.

"Don't short yourself, Ian. Putting your life on hold is pretty generous, even for a parent."

"Thanks. I appreciate that."

"Have things improved since you've been here?"

"Between the two of us, no. He's going to school and doing the things he's supposed to be doing. He swore to me that the drugs had never been a problem and wouldn't be in the future. I have to believe him."

She found him appealingly vulnerable in this moment of admission, knew it hadn't been an easy thing for him to talk about. "Well, as for Luke getting used to being here, give him time. He'll adjust." No sooner were the words out than she realized that she'd offered him the same platitudes people had been giving her about Lena for the past two months.

"So, now that I've pulled all my skeletons out of the closet, what's the problem between you and Lena?" he asked, looking down at her.

"Hah. Now there's a question. It seems like she just woke up one day and decided she didn't like me anymore. I've reached the point where I don't think I can do anything more than take my own cliché advice and wait for things to change again."

"Pretty sad, aren't we?" he asked with a wry smile.

"At least we're trying. All you have to do is open the paper to see what happens to children who don't have parents who care enough to stick with them." She sighed and ran a hand through her hair. "I don't know. The older I get, the more I realize that being a good parent, a good human being, is just plain hard work. I'm human enough to wish I could be selfish and say the heck with it sometimes. But that's not what I want to teach Lena. And from what I can tell, it isn't what you want to teach Luke."

Ian watched her silently, his gaze lingering on her face. In that moment, she felt the forging of a bond that had been developing between them since the moment they'd met. It scared the devil out of her. She stepped back and motioned toward the door. "I'm sorry. I didn't mean to get on my soapbox. It's late. I'd better get going."

"You didn't. I've enjoyed the evening. Might have actually learned something," he said, his gaze direct, warming her in a multitude of places. Clearing her throat, she made her way toward the door. He followed her outside to her truck.

"Good luck with Luke," she said, stopping at the driver's side door. "I hope things will work out for us both soon. With the kids, I mean," she added hastily, and then felt like an idiot.

"I hope you're right," he said in that steady, even way of his.

She made a valiant effort not to look at him again as she started the truck, backed out of the parking space and headed toward the exit. But as she pulled out onto the street, she couldn't resist one last glimpse in the rearview mirror.

He stood beneath the lamppost, staring after her.

26

Throughout the next week, Ian attempted to put some of the information he'd gained at the parent-teenager lecture to use.

Teenagers are no longer children. Consult with them. Ask their opinions. Suggest. Don't order.

While Ian felt sure of the validity of Dr. Watson's advice, he wondered if things were too far gone for any of it to make a difference with Luke and him. He thought about what Colby had said about parenting being plain old hard work. She was right. Rebuilding his relationship with Luke meant working at it each and every day, chipping away at the boy's anger, hoping to move a little closer to his goal with each attempt.

One afternoon when Luke got off the school bus, Ian was outside with a ladder and a bucket of paint, giving the trim on the house the facelift it needed. He spotted Luke coming up the driveway, his stride long and relaxed until he looked up and saw Ian watching him. Insolence made him slow his walk and frown.

Ian dipped his brush into the bucket on the tray at the top of the ladder, then carefully stroked the paint across the chipped trim beneath the roofline. The boy's aloofness stabbed deep, but Ian refused to let him see it. When Luke reached the top of the drive, Ian waved and said, "I've got an extra brush handy if you're interested."

Luke didn't answer for several seconds. "What are you trying to prove, Dad?" he finally asked, his voice filled with condescension. "Do you really think moving me out to the country and pretending to be something you're not is going to change us?"

The anger in Luke's voice sent a wave of despair through Ian. Did his son's resentment run so deep that he might never get past it? The thought scared him more than anything in his life ever had. What if it was too late to make up for his mistakes? He couldn't let himself believe that. They just needed time. Something Ian had plenty of right now.

Refusing to let Luke see that he'd rattled him, he said, "If you change your mind, the extra brushes are at the foot of the ladder."

Luke swung around and stomped inside without answering.

27

Unbelievable.

Unbelievable!

Luke dropped his book bag at the foot of the stairs and stomped down the hallway toward the kitchen. No way was that his dad out there on that ladder. It had to be someone impersonating him. His father never had time for things like house painting. He hired people to do that kind of stuff. For as far back as he remembered, Luke hardly ever saw his dad in anything other than a suit. Since they'd moved here, he practically lived in blue jeans and running shoes.

His dad looked like a different person. And he acted different, asking Luke to help with things, wanting to spend time with him. Luke couldn't get used to it. He didn't want to, because it wouldn't last. He knew it wouldn't. It never had before. He thought about the times his dad promised to come to a soccer match, only to be sidetracked by a last-minute meeting. Or the surprise birthday party he'd arranged for him and then been two hours late getting to. From the moment he'd been born, he'd been nothing but a burden to his father. He just wished his dad would stop pretending otherwise.

Inside the kitchen, the smell of Mabel's homemade chocolate chip cookies still hung in the air. A note on the table said:

Luke,
I've gone to the grocery store. Four cookies before dinner and no more. Back soon.

Mabel

Luke rolled his eyes and grabbed a handful of cookies from the glass jar she kept on the kitchen counter. Why was someone always telling him what to do? His dad, who never cared until he decided it was his duty to reform him. Mabel, who acted like his mother or something. And his teachers, who called him capable of far more than he showed in school. What did they know?

Pulling a glass from the cabinet, Luke poured himself some milk and sat at the kitchen table. No one here really knew him. If he had anything to do with it, they wouldn't be here long enough for it to matter.

He hated it here.

He'd met a couple of okay kids. Football players who were actually more concerned about getting college scholarships than getting high. And a couple of cheerleaders who'd made it clear they'd like to get to know him better.

But they were all boring compared to the kids he'd hung around with in the city.

And that Williams girl. Lena. Cute. But she looked at him as if she had no idea what to say to him. As if they were from different planets—and they might as well have been. He'd passed her in the hall several times. He'd wanted to stop and talk to her, but he had no idea what to say. Not his type, anyway. He liked girls who knew the score. Girls who didn't expect to wear his class ring after the second date.

All the kids at Jefferson High were just too straight for him. He wanted to go back to the city, where he knew how things worked. He belonged there, not here in this stuck-in-the-fifties town.

If he played his cards right, it wouldn't be too much longer before his dad gave up on him. He knew his father's interest in him amounted to nothing more than a guilt trip. Until he'd gotten into trouble, they'd merely lived in the same house. His father left for work before he got up and usually didn't come home until he'd gone to bed.

And now he acted like Ward Cleaver. Painting the house. Fixing up the barn. He'd get tired of it before long.

He finished his fourth cookie, reached for a fifth, then glanced at Mabel's note and put it back in the jar. For the briefest of seconds, he wished that this whole fake life his father had created was true.

That he really had grown up in a house like this, that he and his father had the kind of relationship where he went out and climbed up on a ladder beside him, where he told him about the play they'd read in English class that day. But they didn't. And they never would.

28

On the following Friday afternoon, Colby made an emergency call out to the Bowers farm. A horse had gotten into a half-full grain bin and eaten almost enough of the sweet feed to kill her. Luckily, Lou Ann Bowers caught the mare before she finished it off. As good as the grain might have tasted, Colby doubted the horse enjoyed the dose of mineral oil that followed it.

It was almost six o'clock by the time Colby unenthusiastically headed back toward town. With the end of September, the leaves were beginning to turn bright red and gold on the mountains in the distance. But Colby felt too down to appreciate them. Lena had her campout tonight, so she had an empty house waiting for her.

She passed the Walker's driveway without stopping. Normally, she would have stopped to visit, but Phoebe called the night before, needing to talk to her about Frank. Things still weren't normal between them. She'd stayed on the phone with Phoebe for more than an hour, and, although she tried to sound optimistic, Colby thought maybe her friend had cause for concern. She suggested that Phoebe try to get a sitter tonight so that she and Frank could have some time alone.

Just past Phoebe's house, Colby spotted a large yellow dog in her lane, barking as if it had just cornered a T-bone steak. She caught a glimpse of a smaller animal disappearing into the brush. Slowing to a stop, she recognized the dog as Smidge. The McKinleys' dog.

She pulled over and got out of the truck. "Here, girl."

The dog looked up, then trotted toward Colby, her tongue lolling to one side of her mouth.

"What are you doing way out here by yourself, Smidge?" From ten feet away, Colby realized that the T-bone had in fact been a skunk. And Smidge came out the loser in the confrontation.

"I have a feeling you're going to be in big trouble, girl," Colby said, holding her nose. "Come on. In the back. As much as I like you, I'm not up to sharing the front seat with you."

Colby let down the tailgate. Smidge jumped up and sat with her head over the side, panting. Pulling back onto the road, Colby considered taking Smidge home with her and calling Ian to come and get her. The entrance to Oak Hill loomed just ahead on the right.

Friday night, and she didn't relish the idea of running into his fiancée again if she happened to be visiting. Ridiculous, though. So what if the woman was there? She'd picked the dog up off the road, and now she would take her home. She would have done the same for anyone in Keeling Creek.

Nonetheless, she swung onto the drive with the hope that she could drop Smidge off and leave unnoticed. No such luck. At the top of the driveway, she spotted Ian on a ladder at the side of the house. He turned around at the sound of her truck, looking surprised to see her. Reluctantly, she got out while he climbed down to meet her. He wore a paint-splattered shirt with jeans. His hair looked appealingly disheveled, and when he ran his right hand through it, she experienced the urge to do the same.

"I'm returning your wayward dog," she called out. "Although I'm not sure you're going to want her anytime soon."

Smidge bounded out of the back and greeted Ian in typical dog-love fashion. Tail wagging, she lunged and planted her paws on his chest, her tongue swiping at his jaw.

"Wait! Smidge, don't—" Colby tried to stop her, but too late.

"Good grief," Ian exclaimed, leaping back. "What on earth did you get into?"

Colby shouldn't have laughed, but she couldn't help herself, the look on Ian's face just too comical. "She had a one-on-one with a skunk," she said, trying to cover up a smile. "As you can smell, the skunk won."

"You sure you don't want to take her home with you?"

Colby smiled again. "Not tonight, I don't think."

Ian shot a disgruntled look at Smidge, who looked offended by his less-than-enthusiastic reception. "How do you get rid of it?"

"It's mostly a wear-off thing."

Ian shook his head. "It looks as if you're going to be sleeping in the barn, girl."

Smidge whined and plopped down on the ground, still panting from her adventure.

Colby should have said goodbye then and left Ian to his own devices. But she found herself lingering. "There is one thing that might help."

"Hey, I'm willing to try anything."

"Tomato juice."

Ian looked at her as if she'd just suggested the dog could fly to the Moon. "I'd like to see you make her drink tomato juice."

Colby laughed. "You don't make her drink it. You bathe her in it."

"Bathe her in it? She weighs eighty pounds."

Colby shoved her hands into her pockets and rocked back on her heels. "Yep. We would need a lot of juice."

Ian eyed her skeptically. "Are you serious?"

"It won't get rid of it completely. But it might make her bearable."

The breeze threw a pungent whiff of skunk in their

direction. "I'm desperate enough to try that," he said. "If I offered a pizza as compensation, would you hang around and help me de-skunk my son's dog?"

If a couple of minutes ago had been the time to not involve herself further, now would definitely be the point to say she had to go. The words formed but didn't make it past her lips. There was something about the way he looked so darned appealing in his paint-splattered shirt and the thought of the empty house waiting for her that made her say, "Sure. Why not?"

He looked pleased by her agreement. "Okay. Give me a minute to put Her Smelliness in her fenced yard, and we'll go in search of tomato juice. I don't have any. I sure hope the stores around here do."

He reappeared in less than a minute, car keys jangling in his hand. "I'll drive."

Colby slid onto the passenger seat, and they were off down the driveway. He had the windows down, and the fall air teased the ends of her hair. She suggested they try Smitty's Market first, only a mile or so away. He took a right, and something about rolling down a country road with this man on a late September evening felt free and good. Too much so.

At Smitty's, they both hopped out and went inside. They searched an aisle or two before locating three quarts. They bought them all, then headed on toward town.

"How much do you think we'll need?" Ian asked.

"A lot more than three quarts," she replied.

They hit five stores in all, cleaning each one out.

They both laughed at the last stop when the cashier asked if they were having a Bloody Mary party. "I wish," Ian said.

Just outside the store, he added with a grin, "I hope there's not a run on tomato juice in the next couple of days. We've just depleted the town's supply."

She smiled. "Definitely created a shortage."

Back at the house, Ian followed Colby's instructions and procured a large tin tub from the barn. They placed it near the water hose at the back door of the house. One by one they opened the jars and filled the tub with the juice.

Ian rolled up his sleeves. "I'm glad I don't have to climb in there."

"Oh, this is probably a terribly expensive skin treatment at some swanky spa in California."

Ian shook his head. "I wouldn't doubt it."

Shoving up her own sleeves, she said, "All right. We're ready for her."

"But is she ready for us?"

"Probably not," Colby said, smiling.

Ian let the dog out of the yard and led her toward the tub. Halfway there, Smidge must have figured out what was going on. She promptly put on the brakes, her legs stretched out in front of her like a balking mule. "You asked for this, you know," Ian said.

At the tub, Colby helped him lift the reluctant dog and place her in. She had never seen a more offended-looking animal. The dog stood with one paw in the air as if to say, "You don't really expect me to do this, do you?" While the skunk hadn't seemed to bother

her at all, the tomato juice apparently ranked as a grave indignity.

They used cups to douse her with the liquid. She stood statue-still, turning her nose toward the rising Moon and letting out a protesting howl every minute or two.

"Okay. She needs to soak for a while," Colby said once they'd thoroughly doused her. She pushed the dog's fanny down so that most of her skunk-scented fur was submerged.

"So, how'd you discover the tomato juice secret?" Ian asked. "Did they teach you that in vet school?"

"Nope. That came from my grandmother. Actually, I kind of had the same thing happen when I was seven. I was waiting for the school bus and spotted a mother skunk with three babies. I thought they were cute, and naturally I wanted to pet them, but mama skunk had different ideas."

"So you know exactly what Smidge is going through?" he asked with a grin.

"I don't think she minded as much as I did."

Ian smiled again, and they stood there watching each other. The Moon hung high over his left shoulder, throwing shadowed light on his well-defined face. Nine o'clock on a Friday night, and she was helping Ian McKinley wash his dog and having more fun than she'd had in ages.

The moment shattered when Smidge decided she'd had enough. Standing in the tub, she shook, nose to tail, sending tomato juice flying in all directions. Colby yelped and jumped back. Ian sidestepped the onslaught too, but not in time. They were both covered. Faces, shirts, arms, pants.

Colby looked at Ian and started laughing. She couldn't help it. Even his long, dark eyelashes were dripping with tomato juice.

Judging from his expression, she didn't look any better. His face broke into a grin, and then he started laughing.

With their attention diverted, Smidge hopped out of the tub and took off across the grass, running circles around the scattered old oak trees, a reddish-black streak in the moonlit yard.

Colby collapsed onto the ground, still laughing, holding her stomach now.

It took them a minute or two to regain their composure. Ian tried calling Smidge back a couple of times, but he failed to muster any sternness, and the dog definitely wasn't taking him seriously. She wanted to play. She raced forward, stopping just short of him, barking and then taking off in a flash, fanny tucked low to the ground.

"All right, have your fun," he finally said, "but you've got the rinse cycle to go yet."

Colby got up from the ground, wiping her eyes. She lifted one side of the tub and helped him pour out the juice. He turned on the water hose and refilled the tub. The water level rose slowly, and again, Colby found herself studying him discreetly, his hair tousled and damp at the temples. His shirt was plastered to his chest, now polka-dotted with tomato juice, as well as paint. His blue jeans were in similar disrepair, damp and molded to his long legs in a way that did nothing for her peace of mind.

She jerked her gaze upward and found him giving her a like perusal. Her hand went to her hair, smoothing it back. No doubt she looked a mess. But that wasn't the message she saw in his eyes. He stared at her as if he liked what he saw. The realization did crazy things to her insides.

An unexpected feeling of longing swept through her, a longing for something she'd claimed not to need, not to want. But she realized in that instant what she had been missing out on. Companionship. Simple, basic companionship. Someone with whom she could do silly things. Someone with whom she wanted to let down her guard. Be herself. She thought of all her awful dates in past years. The stiff dinners for two, the awkward silences at her door. None of them had ever felt like this. Maybe if they had, she would have been able to put Doug behind her long ago.

Shocked by her own thoughts, she turned away and called Smidge. The dog slunk toward them, her head bowed. They lifted her over the edge of the tub, silent now. They rinsed and rinsed until all traces of the juice were gone.

"I think it really helped," Ian said, sounding surprised.

"It's still there, but at least it's a little more subdued."

"The miracles of modern medicine," he said.

"Sometimes the simplest cures are the most effective."

It felt so good, standing in the moonlight with a giant, wet, yellow Lab between them. The realization was unsettling and more than a little disturbing. Enough so that she stepped back and said, "I'd better get going."

"Hey, I promised you a pizza. That's the least I can do, considering how you just spent your Friday night."

"I won't hold you to that. It's late—"

"Don't tell me you didn't work up an appetite after all this. Come on. I'll call it in and you can get cleaned up."

To stay longer would be to invite something different from what they'd shared so far. If not on his part, then certainly in her own mind. But she really didn't want to go. Shirking common sense, she said, "Okay. Pizza it is."

"Good," he said, looking pleased. He turned Smidge loose. The dog took off again, cutting circles around the house in obvious appreciation of her freedom. Colby followed Ian inside, where he said, "You'll have to pardon the construction. We've got a little more to do yet."

She'd never seen the inside of the house. It did, indeed, need work, but the actual layout was every bit as magnificent as the outside promised. The foyer was two stories high, and a mahogany staircase wound from the first floor to the second.

"Would you like a tour?" he asked.

"I'd love one."

He led her through the house, stopping at the living room first, a grand room of enormous proportions with a stone fireplace as large as a small room. The kitchen was equally big, with windows on two sides. A butcher block sat in the middle; copper pots hanging above it. Someone, probably Mabel, had placed potted herbs on the sill above the sink. A small greenhouse opened up off the kitchen, the perfect place to raise tomatoes and flowers year-round.

"As you can see," Ian said, "I don't have much of a green thumb. Mabel's been after me to buy some plants."

"I think even I could grow them in here," Colby said. "And I'm known for my brown thumb."

"Couldn't be browner than mine." He led her upstairs to what was apparently his bedroom. This room was also in need of redecoration, the paint on the walls circa 1960. The hardwood floor needed refinishing. But a beautiful cherry sleigh bed sat in the center of the room. Two matching nightstands graced the sides of it. A dresser in the same wood sat near the window. Judging by his choice of furniture, he had excellent taste.

"The bathroom is through there." He tilted his head toward the open door on the other side of the room. He opened the closet and pulled out a dark blue shirt. "This will be too big, but at least it's free of tomato juice. I'd offer you some pants, but I don't think they'd fit."

"This is fine," she said, taking the shirt from him,

feeling suddenly uneasy with the thought of wearing his clothes. It seemed personal in a way that brought to mind things she shouldn't be thinking about.

Their gazes caught and held. Outwardly, they were guilty of nothing. She was standing in his bedroom, holding one of his newly laundered shirts. Nothing wrong with that. So why did it feel as if there was?

"Well, I'll clean up and meet you downstairs," she said, breaking the silence.

He stepped back as if jolted from a trance. "Sure. I'll just go order the pizza. What do you like on yours?"

"Mushrooms and black olives?"

"You got it." He stopped at the door. "When you're finished, there's something I'd like to show you."

And he left her then to wonder what it was.

29

He stood waiting for her at the foot of the stairs when she was finished showering and changing. His hair was wet, and a few drops of water still clung to his neck after his own shower. He'd found a fresh shirt and a pair of faded jeans somewhere, not a spot of tomato juice in sight.

He waved her toward the back door off the kitchen. "The pizza is on its way."

More than a little curious, she followed him outside to the barn. He opened the large, faded red door and motioned her toward a stall a few yards away.

Standing before her was a black-and-white calf, which she immediately recognized as one of the twins she'd delivered at Harry Pasley's. She opened the stall and went in, dropping down on her knees to rub the calf's forehead. "Hey, little girl. How'd you get here?"

She heard Ian move in behind her and looked up to find him with one shoulder against the doorframe. "You said she wouldn't be of much use to Harry. I kept thinking about how she almost hadn't made it and what you said that night after the lecture about how easy it is to ignore things that make our lives more complicated. I've been pretty good at that. I couldn't stand the thought of her being sent to the stockyard. Harry brought her over in his truck for me."

Colby stood perfectly still, so touched by what he'd done that words eluded her. Finally finding her voice, she said, "Well, I bet you surprised the devil out of Harry."

"Luckily, he hadn't let her go yet, and when I told him I'd like to have her, he seemed pretty pleased. He's keeping the other little guy. He said the father was one of his good bulls."

"So what did you name her?"

"Mabel thought Matilda suited her. What do you think?"

"I think. . .Matilda is a lovely name," she said, swallowing the lump in her throat and stroking the calf's soft fur.

"I'm feeding her by bottle three times a day. Harry showed me how to mix up the formula. She seems to like it."

The calf let out a bleat and butted its nose against Ian's leg.

"She likes you," Colby said.

Looking a little embarrassed, he said, "She's just hoping I'll give her an extra bottle. Actually, she's won us all over. Mabel's down here every hour or so checking on her. Luke didn't say much about her at first, but I've noticed that he heads straight for the barn every day when he gets home from school."

"What will you do with her when you and Luke move back to the city?"

He didn't say anything for a moment, as if he hadn't yet considered the question. "I guess I haven't gotten that far yet. But I fully intend for her to get old and fat."

A horn sounded from outside.

"That'll be the pizza." Ian hitched a thumb back toward the house and stepped out of the stall.

"I'll be right up." Once he'd left the barn, Colby turned and stroked Matilda's soft forehead with the backs of her fingers, thinking about what he had done. She felt strange, as if the room had tilted, and she didn't quite have the balance to stand.

Matilda looked up at her with enormous round eyes, swiping her hand with her rough, pink tongue. Colby rubbed a thumb across the calf's moist nose and said, "If we're not careful, Miss Matilda, you and I are both going to be in a heap of trouble."

A few minutes later, Colby sat on the couch with her pizza-filled plate. She'd felt decidedly awkward after returning to the house. She sensed that he did as well. They said very little while he gathered their plates and silverware and carried it all to the living room. She watched him when she was sure he wasn't looking. Saving Matilda from the stockyard wasn't the kind of thing she would have expected from a man whom she initially likened to Doug. More and more, she realized just how wrong she had been. Not sure what to make of that, she said, "So tell me about your work in New York. I know it had to be more exciting than painting houses. Not that you aren't good with trim."

"Thanks." He smiled, wiping the corner of his mouth with a napkin. "I'm keeping my finger in the pie from here."

"Do you like what you do?"

He considered the question for a moment. "It's pretty consuming work. Or rather, I let it be. I think the answer to your question is yes. When this whole thing with Luke happened, I'd just brought in the biggest client ever for the firm. It was a moment I'd spent a lot of years working pretty hard for. But somehow it wasn't everything I thought it would be."

"What do you mean?"

"I don't know exactly. It just felt like something was missing. That was the night I found out about Luke being in trouble. That was when I realized what a lousy father I'd been, that I hadn't really been there for him any more than mine had been there for me."

"I can't imagine that being true."

Ian stayed quiet for a few moments. "I grew up pretty poor," he said at last. "Really poor, in fact. My father left my mother when I was six. She spent most of her adult life trying to make ends meet. For as long as I can remember, I wanted to make something of myself, to make her proud of me. She encouraged me, even though I think it was hard for her to believe I could really do it."

Astonished that his childhood had been nothing like his life now, Colby realized she'd once again jumped to conclusions where he was concerned. "Is she still alive?"

He shook his head. "I had just found out about my scholarship to Columbia when she died."

"She must have been very proud of you," she said, saddened that his mother hadn't been able to see what he'd done with his life.

"I think she was. That's always given me comfort, even if it is selfish comfort."

"It's not selfish at all," she said softly. "We all want our parents to be proud of us." Colby put her plate on the table and sat back on the couch. "Did you get married in college?"

Ian shook his head. "I met Sherry, Luke's mother, my freshman year. We got married right after graduation. We had Luke a little over a year later. She died a few days after he was born."

Colby didn't know what to say. "I'm sorry. I shouldn't have asked. I just assumed you were divorced or—"

"It's all right. Really."

"Those were some pretty tough blows to be dealt at such a young age."

"Yeah. Life has a big fist sometimes."

She had to agree with that. "You were a single parent from the beginning too, then."

He nodded. "And I was so determined to be

different from my own father, to give Luke the things mine had never given me, that I messed up my priorities."

"You're being hard on yourself."

"I don't think so. One thing I've realized since being here is that CCI hasn't fallen to pieces without me. I could have spent more time with Luke."

"Don't do that," she said. "Those 'maybe' games can get you into trouble. Believe me, I know."

"So, why aren't you married? I know it can't be for lack of offers."

"I guess I just never found the right man. Once the toads started outranking the princes ten to one, I decided it wasn't worth the trouble of looking."

Ian laughed. "That bad, huh?"

"That bad."

"What about Lena's father?"

Colby sobered. "That didn't work out."

"I'm sorry."

"Most men with a baby would have remarried," she said, turning the conversation back to him.

"I never wanted to make that kind of commitment to anyone again. The thought was too painful."

He had obviously loved his wife very much. She heard it in his voice. And she respected him for that. "Rachel must be a very special woman."

He hesitated. "It's not the same kind of marriage. But our lives complement each other's."

"I see," she said, not sure she really did. Didn't he love Rachel? Would their marriage be based on compatibility rather than passion?

He watched her, not saying anything. Colby again felt somehow off balance, unsure of her footing. How long they sat there, she didn't know. But she did know that it was getting more and more difficult to pretend indifference to this man. The more time she spent with him, the more dimensional he became, the more she identified with him. "I should go," she said, breaking the silence. "I can help clean up before I leave."

"I can handle throwing away a pizza box and sticking a couple of plates in the dishwasher."

She smiled. "Okay, then. Thanks for the dinner."

"Thanks for the help."

"Let's just hope it worked."

He walked her outside. The Moon hung high in the sky, throwing shadowed light across their faces. They stopped at the door to her truck and then stood there, uneasy with each other. Colby felt the electricity between them. She might not have been the most active member of the Keeling Creek dating circuit, but she could tell when a man was thinking about kissing her. Unless she was way off, Ian wanted to kiss her.

The scary part? She wanted him to. Unwise and highly unadvisable, though it might be. She opened the door and got inside. The sooner she left the better. "Good night, Ian. Thanks again."

"Good night, Colby."

She drove away then, her only consolation the note of regret in his voice.

30

Throughout the week, Lena hadn't been able to muster much enthusiasm for the campout on Friday night. All of her friends were going. But the problem was, every one of them would be hooking up with a guy once they got there. Everyone except her. She was beginning to think something was wrong with her.

They'd just finished setting up the tents when Tim Anderson's Wagoneer rolled to a stop above the pond where they were camping.

Millie tapped Lena on the shoulder. "Looks like it might be your lucky night."

Lena's gaze followed her friend's to the Wagoneer at the top of the hill. Luke McKinley had just gotten out of the passenger side and made his way around to the back of the vehicle. He and Tim pulled out a couple of duffel bags and headed toward the campsite.

Jefferson County High had its share of good-looking guys. Football players with big muscles and broad shoulders. But Luke McKinley was tall and lean and different from any boy she'd ever known. His walk was loose-limbed and hinted at attitude. She couldn't find her voice. When she did, it came out much higher than normal. "I don't know what you're talking about."

"Oh, right, Lena. I've seen the way you look at him in the halls. You're crazy about him."

"I don't even know him," she said, with what she hoped sounded like indifference.

"So? I didn't say you knew him. I said you were crazy about him."

Lena ignored Millie's baiting and went over to the campfire to help grill the burgers. What if she thought he was cute? That didn't mean she wanted to make a fool of herself.

For the next two hours, she did an admirable job of not looking at him. It had to be her overactive imagination that she felt his gaze on her, though. That or wishful thinking.

The Fellowship of Christian Athletes was one of the school's most popular organizations. Jim Bevson, the economics teacher who headed the group was largely responsible for that. Regarded as the coolest teacher at Jefferson County High, all the kids loved him. His wife, Theresa, was just as cool. She went with him on all the field trips. Lena often thought if she had a dad, she'd have liked him to be like Mr. Bevson. The Bevsons had the best marriage she'd ever seen. Except for Aunt Phoebe and Uncle Frank, of course. Nobody had a better marriage than theirs.

Lena sat at the edge of the campfire and listened while Mr. Bevson told them a story about a boy paralyzed from the neck down after diving off the high board at a swim meet. The boy had pretty much given up on life until, one day, someone brought him a computer he operated with his voice. He began to write stories with it and went on to write a prize-winning novel called *When All Is Black*.

Mr. Bevson's stories always had a point. "Every one of us has something in our lives that would hold us back if we let it," he said when he'd finished. "The key is to deal with it, then find a way around it."

Lena looked into the campfire flames and thought of the father she'd never met. Anger smoldered inside her when she let herself think about how her mother had lied to her. Could she ever find a way around that? Could she ever forgive her?

The group around the campfire began to break up, interrupting Lena's thoughts. They didn't have to be in their sleeping bags until midnight, so when someone suggested a walk, everyone agreed. For the couples, it would be a perfect opportunity to sneak off and make out for an hour or so. Sure enough, ten minutes into the walk, both Millie and her date disappeared. Lena tagged along after the rest of the group, feeling like a fifth wheel. She might as well go back to the camp. She didn't want to end up one of the few geeks who didn't have a make-out partner.

Just as she turned to head back, she bumped into someone. She looked up and found herself staring into a pair of narrowed blue eyes. Luke McKinley's blue eyes.

"Hey," he said.

"Hey, Luke." The greeting sounded as if she'd just run five miles.

"You headed back?"

"Uh, I guess so."

"I'll go with you."

"Sure." She shrugged as though it didn't matter one way or the other.

They turned and walked up the moonlit pavement. The rest of the group continued on, their laughter fading in the distance. They walked for a minute or two without saying anything. Finally, unable to stand the silence any longer, Lena said, "I didn't expect to see you here. I mean—" She gave herself a mental *thwap* and then chastised herself. *Great, Lena. Now he thinks you were watching for him.*

"I didn't expect to come. Anderson said it would be a good time. So far, it's seemed pretty lame to me."

Lena immediately took offense. She stopped in the middle of the road. "I suppose there's a lot more action where you come from."

Luke stared down at her with his seen-it-all eyes. "Yeah, you could say that."

"So why'd you come here?"

He swung away from her and dropped his head

back to stare up at the star-speckled sky, his hands in his pockets. "It wasn't my idea."

"Your dad made you?"

He shrugged.

"Why didn't you go live with your mother?"

"I don't have a mother."

"Oh." Lena considered that for a moment. "I don't have a father."

"Aren't we the pair of bookends?"

He had a smart mouth. But she had a feeling he did that to cover up something. What, though?

They continued up the hill, not saying anything for a couple of minutes. Lena stopped again halfway up. "So why *did* he make you come here?"

Luke hesitated, and then told her, "Because he thinks he can reform me."

The words were blunt and to the point, as if he wanted to shock her, or maybe scare her away. Determined not to let him, she kept her voice nonchalant when she said, "For what?"

He looked down at the ground and scuffed a sneakered toe in the dirt. "I got caught with some drugs at a party."

"Were you using them?" she asked, somehow unable to picture him as a druggie.

Luke looked at her for a long minute, as if trying to decide how to answer. "Would you believe me if I said it wasn't something I made a habit of?"

She held his intense gaze, considered the question and then said, "Yeah, I would."

"I don't know why I just told you that. I haven't told anybody else."

"Your secret's safe with me." She tilted her head back and said, "Do you believe in haunted houses?"

"No," he said, looking surprised.

"Wanna see one?"

He shrugged. "Sure. Why not?"

Lena took off at a jog, cutting through the cornfield to their right. The Moon slanted a path of light across the rows of corn stubs. She jumped each one with ease. She congratulated herself for not looking back to see if he was still following her.

At the edge of the field, she slowed to a stop.

"You run track or something?" he asked, coming up behind her.

"As a matter of fact, I do," she said, then took off again.

"Wait!"

She kept going until she reached the fence surrounding the property. Luke was right behind her. They leaned against the rickety railing, their breathing short and raspy.

"This is the old Hathaway place. Spooky, huh?"

"Looks like a house to me."

The brick two-story sat some one hundred yards away, eerie in the moonlight. One side of the porch sagged like a lopsided smile. The roof had holes in it, and the breeze brushed a tree limb back and forth against a broken windowpane, the sound almost mournful.

Lena had a moment of doubt as to whether they

should go farther, but squashed it at the thought of Luke's earlier statement about the campout being so lame. She'd show him lame. "Come on. Let's go inside."

He looked at her as if he thought she'd lost it. "Why?"

"Why not?"

She hopped over the fence and bounded across the yard before she lost her nerve. She stopped at the front steps. They, too, were in terrible shape, partly rotted on one side. The Moon shed little light on the house. Lena tentatively touched a foot to the bottom step, then ventured up.

The door moaned as she gave it a shove inward. Adrenaline shot through her veins. She was crazy to go inside, after what she'd heard about this place. None of the kids she knew would come anywhere near it. But the desire to impress Luke prodded her on. She glanced over her shoulder. He was still behind her.

She stopped inside the enormous hallway. Moonlight shone in from the windows, but it was hard to see. To their right stood a winding staircase. The banister at the top hung precariously loose above them.

Lena pointed at the doorway to their left. "That's where they used to lay people out. It was called the viewing room."

"What do you mean 'lay people out'?"

"They didn't have funeral homes in those days, so people came to the house for the viewing."

Luke didn't say anything, but shifted from one foot to the other. His uneasiness gave her courage. She ventured forward. Boards creaked. From somewhere above, a bird flew out of its nesting place.

Lena stopped, hiding her own fright with words. "This used to be an old plantation. One of the biggest around."

"What kind of plantation?"

Lena shrugged. "I dunno. Probably cotton or tobacco. Later on, it became a boardinghouse, but people eventually stopped staying here because of all the things that kept happening."

"Like what?"

"Doors opening and closing in the middle of the night. There was this one chair that no matter where it was moved in the house, it always turned up in front of the living room window. No one could ever explain how it got moved. But it was rumored to be Mrs. Hathaway's favorite spot to sit."

Luke snorted in disbelief. "Must have been some explanation."

Ignoring his skepticism, Lena said, "They say she locked him in the cellar."

"Locked who in the cellar?" Luke asked, his voice the slightest bit rattled.

"Mr. Hathaway," Lena said, enjoying herself. "The story goes that he was in love with a young woman who worked for them. They'd planned to run away together, but Mrs. Hathaway found out and put an end to it."

"She killed them?"

"That's what they say."

"What'd she do with the bodies?"

"Some people say she buried them in the cornfield. Others say she buried them in the cellar."

"Sounds like a tall tale."

"Maybe. I don't know." Lena shrugged and continued down the hallway. It led into the kitchen. Luke went over to the old dry basin and worked the pump handle. It squeaked in protest and shot out a puff of dust. At the back of the kitchen, a door stood ajar. Lena pointed at it. "That must be the cellar."

Luke went over and opened it farther. The bottom scraped against the floor. Lena jumped. Luke stuck his head through the doorway and peered down the steps. "It's pitch black down there."

"I think this is as far as I'm going," she said.

He swung around and gave her a cocky grin, the tables suddenly turned. "Whatsa matter? You scared?"

"If I'd been scared, I wouldn't have come in here in the first place."

"No, I guess you wouldn't have. I don't know any girls who would come this far," he admitted.

Almost a compliment. Lena's courage reasserted itself. She moved to the door and peered down the steps. She couldn't see a thing. A board beneath her foot collapsed, and she pitched forward.

A pair of hands grabbed her shoulders and yanked her back to safety against a solid chest.

Lena's heart beat so fast she thought it might actually explode. Luke turned her around and said, "You okay?"

"Yeah. Thanks," she said, her voice all breathy again. She ridiculed herself for not being a better actress.

They stared at each other while Lena tried to regain her bearings. Feelings of another sort momentarily replaced her fear. In the dimness, the planes and angles of his good-looking face were even more compelling. His hands were still on her shoulders. She didn't want him to let go.

How long they stood there, she didn't know. Probably only a few seconds, but it seemed like forever. She didn't think forever would be long enough.

"We'd better get out of here," he said finally.

She nodded, not trusting her voice. He led the way, while she followed. They'd almost made it back to the front door when they heard a loud noise from upstairs. They turned around just as a piece of the banister railing fell from the stairway onto the hallway floor.

Lena looked at Luke. He looked at her. Without saying a word, they tore out of the house and ran for all they were worth. Across the porch. Down the steps. Flying through the yard. They didn't stop until they'd reached the edge of the cornfield, where they collapsed on the ground, their backs to the fence. They were both breathing as if they'd run a marathon.

They were silent for a minute or two, their rasping breaths the only sound in the stillness. They turned to look at each other. Smiles broke out on their faces.

"Chicken," Lena said.

"Like you weren't," Luke said, grinning.

"It's not so lame around here, after all, is it?" she asked, her own smile widening. If she had planned this night from the start, it never would have been as good as this. Not in her most outlandish imaginings would she have come up with the two of them ending up alone in a haunted house.

Silence hung between them again, the air full of newfound attraction. And a tension Lena had never before experienced.

Luke turned then, his shoulder against the fence. His head lowered toward hers. He was going to kiss her!

His lips brushed hers. He pulled back and said, "Your eyes are open."

"I know. I want to watch."

Luke smiled, cupped the side of her neck with his hand and kissed her again. She did watch for a second or two, but never-before-experienced feelings flooded her, and her eyes drifted closed. She savored every single sensation. There were so many. The smell of him, warm and overheated from their run across the field. The feel of him, big, broad, the very essence of him male and thoroughly intriguing.

His head tilted, and he deepened the kiss. Shock waves of surprise and pleasure ricocheted through her. Somehow, they managed to get closer. His arms went around her waist, and she found herself pressed close against his chest. It felt so good. Better than she'd imagined. Better than she'd ever dreamed.

She'd been kissed a couple of times. But never like this. Not quite sure what to do, she let instinct guide her, hoping she wasn't opening her mouth too wide, following his lead when his tongue brushed against hers.

They kissed for long, pulse-pounding minutes until Luke lifted his head. "When you set out to prove a guy wrong, you pull out all the stops."

Lena smiled. "I like to win."

"Yeah. I can see that." His thumb caressed her chin, lingering at her bottom lip, filling Lena with a yearning for something she didn't quite understand but wanted more of nonetheless.

"I think we'd better get back," Luke said in a reluctant voice.

Disappointment tumbled through her. She straightened her clothes, feeling as if she'd done something wrong. "Yeah. Someone will have missed us by now."

"Hey." He reached for her arm and stopped her jerky motions. "Lena, I didn't expect . . . I mean—"

"Please don't say you're sorry," she said. Being with him made her feel better. For a short while, she'd even become her old self, not the bitchy brat she'd been since she'd discovered her mother's betrayal. Being with Luke made her feel wanted and worthwhile. Being with him made her forget about the father who hadn't wanted her. She didn't want to hear that he wished it hadn't happened.

"I don't know what you're thinking, Lena." He reached out and curved his hand around her neck. "But the last thing I want to do is go back."

In the span of a couple of hours, her whole life had

changed. She knew without a doubt that she would never be the same again.

Once he'd made sure Lena had reached the campsite, Luke climbed the hill to Tim Anderson's Wagoneer and pulled a sleeping bag out of the back. He made his way to the tent the two of them had pitched earlier.

Tim was already inside. Opening the flap, Luke ducked in, trying not to wake him.

"Where you been?" the other boy asked, lifting up on one elbow.

"Went for a walk."

"Some walk. Who went with you?"

"Nobody."

Tim grinned. "Yeah, I believe that."

Luke rolled out the bed, then lay down on it, ignoring the other boy's baiting.

"Somebody said Lena Williams wasn't back a little while ago. She wasn't out walking with you, was she?"

"'Night, Anderson," Luke said, rolling over on his side.

Tim chuckled. "I'll take that as a yes."

Luke couldn't fall asleep, his mind wide-awake with what had happened between Lena and him. Everything about it surprised him.

Lena Williams was nothing like the girls he'd hung around with in the city. Most of them would have eaten her alive. But something about her appealed to him. She had guts, that was for sure, but kissing her had been the biggest surprise of all. It had just happened as if it were supposed to all along. And he'd enjoyed it. More than he wanted to admit, even now. He'd liked the way she felt against him. He'd sensed that she hadn't done a lot of kissing. He'd gotten used to girls who showed him things. He'd liked being the one to show her. It was a rite of passage for all guys to brag when they'd been with a girl. So why hadn't he wanted to tell Tim?

Lying there on his sleeping bag, Luke avoided answering that question. He stared up at the top of the tent and let himself admit that maybe Keeling Creek wouldn't be so bad after all. Something about the place had kind of started to grow on him. It was even getting to his dad. He'd actually gone out and bought a calf a few days ago. A calf, of all things! When Luke had come home and found it tied under one of the oak trees in the front yard, he'd thought for sure his father must be losing it. Luke questioned him about it, but he'd just said a farm needed animals.

Luke still couldn't get over it. Even though he hadn't let on as much to his dad, he thought it was pretty cool. This place was definitely having a weird effect on his father. And maybe on him too.

31

After leaving the clinic on Saturday morning, Colby stopped by her parents' house for lunch since Lena wouldn't be home from the campout until later that afternoon.

She knocked at the back door, sending a glance around the familiar yard. Samuel and Emma Williams had the neatest house around. They weren't wealthy by some standards, but they took great pride in their things. They loved working in the yard together, planting bulbs in the spring and fall, pruning bushes and keeping the lawn as closely mowed as the golf course at the Low Valley Country Club. People drove from as far as seventy-five miles away just to see her mother's flower garden. An enormous old magnolia tree stood in the front yard. In the spring and summer, red impatiens encircled it, thick as clover in a hayfield. Fall brought out different flowers, the driveway now lined with burgundy mums, four plants wide on each side.

Standing there on the brick walkway, Colby realized, not for the first time, that if things had worked out differently for her, theirs was the kind of marriage she would want. A partnership. Someone to share things with, do things with. After Doug, she'd been so busy trying to prove that she could accomplish on her own all the things in life that really mattered that maybe she'd never really given anyone a chance. The hurt he'd caused her shaped her adult life, and she wondered now if she'd been wrong to let him have that much power over her.

Her mother appeared at the door, a pleased expression on her face. "Colby. You're just in time for lunch, dear."

"I'd hoped I would be." She stepped inside and gave her mom a hug. "Sorry I didn't call first."

"As if you need to. Your father's golfing this morning, so he won't be back for a while yet. Let me grab another bowl, and we'll sit down."

Colby washed her hands and tested the soup on the stove. "Um, that's good."

"Vegetable soup. Every one from my summer garden." She poured them each a glass of iced tea, and they began eating. The soup tasted perfect for an early fall afternoon.

"How's Lena?"

"The same."

"Maybe I should talk to her, honey."

"Thanks, Mom, but this is something I need to handle on my own."

"I understand, and you're probably right. But you know it's a mother's nature to want to fix whatever's wrong in her daughter's life."

"I know, Mom. And I appreciate it," Colby said, stirring some sugar into her tea.

"While we're on that subject, I ran into Phoebe at the grocery store this week. She told me she'd fixed you up with Mr. McKinley."

"It wasn't a date. You know Phoebe. She thinks I'm desperate for a husband."

"Well, he is awfully handsome."

"Handsome and engaged," Colby said pointedly.

Emma's expression fell. "She forgot to mention that part."

"Phoebe's an optimist. She considers that a minor hitch in her plan."

Emma chuckled and shook her head. "Your father said he saw your truck at Oak Hill last night, though. We thought you might have had a date."

Colby reached for some crackers and crumbled them into her soup. "Actually, I helped him de-skunk his dog."

"Oh."

"Not the answer you'd hoped for, I gather."

"Now, honey—"

"Mom, even if I were interested, which I'm not," she emphasized, trying not to think about last night, "the man is not up for consideration. You and Phoebe both might as well accept that."

"All right, honey. Whatever you say," she said, a curious look in her eye that Colby determinedly ignored.

IT WAS ALMOST dinnertime when Mrs. Mitchell's car pulled up in front of the house, and Lena got out, wearing faded jeans and a multicolored sweatshirt. From her position at the living room window, Colby noticed that she was smiling and looked happier than she had seen her in months. The sight of it both lifted her heart and sent it plummeting.

How long since Lena had smiled at her that way?

A minute later, Lena bounded through the door, her hair tousled, her cheeks bright with color.

Colby tried to keep her voice light when she said, "Hi. How was the campout?"

Lena looked up, her expression closing immediately. "It was okay."

"Did they have a good turnout?"

"Yeah." Lena headed for the stairs without looking back.

"Lena?"

She stopped midway up and said, "What?"

Sighing, Colby decided then and there to take the bull by the horns. This couldn't go on any longer. She'd done everything but stand on her head to try to mend a rift she didn't even understand. "Come down here. I think we need to talk."

"I've got stuff to do," she called back with attitude.

"This can't wait," Colby said, her voice unusually firm.

Lena turned and clomped down the stairs, the heaviness of her footsteps echoing her reluctance.

Colby went into the den and stood by the window. Confrontations had never been a part of her relationship with her daughter, and she wished fervently that they weren't now. "I want to know what's wrong, Lena. And don't say 'Nothing.' I've tried to be patient, hoping that whatever it was would blow over. But obviously, it isn't going to. So tell me what's going on."

Lena folded her arms across her chest and glared at her. "There's nothing to talk about."

"I don't believe that."

"Believe what you want."

Anger and hurt were neck and neck among the emotions galloping through Colby's insides. She subdued them both and said, "We used to be able to talk about everything, Lena. What's changed?"

"Nothing."

"Yes, it has. Why is it different now?"

For a long time, Lena didn't say anything. She kept her gaze locked somewhere over Colby's left shoulder. When she spoke, her voice rang out harsh with anger. "Why did you lie to me?"

"About what?" she asked, caught off guard by the question.

Lena turned and stomped up the stairs without answering. Stunned, Colby stayed where she was. What on earth was she talking about? Just when

Colby started to go after her, Lena tramped back downstairs with a piece of paper in her hand. She held it out to her with a look of condemnation in her eyes.

Colby took it, glanced at it, and then felt the color drain from her face when she realized what it was. "Where did you find this?" she asked in little more than a whisper.

"In your old room at Grandma's."

Dread marched down Colby's spine, followed by a crystal clear understanding of what brought about the changes in her child. "Lena—"

"Why couldn't you just tell me the truth, Mom? That he didn't want anything to do with either one of us."

"Oh, Lena, it's not what—"

Tears running down her face, Lena ran back up the stairs. Her door slammed. Colby flinched. She groped for the chair behind her and sat down, feeling shell-shocked. How had this happened? All these years, she'd kept the truth from Lena, not wanting to hurt her. And now, because of one stupid letter she should have thrown away long ago. . . .

Why hadn't she? But she knew why.

She'd kept it as a reminder to herself that she'd done the right thing. That Doug made his choice, and he was the one who would come out the loser.

She now understood Lena's rebellion, her anger. She'd been keeping this inside, letting it build until the wall between them had become so high that they might never get past it.

How did she explain this to Lena? Tell her that Doug wanted her to terminate the pregnancy? That he'd had no understanding of Colby's refusal to do so? She couldn't. She wouldn't. Right now, she feared what that might do to her daughter more than any resentment Lena felt for her.

She sat there until all the sunlight disappeared from the room, torn between the need to go to Lena and the fear that she wouldn't be able to find the right words to say. Finally, unable to avoid it any longer, she got up and climbed the stairs to Lena's room, feeling as if her feet were weighted with lead.

She knocked at the door. "Lena?" No answer. She turned the knob, surprised to find it unlocked.

Lena sat on the side of the bed, staring out the window that looked onto their backyard. Colby went over and sat down beside her, close but not touching. "Baby, we need to talk," she said, unconsciously reverting to the endearment Lena recently demanded she stop using.

"What's there to talk about?"

"For starters, the fact that I love you more than life itself and the last thing I ever wanted to do was hurt you."

"Why did you tell me my father was dead, then? He's not, is he?"

Colby looked down at her hands and shook her head. "No, he isn't. At least not that I know of."

Fresh tears gathered in Lena's eyes. She swiped at them. "All these years I've wondered what he would have been like, if he would have been the kind of father I'd have wanted to take to parents' day. . .if I looked like him."

The lump in Colby's throat thickened. How she wished that he had been. How she would have liked for him to deserve this child's grief over not knowing him. But he *didn't* deserve it. Not once had he ever called to see whether they had a boy or a girl. Not once in all these years had he ever tried to contact them. Lena deserved better than that. So much better.

"Honey, your father and I were so young. He. . .he wasn't ready for that kind of responsibility. I wish things had been different, but. . . ."

Lena jumped up from the bed, cutting her off and turning to stare at her with angry eyes. "Why didn't you just tell me that? That the two of you broke up? At least I would have had the option of seeing him."

"Lena, it's not that simple."

"Will you find him for me?" she asked, her eyes defiant.

"Oh, Lena." Colby didn't know what to say. When she'd heard years ago that Doug had married, the news hadn't bothered her in the least. Whatever love she'd thought she held in her heart for him died the day he'd renounced any obligation to their unborn child. But for Lena's sake, she feared opening that can of worms. It was already done, though, and she couldn't close it again. "Is that what you really want?"

"Yes," Lena said, her expression set.

In that moment, Colby realized that Lena wanted to hurt her. To pay her back for keeping the truth from her. And she had found the most effective way of doing it. With a sigh of resignation, she said, "Then I'll do whatever I can to find him."

Sleep proved a futile effort that night. Colby lay awake thinking about what calling Doug would mean, dreading it more than she had ever imagined she would. She had no idea whether he still lived in Philadelphia, but she would start there.

Up before the sun rose, she sat at the kitchen table drinking coffee until almost eight o'clock when she picked up the phone and called Phoebe. She needed to talk to someone. She didn't want to call her parents. This would upset them too much.

Phoebe's hello sounded cheerful enough that Colby knew she hadn't gotten her out of bed. She told her, in as few words as possible, what had happened last night.

"Oh, Colby," Phoebe said when she finished. "That's what's been wrong with her, then?"

"Yes," she said, miserable.

"So are you going to call the slime bucket?"

"I don't have a choice."

"She'd resent you forever if you didn't."

"How'd I turn out to be the bad guy in this? That's what I want to know."

"Give her a chance to judge him. You'll come out smelling like a rose. Trust me."

She hoped Phoebe was right. She would never forgive herself if this permanently marred her relationship with Lena.

She waited until nine o'clock and then dialed information.

"Directory assistance. What city, please?"

"Philadelphia. Douglas Jamison."

"I have a Douglas A. and two Douglas C. Jamisons."

Colby asked for the first Douglas C, since she had no way of knowing which was the right one. She punched in the number. After three rings, a woman answered.

"May I speak to Doug Jamison, please?" Colby asked.

A pause of silence, and then the woman said, "My husband is no longer alive."

"Oh. I'm sorry," Colby said. "I have the wrong number." She hung up, a knot in her stomach. The woman sounded too old to be Doug's wife. Maybe that had been his parents' home, and his father had died.

Colby tried information again and asked for the second Douglas C.

Before she lost her courage, she picked up the phone and dialed the number. It rang twice, and then she heard his voice for the first time in more than sixteen years. She couldn't say anything for a moment, frozen with too many emotions to identify.

"Hello? Is anyone there?" he asked, irritation marking the words.

"It's Colby, Doug," she said finally.

Silence, and then the click of a door closing.

His voice sounded lower when he said, "Colby. Where are you?"

"I'm at home. In Keeling Creek."

"Oh." He paused. "You're the last person I expected to hear from."

"Believe me," she said, "this isn't a social call."

"What is it, then?" he asked warily.

"It's about our daughter. . .she wants to see you." Blunt, but what point was there in beating around the bush?

"What do you mean?" The words held an edge, as if he were being backed into a corner.

"I had a girl, Doug. I never told her the truth about you. She found out recently, though, and she's understandably upset."

"What did you tell her?"

"What difference does it make? You weren't a part of our lives." She couldn't keep the accusation from her voice.

He was silent a moment, then said, "You can't just spring this on me and expect me to—"

"Calling you is the last thing I ever wanted to do. But Lena is hurting over this. She's confused and—"

"I have a family, Colby."

On some level, she had known that he would. But hearing him say it somehow brought back a pain that she'd thought long ago put away. He had been nineteen when Lena was born. He hadn't wanted marriage and a family. It hurt somehow to think that he eventually chose them with another woman, other children. For the first time since her confrontation with Lena, she thought she truly understood how her daughter must feel. "Are you saying you don't want to see her?"

"I don't know," he said, the words sounding as if they'd been issued through clenched teeth. Just for her own satisfaction, she pictured him fat and sweating.

"Look, Doug, I'm not asking anything of you," she said, her voice cool. "But I will not allow you to hurt her. If you don't want to see her, just say so, and I'll think of something to tell her."

"This is too sudden, Colby."

Colby laughed. She couldn't help it. It was such a ridiculous statement, and typical of the selfish person he was. "You're right. Sixteen years is a bit sudden." As soon as the words were out, she wanted to take them back. She didn't want him to think that she'd ever spent a moment yearning for him.

"I made my decision about this before she was born," he said, his voice ice-cold and impersonal to the point that she wondered if she'd ever known him. "You know what my choice was. I didn't want this child. I wanted you to have an abortion. You chose not to do that. I hardly think it's fair for you to call me up out of the blue and—"

"Fair?" she interrupted, anger scalding through her. How dare he sit there, blithely talking about an abortion as if Lena didn't exist? As if he had any idea what he had missed in not knowing her as his child? How had she ever imagined herself in love with him? "I'm sorry to see that you haven't changed one bit, Doug. Give me a call when you've had enough time to think about this. Personally, I don't think you deserve to know our daughter. I won't tell her we talked until

I hear from you." She gave him her number and hung up without saying goodbye.

She tore off the piece of paper on which she'd scribbled his number and shoved it in her pocket. To her disgust, her hand shook, and she hated herself for letting him get to her that way.

Many different emotions assaulted her at once, anger and protectiveness at the top of the list. A few minutes spent talking to him brought back all the old insecurities with which their relationship had left her. Doug Jamison would be a disappointment to his daughter. She knew that. How would Lena handle his rejection? Be anything but devastated?

Colby glanced at her watch. The eleven o'clock church service would be starting in an hour and a half. But she didn't feel like going this morning. She needed to pull herself together. Deciding to let Lena sleep on, Colby wrote her a note, then grabbed her keys and left the house.

32

It had become a ritual for Ian to drive into town for the Sunday paper. He arrived at Cutter's Grocery about eight-thirty. Located in the middle of town, Maude Cutter and her husband, Harvey, ran the place. Since Ian had first set foot in the store, he'd been unable to resist Mrs. Cutter's homemade cinnamon rolls, which she made fresh every day. The tantalizing aroma predictably tempted him as he stepped inside and poured himself a cup of coffee from the pot on the counter. He nodded at Dillard and Willard Nolen, who were sitting on the bench by the door swapping sections of the paper.

"Morning, Mr. McKinley," Mrs. Cutter said from behind the counter. "Looks like we're gonna have a nice week."

"No rain in the forecast?" he asked. This, too, was

part of the ritual—Mrs. Cutter's weekly weather bulletin.

"Doesn't look like it. We might get a few clouds by Wednesday, but they don't talk like it'll turn to rain."

"Good. I've got some work to do on the barn. Then there's all that hay that needs cutting," he said, some inner devil urging him on. Dillard and Willard both peered over their papers at him, nodding in approval. Obviously, they hadn't heard about his tractor mishap or they would have known he wouldn't be going anywhere near one. He smiled to himself and picked up the paper. "I'll take some of those cinnamon rolls too. You've ruined my willpower, Mrs. Cutter."

The older woman beamed. "It's nice to know I can still tempt a young looker like you."

Ian chuckled and paid her, enjoying their banter. He leafed through the financial section while he drank his coffee. A little while later, he left the store with a fresh cup of coffee in his hand.

The morning felt crisp and cool, the sky cloudless above him. He climbed into his car, thinking of how different his Sundays had been in New York. Trying to get ahead on his work, never catching up from one week to the next, but continuing the race until the days and months ran together, he had forgotten how to stop and smell the roses altogether. He was relearning how to do that here. He hoped he never forgot again.

On his way out of town, he spotted the tail end of Colby's truck behind her clinic. Common sense told him to keep on driving, but given that he hadn't been listening to that a lot lately where she was concerned, he swung the Mercedes into the parking lot and sat there, debating whether or not to go in.

Since the moment she'd left his house on Friday, he'd been comparing her to Rachel in ways he shouldn't have. The two of them couldn't have been more different. Not in a million years would he have imagined doing with Rachel what he'd done with Colby. Rachel would have been horrified at the thought of helping him bathe Smidge in tomato juice. She'd have thought he'd lost his mind for buying Matilda. And she didn't eat pizza. Under any circumstances.

The mere fact that he compared the two of them should have made him turn the car around and drive away as fast as he could get the thing in gear. Instead, he got out and crossed the parking lot to the back door.

It had been left open an inch or two. He knocked. "Colby?"

No answer. He went inside and called her name again.

"I'm back here."

He followed her voice. Several dogs barked in unison, aware now that they had company on an otherwise quiet morning. He found her at the back of the building, sitting on a crate in the middle of what looked like a supply room. A bunch of smaller boxes surrounded her. A clipboard lay across her lap.

"Putting in some overtime?" he asked, leaning against the doorjamb.

She kept her face averted, running a thumb beneath each eye and not quite meeting his gaze. "I. . .not really. Just doing some inventory."

Her voice sounded funny, raspy and uneven. "Thought you'd be in church," he said.

"I asked God for a raincheck," she said with a bad attempt at a smile.

There was something wrong. He saw it in the tenseness of her expression. "Are you okay?"

She nodded, focusing on the clipboard in her left hand.

But he could see she wasn't. He went over and sat down on the crate beside her, careful not to touch her. "You want to talk about it?"

Her shoulders lifted in a shrug. "There's nothing to talk about—"

"Why don't I believe you?"

Tears welled in her eyes. She tossed the clipboard on the floor and wiped the back of her hand across her cheeks. "Oh, shoot!"

"What is it, Colby?" He put a hand on her arm and tried to ignore the shock of awareness that touching her sent through him.

She didn't answer for several moments, visibly struggling for composure. "It's a long story. You don't really want to hear it."

"Hey, I don't have anywhere else to be."

She sat there, not saying anything for a while. He just waited, knowing she would get around to it when she felt ready. She let out a heavy sigh and then said, "I found out why Lena's been hating me the past couple of months."

"And?"

She dabbed at her eyes with her shirtsleeve and sighed, her shoulders slumping. "I had her when I was in college. I wasn't married."

She looked up at him as though she expected him to be shocked or disgusted. He was neither. He knew she must have been young when Lena was born. But he'd assumed she'd married and divorced.

"That was a long time ago," she said, before he could respond. "Lena never knew her father. I told her he was dead."

Surprised, Ian didn't know what to say. "Why?"

She got up from the crate and moved to the window that looked out on the back parking lot, arms folded across her chest as if she were physically holding herself together. "We were young and when I first found out, I had no idea what to do. Doug wanted me. . .he wanted me not to have the baby. I almost let him convince me it was the right thing to do. . . ."

"But you didn't let him."

She shook her head, pain clear in her face.

Colby Williams was the strongest woman Ian had ever known, and the unfamiliar fragility he sensed in her now bothered him in ways he couldn't explain. He wanted to pull her into his arms and give her the comfort she so clearly needed. He subdued the impulse with hard-won restraint. "And that's why you two didn't stay together?"

"That pretty much ended things."

Ian didn't know what to say, amazed at the guy's heartlessness. "He didn't want to be in her life?"

"No. And I could never bring myself to tell her that."

"So how did she find out about him?"

"She found a letter from him to me in my old room at my parents' house. That's why she's been so different lately. Not that I blame her. I can't believe I was stupid enough to keep that letter. I've called him, asking him to speak to her, but I haven't told her in case he still doesn't want anything to do with her."

"Hey," he said, tilting her chin up and forcing her to look at him. "Don't blame yourself. She's lucky to have you for a mother."

He felt her distress as if it were his own. They stood there, staring at each other, caught up in something Ian didn't want to name but couldn't deny. Consoling her wasn't his right or his place. But she needed comfort. And he was here. He told himself that was all there was to it as he pulled her against him. He actually believed it until the reality of her breasts against his chest shot that theory all to pieces.

It felt as if she melted against him; she wrapped her arms around his waist, her hands splayed across his back.

Ian closed his eyes. His hands hung suspended behind her until the need to touch her overrode all the reasons why he should not. He let one hand rest in the center of her back while the other stroked the length of her hair. Soft and straight, it felt like silk against his palm.

Something shifted inside him, cutting him adrift from everything he had felt certain about just moments ago.

His first thought? They fit somehow. Like two interlocking pieces of a puzzle. Colby was a woman able to take care of herself. A woman who didn't need a man to complete her. But with her in his arms, he felt a sense of completeness that was distinctly unnerving, if equally welcome.

For long, uncountable moments, they stood, simply holding each other. When she looked up at him, her eyes were questioning and needy in a way that he could not ignore. He felt the shift inside him again, and, of its own volition, his hand moved to smooth a strand of hair from her face. He was sure the uncertainty in her expression reflected his own. Kissing her suddenly seemed like something he had to do. He leaned down and brushed his mouth against hers. She made a soft sound somewhere between protest and acquiescence.

He deepened the kiss, cupping his hand around the back of her neck, holding her closer. He was aware of the curves and lines of her, surprised by how right that felt too. It was the first time he had held her this way, and yet there was nothing strange or unfamiliar about it.

The kiss grew more hurried, greedier, Colby as insistent as he. What began as consolation became something else entirely. Yet, he didn't want to stop. Didn't want to. Reason and logic deserted him, and he wanted more of everything. Her mouth. Her skin. The soft sounds of pleasure coming from her throat.

The phone rang, the answering machine out front picking up the call. The noise sufficient to bring some semblance of sanity to what was happening between them.

Colby pulled away and touched the back of her hand to her mouth.

"Colby, are you there? We didn't see you at church, and I got a little concerned. No one answered at your house, so I thought I'd check here. If you get this message, give me a call."

"My mom." Colby pressed her lips together and avoided his gaze.

Ian nodded and stepped back, shoving a hand through his hair. Colby moved to the window, looking out, her breathing still erratic. He wondered what he was supposed to say about what just happened when he had no idea why or how it had.

"We shouldn't have done that," she said, her voice oddly uneven.

She was right. They shouldn't have. He had no right to kiss her. But if anyone should be blamed for this, he should. "It wasn't your fault. I—"

She turned to face him and raised a hand to interrupt. "Please. You were just being nice. I took advantage of that."

"You didn't take advantage of anything, Colby." Confusion settled over him like fog over San

Francisco. He should feel guilty, but of all the other emotions churning inside him, that one was absent. In all honesty, he had wanted to kiss her for a long time now—on the day she'd brought him home from the hospital and then again on Friday night when she'd left his house. From the first day he'd met her, something had been simmering beneath the surface between them. He couldn't deny that. But he'd never expected the kind of heat their kiss generated.

"Okay, let's be rational about this," she said, one hand in stop sign mode. "You and I both know what just happened wouldn't have happened if I hadn't been upset. You were only—"

"Colby."

"—trying to make me feel—"

"Colby."

She stopped, meeting his gaze with what looked like a sincere attempt to convince them both that this whole thing had been nothing more than a fluke brought on by need on her part and martyrdom on his. As much as he would have liked to believe that, his gut didn't buy it. "Let's put this on rewind. Stay right there."

He backed out of the room while she watched him, a curious expression on her face. He retraced his steps to the door that opened into the parking lot and called out, "Colby?"

"In the back," she answered, sounding puzzled.

He wound his way down the hall, across the room to the window, where she stood looking at him as if she thought he'd lost his mind. "So this Doug," he said.

"He's a real jerk, right? Well, I think you're doing the right thing in waiting to tell Lena that you spoke with him. That kind of thing might do a lot of damage to a fifteen-year-old's self-image. And if you ever need anyone to talk to about this, just pick up the phone and call, okay? After all, that's what friends are for."

Colby's face broke into a smile, her eyes still moist from the earlier tears.

"All right?" he prompted.

"All right," she said.

"I'm going to go now." He backed away from her, slowly, their gazes snagged, until he turned abruptly and left before he changed his mind.

33

The smile lingered on Colby's lips long after Ian had gone.

An hour ago, she'd thought she might never smile again.

She sank back down on the crate and sighed. No matter how they colored it, what happened here had been a mistake. Of the screwing-up-your-life-in-a-big-way variety.

Logically, she knew that to be true. So why hadn't she wanted it to stop? Why had she been sorry to see him go even as she'd been telling him he should?

Being friends with Ian McKinley might not work out exactly as she'd thought it would. Maybe she'd been crazy to think it possible.

Considering everything going on with Lena right now, she hardly needed to set herself up as the other woman.

No, the friends thing definitely wasn't working. But it wasn't too late for damage control. She would just stay away from him. No more complicated than that. The right thing to do. The only thing to do.

IN THE WEEK following the incident at Colby's clinic, Ian was tempted to call and find out whether she'd heard from Lena's father yet. The way he saw it, the jerk didn't deserve a chance to be part of Lena's life. But he didn't call. His reasons for wanting to weren't as pure as they should have been. And he knew it.

He worked in his office each morning, then spent his afternoons puttering around the barn and the outside of the house. The leaves had begun to brighten toward full color now, the oak trees lining the driveway streaked in yellow. Somehow, in the city, the beauty of autumn always escaped him. Here, he reveled in it. He brought Matilda out in the afternoons and let her nibble at the grass while Smidge raced circles around her, wanting to play.

Even though he didn't see Colby, she was never far from his thoughts. He'd gone over that Sunday morning so many times, it played like an old movie running through his head. As much as he tried to rationalize it to himself, a voice in his gut told him that a happily engaged man didn't do what he'd done with Colby Williams. Be that as it might, he found reassurance in the realization that it didn't have to . . . wouldn't . . . happen again.

When Rachel called on Wednesday and said she

would like to come down for the weekend, he said all the right things. Of course he wanted her to come. He would be glad to see her. But when she called back on Thursday and said something had come up at work and she would be tied up all day Saturday, he felt more than a little unsettled to find that he wasn't disappointed.

Then he ran across a letter from Colby on the editorial page of Friday's paper. The sight of it made his chest tighten and blew to pieces any notion that he'd put what happened between them from his mind. Without taking his gaze from the page, he set down his cup of coffee and began to read.

Dear Editor,

On my way to work today, I found a black-and-white beagle puppy lying in the middle of the road at the top of Nolen Hill. His small body was twisted and broken, rain pelting off his fur. It was too late for me to do anything to help him.

A few yards away, his brother and two sisters sat huddled together on the shoulder, looking as if they were sure the person who had left them there would soon return to take them home.

This isn't the first time I've seen dogs and cats who, no longer wanted, have been dropped off and left to sit by the road in that same way, just waiting.

I have to wonder how someone left those puppies, knowing that they would either starve to death or be hit by a car. Their fate was certain to be one or the other.

As anyone who has ever been to my clinic knows, I encourage the spaying and neutering of pets so that unplanned-for puppies and kittens won't be brought into the world. If such a thing should happen, though, please don't abandon them to the kind of fate I've just described.

I plan to one day be part of bringing a No-Kill shelter to this county where unwanted pets can stay until they are adopted. Until then, I hope I never see another animal abandoned this way.

Colby Williams, DVM

The editor included a note below the letter that read: "For anyone interested in adopting a pet, the county shelter will be holding Adopt-A-Pet Day on the lawn outside the courthouse on Saturday from 1:00 to 4:00 p.m."

Ian put down the paper and turned his chair to stare out the window. His throat felt tight, and it was hard to swallow.

The letter made him think about the choice Colby made sixteen years ago. She had accepted responsibility for her actions. Had a child and raised her by herself. Not an easy task for someone trying to get through college and then vet school. She was the same woman today that she had been then. A woman with values that she not only spoke, but practiced. Her own life couldn't exactly be a bed of roses at the moment, and yet she'd taken the time to write this letter.

He read it again, and if he'd had any doubts before, he no longer thought that putting Colby Williams out of his mind would be easy.

34

Without looking up, Colby knew exactly when Ian walked through the gate to the Adopt-A-Pet Day on Saturday afternoon. She glanced up and found him smiling at something Stacey Renick was saying to him.

It had been almost a week since she'd seen him, and yet her awareness of him was as pronounced now as before. She felt as if she had a divining fork inside her, and he was the only water in a bone-dry desert.

She'd been tempted to call him, to apologize for unloading on him last Sunday, but when she'd picked up the phone, cowardice won out. She hadn't trusted her own declarations of indifference.

She still didn't.

For the next hour, she deliberately put herself as far away from him as possible. At one point, she looked up and found him staring at her. She swallowed, caught up in remembering the heat of their kiss, and almost, almost, lost her resolve to keep her distance.

Phoebe walked up just then. "Well, aren't you going to go over and say hi?"

"No, Phoebe, I'm not," she said, and inserted herself in a debate between a young husband and wife trying to choose a kitten. Colby convinced them to take two, since the couple had a nice barn in which the cats earned their keep by keeping the mice away.

At four o'clock, she made her way back to the gate, where Stacey said, "Boy, this was a great day. I think your letter to the paper pricked a few consciences."

Colby smiled. "Good. Who took our last little beagle?"

"Mr. McKinley. You should have seen them leaving. That little fella was as happy as a bee in clover."

"That's great," Colby said, caught off guard by the news.

Stacey laughed. "Yeah, I'd be happy if he took me home with him too."

Colby aimed for a laugh herself and failed noticeably. She tried not to think about him, but he wasn't helping matters any. Sooner or later, he would do something to tarnish his image. Sooner or later, all men did.

35

Having a puppy was like having a newborn baby in the house.

On the way home, Ian stopped by the grocery store and bought several different varieties of puppy food, wanting to make sure he found one the puppy would like.

Ian felt guilty about not taking every single animal home with him. Seeing those pets, each of which once had a home to live in, staring up at every person who walked by with hopeful looks on their faces, made him feel sick inside.

That explained why he'd ended up driving home with a grateful little beagle in the front seat. A beagle, of all things. Beagles weren't New York City dogs. They liked to run. And chase rabbits. Didn't they? There weren't any rabbits on Park Avenue.

First a calf and now a beagle. What was happening to him?

He thought about the office he'd left behind in New York and the no-nonsense person he'd been. Would any of those people even recognize him? Would his own fiancée recognize him?

He didn't think so.

He didn't recognize himself.

Back at the house, Mabel fussed over the puppy and fixed him a bowl of warm food, clucking and persisting until he'd finished every morsel.

"Pretty soon we'll have more animals roaming around here than Colby has at her clinic, won't we, Mr. McKinley?" she asked with a knowing smile.

Ian pretended to miss the innuendo behind Mabel's seemingly innocent remark and went to the sink to rinse out the puppy's bowl.

Mabel left just after six, leaving Smidge and him alone with the latest addition to the family. The puppy refused to stay in his bed. He trotted around the house and acquainted himself with his new surroundings while Smidge followed, curious and a little miffed by his presence. Ian suspected the two would soon be devoted buddies.

That night, Ian left them in the kitchen together. Luke had gone out with friends, and he didn't expect him back until late. Ian had hoped he would get home in time to meet the new puppy, but it would have to wait until morning.

He fixed a basket with a towel inside it and a ticking alarm clock beneath it. He'd once heard the noise comforted puppies recently taken from their mothers. He hoped it would work.

He'd been upstairs no more than five minutes when the howling started. Only it sounded more like crying. Ian gave the puppy a few minutes, thinking he'd adjust. He didn't.

Guilt led Ian to the kitchen, where he scooped the puppy up, basket and all and took him to his room. Smidge stayed in the kitchen as if she didn't want her sleep disturbed again. Ian tucked the puppy back in and kept his hand on the little guy's head until he fell asleep. As soon as he removed his hand from the basket, the puppy started howling again.

Ian finally dozed off at some point after eleven, but came abruptly awake to a pitiful, protesting wail sometime later. "Okay, okay." He bent down to pick up the scrawny little puppy and tuck him beneath the covers. "You win."

"What's going on?"

Luke stood in the doorway, dressed in jeans and a leather jacket. He glanced at Ian and then at the puppy.

"We've got a new member of the family," Ian said. "Come meet him."

Luke hung back for a few moments, struggling not to appear too interested. But curiosity apparently got the better of him. He stepped inside the room and said, "Where did he come from?"

"The adoption event today."

"Why?"

Ian heard the surprise in his son's voice and

realized that it was justified. He wouldn't have done that a few months ago. "He needed a home."

"Is he one of the puppies Dr. Williams wrote to the paper about?"

Ian nodded. "You read the letter?"

"Yeah." Luke rubbed the sleepy puppy's ears. The puppy got up and wagged his tail, then playfully swatted Luke's hand with his paw.

"We need to come up with a name for him," Ian said.

"Like what?"

"I don't know. What's he look like?"

"A shrimp."

Ian smiled. "You think he'd answer to that?"

Luke shrugged and rubbed the puppy's ears again, surprising Ian with his half smile.

"Too bad we can't think of something that means 'doesn't sleep at night.'"

Luke laughed, startling Ian into speechlessness. He stared at his son for a moment, completely taken aback. How long had it been since he'd made his son laugh? Too long. Way too long.

Rubbing the puppy's back, Luke said, "What do you think about Rebel?"

The puppy licked his hand and wagged his tail like a windshield wiper on high speed.

"He does have a bit of a James Dean look to him, doesn't he?"

"Yeah, he does." Luke picked the puppy up and cradled him against his chest.

Pleasure rose inside Ian and spread outward, love

for his son a pain in his heart. "He doesn't like sleeping by himself. You want to take him with you?"

Luke looked up at him, obviously pleased. "Sure."

"Smidge didn't know what to think of him at first."

"She'll like him. She'll have somebody to play with other than Matilda."

Ian smiled. "Matilda's not much on chasing rabbits."

Luke chuckled again. The sound filled Ian with gratitude, and he knew that anything he'd sacrificed in coming here had been worth it. This was the boy he'd missed. "You can have the basket," he said, hearing the waver in his own voice.

Luke scooped the basket up with one hand and headed out of the room. "'Night, Dad," he said.

"Hey, Luke?"

"Yeah?" he said, turning around.

Ian searched for words and prayed that his timing was right. "Remember what you said that night at the police station? About me blaming you for your mother's death?"

Luke held the puppy a little closer and nodded.

"I want you to know that was never true. You were what kept me going then. I don't know what I would have done without you. I'm the one who's made some mistakes. It's kind of hard to explain why people do the things they do, but I guess I used my work as a way to get through the grief. After a while, working became a way of life. I wanted to give you all the things my father never gave me when I was growing up. I didn't realize that I wasn't there for you in the ways that count. I hope you can forgive me for that, because I really want to make it up to you."

Luke looked down at the puppy. When he glanced back up, his eyes held a sheen of tears. "I haven't exactly been the world's greatest son."

"With both of us trying, we're bound to get things right sooner or later," Ian said.

Luke nodded, not quite meeting his gaze. "See you in the morning."

"'Night, son."

Luke turned in the doorway. "Maybe we could make a house for Rebel outside next to Smidge's tomorrow."

Ian felt such love for the boy. "That'd be great, Luke. Really great."

And for the first time since they'd moved to Keeling Creek, Ian went to sleep feeling as if he'd made some small headway in the healing process between him and his son.

Life was good.

36

Curling iron in hand, Lena put the finishing touches on her hair, deciding that maybe her own color—somewhere between blonde and brown—wasn't so bad. She'd stopped putting the purple streaks in it when Luke had said he thought her natural color much prettier.

Because of Luke, Lena actually looked forward to school these days. She lived for the breaks in between classes when the two of them would meet at her locker.

Since the campout, they had spent more and more time with each other. Sometimes, she still wanted to pinch herself to make sure it was true.

Lena had never known anyone like Luke. He was exciting and fun. He made her feel things she didn't understand but wanted to more than anything. When they were together, she didn't think about the fact that her mom hadn't brought up the subject of her father since the night she'd confronted her with the letter.

She and Luke had been hanging out after school every day. Lena even told her mom she was going to the movies and met Luke instead. Even though her mom's rule was that she couldn't date until she turned sixteen, Lena justified whatever guilt she felt by reminding herself of how her mother deceived *her* all these years. This hardly compared.

Luke felt easy to talk to in a way she very much needed since she and her mom were on the outs. She'd found herself telling him about it one day after school when they'd been sitting outside on the school steps. She'd somehow known he would understand. She told him about how she'd gone through her whole life thinking her father was dead. When she'd reached the part about finding the letter in her mother's closet, she'd broken off, her voice cracking.

"Did you ask her about it?" Luke had asked.

Lena nodded. "Yeah, she was pretty freaked out. She's supposedly trying to track him down."

"So, do you want to see him or something?"

Lena stayed quiet. "I don't know," she said finally. "Yes, I want to. But I'm scared."

"Why?"

"What if he doesn't want to see me?"

"Why wouldn't he? He'd be crazy not to."

They'd sat on the grass while a fall breeze hinted at cooler weather. With Luke, Lena felt as if she could conquer all the demons inside her, her anger at her mother, her need to know about her father. He did that to her, made her feel like more than she was. She liked that most about him. That, and the fact that she'd never met a better-looking guy. She felt proud to walk down the hall beside him with all the other girls, even the cheerleaders, looking at her with envy.

Lena unplugged the curling iron now and stood looking at herself in the mirror. She'd never thought of herself as pretty, like her mom, but maybe she wasn't so bad.

She put away her things and headed downstairs, hoping that today would be the day Luke asked her to the homecoming dance.

37

Today was the day.

Luke was going to ask her. He'd been thinking about it for days but hadn't worked up the courage yet. When he and his dad first moved here, he couldn't have imagined ever wanting to go to the homecoming dance. All he'd wanted was to move back to the city as fast as possible.

But things were different now. He and his dad were actually talking. About everything. His schoolwork. The books he read for English class. Luke had started helping him work on the house a few afternoons a week. He'd surprised himself by thinking it was kind of fun. They'd even gone out the afternoon before and bought an old truck for the farm together. His dad needed something to haul stuff around on, and he'd said Luke could drive it when he wanted. They'd named it Pokey because it had about as much power as a twenty-year-old lawnmower.

Things *were* different. At home and at school. Luke liked Lena. She had to be the coolest girl he'd ever known. And he identified with her. She'd had problems with her mom, the same as he'd had with his dad. Whatever the reason, he just liked being with her. He felt as if he could tell her anything, that he could be himself with her.

He opened his locker and threw his books inside. He was supposed to have met Lena in the cafeteria five minutes ago. He slammed the door and swung around, almost bumping into the two guys standing behind him.

"Hey," the tall one said. Luke thought his name was Larry. He had long, stringy hair, and from what Luke knew of him, he spent most of his time in detention hall. The shorter one was Jimmy, or something like that. Like his buddy, he wasn't one of Jefferson County High's finest students.

"Hey," he said, and moved to step around them.

Larry caught his arm and stopped him, glancing over his shoulder before saying, "Hey, man, we heard you were connected."

Luke frowned. "Who told you that?"

The short guy shrugged. "Grapevine. What difference does it make?"

"Are you or aren't you?" Larry prodded.

Luke stepped back, feeling sick inside. Nobody knew about his past except the principal. Mr. Walters had promised Luke's dad that the knowledge wouldn't leave his office. He'd agreed to give Luke a second chance here. That meant there was only one person who had told them. Lena.

"I don't know where you got your info, but you've got it all wrong," he said, and then took off down the hall and out of the school.

38

Homecoming at Jefferson County High always fell on the last weekend in October. Colby had been asked to act as a chaperon at the dance on Saturday night. She felt every bit the fifth wheel as she walked alone into the high school gymnasium at just after seven.

She would probably be the only adult without a date. Being single had never bothered her the way it seemed to lately. Especially during the past two weeks, when she'd done her best to avoid crossing paths with Ian and yet heard about him at every turn. A stop at Cutter's Grocery led Maude Cutter to extol the virtues of her cinnamon rolls based on Mr. McKinley's rave reviews. And a call to Harry Pasley's farm to help out with another problem delivery meant listening to how he couldn't get over somebody like that McKinley fella buying that calf as a pet. Needless to say, it had been impossible to erase him from her own thoughts when everyone else insisted on bringing him up.

She'd planned to drive Lena and Millie to the dance tonight, but that afternoon, Lena announced she was going over to Millie's to get ready and that Mrs. Mitchell would be taking them.

If possible, Lena had become even more withdrawn and upset in the past couple of weeks. Colby still hadn't heard from Doug. She'd told herself she would hold out for a while longer, mainly because she wanted him to contact Lena on his own terms, but also because she didn't know how to explain it to her daughter if he refused to see her.

When Colby suggested picking her up after school one afternoon to look for a dress, Lena refused. And when Colby came home a few nights later to find a new one on Lena's bed, Lena had said she'd gone with Grandma Williams to pick it out.

Lena's deliberate attempts to hurt her were clear. She told herself not to dwell on them. Lena herself was hurting, and someone had to be the target of that pain.

One afternoon when she needed to get away for a while, she drove to Charlottesville by herself, hitting a total of eight stores before she found something suitable for the dance. The dress didn't sparkle, and it wasn't weighed down with frills. Its simplicity caught her eye, black with cap sleeves and a V-neck that hinted at cleavage but didn't actually reveal any. The skirt fit close against her hips, and even though it was totally different from her normal wardrobe, when she'd glanced in the mirror, she'd realized it flattered her.

She caught herself wondering if Ian would like it. But she hadn't bought it with him in mind. He probably wouldn't even be here.

She hung her coat on one of the racks in the cloakroom, making her way to the gym. Ian stood by the bleachers, talking with Randall Walters, the high school principal. He couldn't see her watching him, so she took advantage of the moment. While most of the men here were far more at home in jeans and work shirts than a suit, Ian looked as if his had been made for him. Dark blue with a tastefully muted tie knotted at his throat. His face was tan from the work he'd been doing outdoors. He definitely stood out among the other men, but then, he would have stood out most anywhere.

Memories of the last time she'd seen him alone assaulted her. Her mouth tingled with the recollection of his kiss. Warmth spread through her and set butterflies astir in her midsection.

He glanced up and caught her staring. She looked away too hastily to be anything but guilty. She headed toward a table set up with punch bowls and poured herself a glass.

Lena had helped decorate the gym earlier in the day. Balloons hung in clusters from the ceiling. Banners announcing the names of this year's homecoming queen and king were draped across the front and back of the gymnasium. The one thing conspicuously absent? The band.

Colby wandered over to a group of parents, most of whom she knew. They all greeted her with smiles. She'd been chatting with them for a couple of minutes when the principal approached them, Ian right behind him.

"Evening, folks," Mr. Walters said. "Have most of you met Ian McKinley? His son, Luke, is a senior here this year."

Ian shook hands with everyone. When his gaze finally met hers, she knew that he too remembered that morning at the clinic.

"Our band for tonight went to the wrong state. Right now, they're in Jefferson County, North Carolina," the principal said, shaking his head. "So, we're without music. Ian was nice enough to make a few calls to the local radio stations. Both DJs are booked for wedding receptions. I really don't know what to do."

"Does the school have a music system, Mr. Walters?" Ian asked.

"Yes. A pretty good one," the principal said.

"I'd be willing to play DJ if we can set it up in here."

Looking pleased with the suggestion, Mr. Walters said, "That would be great. You'd be a lifesaver. I'd hate to think what would happen if all the kids showed up, and we didn't have any music. Colby, would you mind helping out?"

A quick refusal sprang to her lips. "I don't know very much about the kind of music the kids like."

"Yes, you do." Mr. Walters smiled. "I'll bet Lena's laptop is full of it."

He was right. It was. It would be silly to refuse Mr. Walters's request simply because she promised herself she would stay away from Ian. "It is."

"Terrific."

"So is Luke's," Ian said. He glanced at his watch and then looked at her. "We could run by our houses and grab them. What do you think?"

Colby had to admit it seemed like a good idea. And since their options were limited, what else could they do? "Sure. I'd be glad to help."

Agreeing that it might be quicker to go separately, Ian and Colby took their own cars. Colby arrived back before he did. Mr. Walters had set up the speakers while they were gone. Once Ian arrived, the principal gratefully left them to it and went off to put out the most recent fire.

They worked in silence, burning CDs of songs they thought would be appropriate for the dance. Within twenty minutes, they had a great mix.

Ian turned to look at her. "Think we can pull this off?"

The question startled her. They hadn't said anything for the last ten minutes, both of them feigning intense concentration on the task at hand. She'd been on pins and needles the entire time. "If we don't, we might have a rebellion on our hands," she said, glancing toward the door where couples were filing in. It was almost eight-thirty. The dance officially started at eight, but no one came that early. "Good thing it isn't cool to get here on time, huh?"

Ian smiled. "Yeah. We might have been reduced to singing."

With the atmosphere between them considerably lighter, Colby laughed. "*That* would have been a disaster."

"And you haven't even heard me sing," he said in mock dismay.

"I was speaking of my own lack of talent."

His gaze lingered on her. "You look incredible tonight, Colby."

"Thank you," she said, realizing how much she wanted him to notice. She would have been lying to herself to deny it. "You look nice yourself."

"No mud or tomato juice on my shirt?"

She smiled while awkwardness descended on them in a grip every bit as crippling as any she had ever experienced as a teenager.

For the next forty-five minutes or so, they played music and made small talk. A couple of their first selections got a few boos, but several songs into the mix, they apparently hit the right combination. The dance floor was packed, and no one seemed to be missing the band at all.

Colby searched the crowd for Lena, finally spotting her on the other side of the gym. She waved, certain that Lena saw her, but Lena turned away without waving back.

Colby restacked the CD cases in front of her, determined not to let it ruin the night.

"They can put a knife through your heart, can't they?" Ian asked in a quiet voice.

Colby looked up, started to deny it, then decided there would be no point. He was right. And she knew he understood. "I never thought being a parent would be this hard. Even when she was a newborn and I was trying to go to college, it wasn't this difficult."

"Caring is what makes it hard. I imagine it would be a lot easier if we didn't love them so much."

"You're right," she said, sighing. "How are things with you and Luke?"

"Better than they've been in a long time. We're actually talking, and it feels really good."

"I'm happy for you. That's terrific."

"Thanks." He paused, then said, "Any word from Lena's father?"

She shook her head. "No."

Ian reached out and squeezed her shoulder in a gesture of comfort. Or at least that's what Colby told herself. That did not explain, however, her own response to it: the instant need it conjured up, the yearning to be alone with him, away from curious gazes, to pick up where they'd left off that Sunday morning in the storage room of her clinic.

He took her arm and tugged her into the crowd. "Come on. What do you say we test our selection?"

Before she knew it, they were in the middle of the throng of dancers, the song a Coldplay number Lena loved, and Colby had no idea how to dance to. She gave it her best shot, though, and after a minute or so, forgot about her inhibitions and relaxed.

As a dancer, Ian surprised her. She'd always thought men of his height and breadth had a disadvantage when it came to looking good on a dance floor. He proved her wrong. They finished out two fast songs. Toby Keith played next with a toe-tapper about the woman of his dreams. "I don't think I know how to dance to this one," Ian said.

"You were the one who wanted to come out here. You're not getting off that easily. Come on. I'll show you the two-step." Colby took his hand and walked him through the motions. When he looked impressed that she knew it, she said, "That was the one thing I got out of my date with Tip LaPrade before he showed me the prenup agreement."

Ian laughed, the sound of it rich and full and undeniably seductive.

He caught on quickly, and she said, "Let me guess. You own stock in a dance studio."

Ian smiled. "Right. I've also got a couple of bridges in Nevada if you're interested."

They finished out the Toby Keith. Kenny Chesney was next, and someone started a line dance. Everyone knew the steps except Ian. "You'll catch on," she told him when he began to look doubtful.

He was a good sport, following her lead but missing every other step at first. His forehead wrinkled with the effort of concentrating, while the line of dancers moved gracefully in one direction and then the other. He started laughing at one point and said, "Clueless in Keeling Creek. That's me."

Colby laughed until tears threatened to ruin her mascara. She wiped at her eyes, smiling and refusing to let him give up. "No, you're not. You've almost got it."

"Doesn't that only count in horseshoes—"

"—and hand grenades," she finished.

They both laughed again, and, by the end of the song, he nearly had the hang of it.

Something slow and bone melting followed. Alarm bells went off inside Colby. Time to get back to work. Distance between them was one thing. Dancing as closely as this song called for something else altogether. Colby turned to head back to the table, but Ian stopped her with a hand on her arm. From the look in his eyes, he, too, knew it wasn't wise, but that didn't stop him from saying, "One more?"

If she'd had an ounce of honor inside her, she would have turned him down. But there in the middle of the crowded dance floor, his gaze held hers, said things that didn't need words for expression. The message couldn't have been more eloquent. Her own response echoed inside her, compelled her to take his hand, to move into the circle of his arms, the last place on earth she should have been.

He held her close, closer than she should have allowed him to.

The music echoed her pulse rate. Sensation heightened her awareness, making her conscious of each and every place their bodies touched in mirror alignment. Her left shoulder to his right, her hipbone to his thigh, their knees grazing with each half turn. She was aware of the silk of her dress smoothing across her skin, the brush of his cotton shirt on her arm.

To Colby, dancing had always seemed an act of intimacy, but this? Another thing altogether. Here in his arms, they might have been the only two people in the room.

Neither of them said a word throughout the entire song. They didn't have to. Their bodies did the talking, and Colby knew there was no point in denying what they were saying. Yet she was dancing with a man engaged to another woman. A man who made her question her own choice to be alone all these years. She couldn't make herself step out of his arms and walk away.

They swayed to the music, their bodies in tune with the rhythm, in tune with each other. The song seemed to go on forever, but when it ended, Colby wished it hadn't. They lingered for a moment under a spell of confusion, but the silence following the song jolted them both back to awareness. The CD player had stopped. Everyone on the dance floor stared at them.

Blushing, she turned and headed back to the table. Ian followed her, pacifying the crowd with a promise that the music would be on in a second.

Luckily for them, the problem ended up being nothing more than an electrical cord someone knocked loose. Ian got the music started again while Colby went off to get herself some punch. She wasn't thirsty, but she needed to collect her thoughts.

She stayed away as long as she could manage without totally deserting him, talking to anyone she recognized. Finally, she returned to the table, where Ian stood watching her with knowing eyes.

"You didn't have to do that, you know," he said.

"Ian, I don't think it's a good idea for us to—" she broke off, thinking maybe she'd assumed too much.

"You're right." He held up a hand. "It wasn't." And with that, he turned around and walked away.

39

No way!

Her mother acting as DJ! With Luke's father! And the two of them dancing together a little while ago. It was awful. The two of them looking at each other as if they couldn't pull their eyes away.

Her mother had to be doing this to deliberately embarrass her. As if she didn't have enough to deal with.

Lena stood in the shadow of a set of bleachers, her gaze on the dance floor where Luke swayed to a slow song with Melanie Cundiff.

She felt as if her very soul were breaking into little bitty pieces, one grain at a time.

What did he see in her, anyway?

Lena glanced down at her dress and wished she could disappear. What a fool she'd been to let Millie convince her that she should show up without a date in the hope that he would also be alone. She deserved to feel this way. It served her right.

Why did girls like Melanie always get the guys? Melanie already had more boyfriends than Lena dreamed of having in her whole life.

But then, she knew the answer to her own question.

Sex. It was always about sex. Melanie put out. Everybody knew it.

Since she'd met Luke, Lena thought about making out a lot. But whenever her thoughts reached the sex part, they'd shied away. She couldn't imagine that it might actually be fun. She'd grown up seeing animals do it, and, to be honest, she'd always felt kind of sorry for the female. How could it be much different with humans?

Luke and Melanie danced into her line of vision again. Melanie's arms were tight around his neck, her breasts to his chest, her thighs against his. Obviously, Lena was wrong. There had to be a lot more to it than she'd imagined.

So maybe she needed to try it herself. She was nearly sixteen. Several of her friends had already done it. The others were talking about doing it. Why wait?

If sex would help her get Luke McKinley, then she would do it.

She wouldn't ever make the mistakes her mother had made though. Not ever.

40

It was almost one o'clock when the last few kids left the dance. Strung tight as a banjo string, Colby should have been tired, but she wasn't. She and Ian had barely said two words to each other since he'd left the table earlier, returning a little while later with a set look on his face. She'd danced with the principal and a couple of other acquaintances, all of whom were married. Each of them teased her about the silent music she and Ian had been dancing to. Colby made light of their joking, while inside cringing at the thought of how it must have looked.

Ian hadn't asked her to dance again. In a way, she was relieved. She didn't think her nerves could handle being that close to him. She wasn't a good enough actress to pretend indifference.

Lena came by the table earlier and said she wanted to spend the night with Millie. The gym was so crowded that Colby barely caught a glimpse of her the entire evening.

Some of the other parents helped them clean up and put away the stereo equipment. Once they'd finished, she collected her purse and coat and deliberately avoided looking at Ian. "I'm calling it a night. 'Bye, everybody."

She'd just reached the parking lot when a voice behind her said, "Colby. Wait up."

She turned around to find Ian walking in her direction, his hands shoved inside the pockets of a long black wool coat that made him look even more appealing than he had earlier. He held her gaze for a moment before saying, "I'm sorry for being such a jerk in there."

"You weren't."

"I was."

"Okay, so you were."

That got a crooked smile out of him.

She looked away. "I have to go. Good night, Ian."

"Would you like to take a drive?"

Tentative though the question was, it surprised her. She met his gaze and shivered in the chill October air. "I really should get home," she said, stepping back.

"Just to talk? For a little while?"

Common sense told her that going anywhere with him at this hour would be asking for trouble. "It's not a good idea."

"Probably not."

Put that way, with that particular look on his good-looking face, Colby ignored logic and walked with him through the parking lot. She climbed inside the vehicle when he opened the door, then sat waiting for him to go around to the other side.

They left the high school and headed out of town, driving without saying anything. The tension between them all but hummed.

Blue Mountain Lake lay some ten miles outside of town. She recognized the turnoff to the dam as soon as Ian swung onto the narrow paved road that led to the lookout. It had been years since she'd been out here. During the day, the views were spectacular. She'd never seen it in moonlight. Until a couple of years ago, it had been closed off at night.

They pulled into the left-hand corner of the lot. Ian cut the engine, and everything went black. He looped his arms over the steering wheel and stared out into the darkness. "I have no excuse for acting the way I did tonight. I had a good time. Maybe too good. And that was the problem."

"You don't have to apologize."

"Yeah, I do." He hesitated and then said, "The only excuse I have is that I wanted to kiss you so much I couldn't think straight."

She considered that, a little shocked by his honesty.

"I still do," he added, turning to look at her.

Colby's pulse began a slow, rhythmic thud. It was cold inside the vehicle, and yet she felt suddenly warm, too warm. She loosened her coat and twisted the ring on her right hand. "Ian . . . you shouldn't be saying that."

"No, I shouldn't."

She felt the force of his gaze on her in the darkness, the heat of it, the directness that told her she hadn't imagined the chemistry building between them throughout the night.

When he moved toward her, she leaned across the seat to meet him, barely conscious of doing so, as if some irresistible force were pulling them together.

His hand slid behind her neck, his thumb caressing the side of her throat.

"I've done my best not to think about you. About this," he said, his voice low and ragged. "And it's been driving me crazy."

They sat there, mere inches between them, suspended between "Should we?" or "Shouldn't we?"

When he eased her against his chest, she realized they'd been headed toward this all night. Pretensions of anything else fell away, leaving nothing between them but raw, honest feelings. All the lectures she'd given herself these past weeks about getting involved with a man who wasn't free collapsed beneath the reality of being in his arms. They kissed like two people who had been thinking about it for far too long, their mouths open and seeking, their arms locked tight around each other.

Colby had been kissed before. She was a grown woman. She had a teenage daughter. But in Ian's arms, she *felt* like a teenager. His touch made her forget all else. Pure, undiluted physical attraction caught her in its grip, full and ripe, like a peach ready to fall from the tree.

Ian had taken his coat off before they'd left the

school, but he still wore his suit jacket. Her own coat suddenly felt too cumbersome, too confining. As if reading her thoughts, he reached for her belt and untied it, slipping his hands inside to curve around her waist.

All the while, they kissed and the clock on the dashboard ticked, ticked.

Colby's hands found their way inside Ian's jacket, around to his back, where she smoothed her palms across corded muscle, then up to his shoulder blades.

His hands cupped her face, tilting her head back while he nuzzled the line of her jaw. "You smell so good," he said, his voice hoarse at the edges.

The words were intoxicating. Colby sighed, and something inside her went warm and liquid. His lips trailed the curve of her neck, paused at the hollow of her throat while his thumb stroked her pounding pulse point.

No one had ever held her with such appreciation, such heat, such wanting. It was heady and gratifying and unbelievably empowering.

His kiss deepened, and the world tilted on its axis. She should stop him. Really. But it had been so long since a man touched her this way. Since she had wanted a man to touch her this way. "Ian—"

"I know," he said. "I know."

She loosened his tie and marveled that her fingers still functioned when her insides were shaking. With the tie out of the way, she undid the buttons of his shirt. Surely she would die if she didn't touch him. Now. Now. Her hands found him. Ah. Hair-roughened skin over contoured muscle. He felt as wonderful as he looked. She tugged the sides of his shirt free from his pants.

"Colby—" Her name on his lips was low and tortured, his breathing as uneven as her own. She couldn't think for wanting him. All the reasons why they shouldn't be doing this slipped out of her grasp. Nothing seemed more important than following the road before them, finding out where it led. Their movements became frantic, as if neither of them could get close enough, touch enough.

Headlights suddenly flooded the car. The sound of crunching gravel hit Colby like a blast of cold air, jolting her back to reality. "Oh, no," she said. "Who is that?"

"I don't know." He adjusted her dress and pulled her coat around her shoulders.

He quickly buttoned his shirt just before a flashlight shone in through the driver's window. She looked up, completely blinded by the glare.

"Jefferson County Sheriff's Department. Step out of the car, please," the voice behind the light said.

Ian opened the vehicle door and slid out. "Is something wrong, officer?"

Fear should have been Colby's overriding emotion. But mortification left it in its dust. She recognized the deputy's voice. Joe Middleton. They'd gone to high school together.

He bent over and directed the beam inside, once again blinding her. "Is that you, Colby?"

"Hi, Joe. I apologize if we were trespassing. We were, ah, just looking for a quiet place to talk."

Joe chuckled, diverting the beam toward the other end of the darkened lot. "Yeah, you and the rest of the homecoming dance."

In the arc of light, she caught a glimpse of a few other cars, teenage boys standing outside the doors while two deputies questioned them. She closed her eyes and pictured the headlines in Monday's paper. "Local Vet Arrested for Parking at Blue Mountain Lake." A second later, she added, "with Engaged Man."

Ian had stepped away from the car with Joe. They talked for a couple of minutes, but she couldn't make out what they were saying. When Ian got back in, Joe leaned down and said, "Night, Colby. See you around."

Joe got into his car, following the other vehicles from the lot.

"I told him we would head out in a few minutes," Ian said.

Colby pushed her hair away from her face. "I've already written the article in Monday's paper. I'd just gotten to the part where I was trying to explain this to Lena."

Ian dropped his head back on the seat, a low chuckle rumbling from his chest.

She laughed too.

He sobered first, and even in the dimness she saw the light in his eyes. He shoved a hand through his hair. "I'm sorry about this. But I'm glad you're the kind of woman who can see the humor in it." He held her gaze for several long moments. "You know, I think I've laughed more with you in the past couple of months than I have in years."

The words pleased her. A lot. "We both got caught up in things tonight," she said, striving for reason. "The dancing. Being all dressed up—"

"I wish it were that simple," he interrupted, his voice serious now. Not knowing what to say, she sat there, fighting a feeling as easy to ignore as a tidal wave coming in from the ocean.

Still looking at her, his eyes dark and intent, he said, "My life's done a one-eighty, and I don't know what to make of it anymore."

The admission took her by surprise. "What do you mean?"

With the engine still running, he slid sideways to face her, his left elbow propped on the steering wheel, his right knee on the emergency brake. "I came here with my life all mapped out for the next year. Since I met you, not one thing has gone the way I planned it. When I'm around you, I find myself doing things I never intended to do. Like asking you to come out here tonight."

"I shouldn't have agreed. You're not entirely to blame."

"I can't think when I'm around you. And when I'm not around you, you're all I think about."

"I. . .I don't know what to say to that, Ian. I conveniently let myself forget that there's another woman in your life. That was wrong. I can't be part of messing up someone else's future. I'm a practical woman. Practical women don't have affairs with unavailable men."

"Colby, I wasn't asking you to—"

"Then what were you asking me? We've agreed to be friends, but friends don't do what we just did. And they don't want to do what we wanted to do but didn't get around to doing." If she hadn't been so frustrated, she would have laughed at herself. But she *was* frustrated and a little angry now because he wasn't hers to want. She *did* want him.

If she let this play out any further, she would lose her heart in a big way. She couldn't afford to do that. She'd tasted rejection once. Hopeless situations were hopeless. "I'd like to go back now," she said.

He didn't say anything, merely watched her a few moments longer. "Okay," he said finally, shifting in his seat and turning the key in the ignition.

Disappointment assailed her as he eased back out onto the main road. The feeling was inexplicable, unjustifiable. He was doing as she'd asked. Why then did she feel so miserable?

The drive to the high school parking lot seemed to take forever. Colby ached for him to touch her, to cover her hand with his, wrong as she knew it to be. She focused on the road ahead, telling herself she'd done the right thing. When he stopped beside her car, she slid out of the passenger side and held the door open. "I think it's better if we don't see each other anymore. For all concerned."

"Colby—"

But she wouldn't let herself stop and listen to him.

She turned to her truck, fumbling to get the key in the lock. He called out again, but without looking back, she tore out of the parking lot while she still had the will to leave.

41

Colby pulled into her driveway at nearly three a.m. Phoebe sat on the front porch waiting for her, huddled up in Frank's old varsity football jacket.

Colby got out of the truck and jogged across the yard. "Phoebe, are you all right? What's wrong?"

Phoebe sniffed and wiped her cheek. "How about what's not? It'll take less time."

Colby sat down on the step and put an arm around her friend's shoulder, almost welcoming the distraction from her own troubled thoughts. "Come on, tell me about it."

"There's not much to say. One day I thought we had a great marriage, and now . . . now everything's a mess," she said with a broken sob.

Colby hugged her closer. "Where are the kids?"
"At their grandma's."

"Come on then," she said, getting up and pulling Phoebe to her feet. "I'll make coffee. You'll talk."

Phoebe followed Colby into the kitchen and sat down. In a couple of minutes, Colby had the coffee made, filling a cup for each of them. She took a fortifying sip. "What happened?"

Phoebe's face crumpled. "He said he had some kind of business dinner tonight. And he wasn't home when I left at midnight."

"He could have had a flat tire. Anything might have happened."

"He always takes me with him if he has business on the weekend."

"Have you talked to him about any of this, Phoebe?"

"I'm afraid to. What if he's having an affair? I don't think I want to know. And, on the other hand, I think I'll die if I don't find out something soon."

"What good does it do to assume the worst, Phoebs?"

"What else could it be?" She sighed, looking miserable. "Our fifteenth wedding anniversary is coming up next week. I never thought I'd be celebrating it like this."

Colby hadn't wanted to believe Frank would ever do such a thing. But maybe she was just being naive. Why was it so hard to believe? Why had she thought him any different from most men? Any different from Ian McKinley, who had kissed her tonight, who had wanted more than that? Ian McKinley, who belonged to someone else.

She'd driven home, ridiculing herself for letting

things get so out of hand. How far would they have gone if they hadn't been interrupted? She would like to think she'd have come to her senses, but who was she kidding?

She forced her attention back to Phoebe. "Did you leave him a note?" she asked.

Phoebe nodded, sniffing.

"Then why don't you stay here tonight? Lena's staying at Millie's. You can sleep in her bed."

"Are you sure I won't be putting you out?"

Colby squeezed her shoulder and said, "Never."

Phoebe stayed until almost ten the next morning. The two of them were up early, though, talking and drinking coffee. Colby listened while Phoebe talked. Hearing the strain in her friend's voice, she realized Phoebe had been holding her worries in, hiding behind her usual front of good spirits. She felt guilty for not having taken Phoebe's concerns more seriously. She'd felt sure there had to be some explanation for Frank's behavior, but now, she honestly had no idea.

Once Phoebe had left, she straightened up the house, admitting to herself that she didn't know about a lot of things anymore. Her relationship with her daughter. Her growing preoccupation with an unavailable man.

What had happened to her steady, if somewhat predictable, life? How many times had Phoebe accused her of being set in her ways? Of refusing to open herself up to the possibility of falling in love? If that meant she didn't have to walk around with a knot in her stomach and a yearning for something she couldn't have, then she'd choose that option any day of the week.

She took a shower, got dressed, and drove to the clinic to check on a Springer Spaniel named Hermie that had been hit by a car on Friday. The dog had been badly hurt with internal injuries and a broken leg. Andrea Morris, the dog's person, as she liked to be known, absolutely doted on the dog. She'd been nearly hysterical when she'd brought him in. Colby opened Hermie's kennel now and stepped inside. He raised his head and looked at her, his eyes noticeably more alert than yesterday. She bent down and rubbed his ears. "Hey, fella. Glad to see you're feeling better."

The dog whimpered again. She stroked the fur beneath his chin, and he tipped his head back a little farther, obviously enjoying the attention. She looked at the cast on his leg, checked his temperature, relieved to see it was normal. He had also eaten some of the food in his bowl, another good sign. She went to her office and called Mrs. Morris to tell her that Hermie was doing much better. The woman's relief was tangible.

"If you'd like to come see him, someone will be here. Just knock at the back door."

"Thank you, Dr. Williams. I'll do that."

Colby hung up, taking satisfaction in knowing she'd relieved the woman's worries. She drove back home and spent the rest of the morning preparing lunch for Lena, who was supposed to be back by noon. But her mind was only half on what she was doing. She kept reliving last night, hating herself for it but unable to stop thinking about Ian. She wasn't naive when it came to chemistry between a man and a woman. There was definitely chemistry. That and then some.

The memory of last night was both sweet and poignant. Poignant, because she knew it couldn't happen again. She was a God-fearing, churchgoing, small-town veterinarian and mother. Women like her didn't have affairs with engaged men from Manhattan who looked as at home in tailor-made suits as she did in manure-spattered rubber boots. It wouldn't be anything more than an affair. And in the light of day, she knew that an affair was out of the question.

The front door opened, then closed. "Lena. Is that you?" she called out.

No answer. Lena appeared in the kitchen doorway, her expression stony.

"Hi, honey," Colby said cautiously. "Did you have a good time last night?"

Lena folded her arms across her chest and stared at her. "I was about to ask you the same question."

She faltered under the criticism in Lena's voice. "What do you mean?"

"Mom, how could you? The whole town's talking about you and Mr. McKinley. Everybody knows he's engaged, and the rumor is that you're moving in on him!"

The attack left Colby stunned. "What?"

"Well, aren't you?"

"Where did you get that idea?"

"Maybe from the way you were hanging all over him at the dance last night. I guess that's why you haven't gotten in touch with my dad yet. You're too busy trying to steal Mr. McKinley from his fiancée to bother."

The injustice of the accusation cut like a knife. Colby had been walking on pins and needles for the past few weeks, waiting for Doug to call, hoping he would want to meet his daughter. "Regardless of whatever resentment you're feeling toward me, Lena, I'm your mother, and I won't tolerate that kind of disrespect."

Lena's mutinous expression wavered a bit. Colby never spoke to her in that tone of voice. But she'd just about reached her saturation point. She turned around and went outside, sitting down in the rope swing attached to the maple in their backyard.

She pushed off with her feet, taking the swing higher and higher. Higher than she'd ever allowed Lena to go. Higher than she should have.

The rebellion felt good. It eased the anger inside her, anger quickly followed by an avalanche of guilt. How had things with Lena gotten so out of control? She ached for the kind of relationship they'd once had. How she would have talked to her about last night. For the lighthearted moments in which she joked with her about bad dates and bad days.

Not once had she ever imagined things would be like this between them.

Lena's accusatory words played through her mind

again. *Maybe from the way you were hanging all over him at the dance last night.*

Had she been hanging all over him? Did the rest of the town a think that, as well? If her face revealed the feelings swirling around inside her, then they couldn't be thinking anything else.

She had fallen for a man who belonged to another woman.

She, who had been perfectly content with her life. She, who had not gone out looking for this. Who considered herself immune to the kinds of feelings she'd known last night in Ian McKinley's arms.

She'd let things get out of hand. Way out of hand. She'd embarrassed her own daughter and made a fool of herself in front of half the town if what Lena said was true.

She stopped the swing with her feet and sat staring at the grass beneath her shoes. She'd made the correct call in telling Ian they couldn't see each other anymore. As much as she might have wished for things to be different, she'd simply met the right man at the wrong time.

42

On Monday, Lena skipped school and hitched a ride to the health department in the next county.

Getting the appointment with a doctor had been a breeze. She'd called that morning, and the doctor would see her at two o'clock.

She arrived at the clinic two hours early and sat in a diner across the street, drinking lemonade and trying to still the butterflies in her stomach.

There were a couple of moments when she nearly chickened out and headed home. But this was the right thing to do. If she wanted Luke McKinley to like her, it was the *only* thing to do.

COLBY HAD JUST gotten in from work on Thursday when the phone rang. She dropped her grocery bags at the door and dashed for it.

"Hi, Dr. Williams. This is Millie. Is Lena in?"

"Hi, Millie. Just a minute. I'll check." She covered the phone and called up the stairs for Lena. No answer. "She must have gone out for a run or something."

"Oh, shoot. You don't see her algebra book anywhere nearby, do you? I need to borrow it if she brought it home with her."

She craned her neck for a glimpse of Lena's book bag and spotted it on the living room couch. "Just a sec." She put down the phone and reached for the backpack. There were two books inside. English Lit and Algebra. She put the bag back on the couch. It caught the side of a cushion and slid to the floor, spilling the contents beneath the coffee table.

She sighed and picked up the phone. "It's here, Millie."

"Great. I'll call her in a little while and come over and get it."

Colby hung up, then picked up the contents of Lena's bag. She dropped to her knees and gathered up what she could readily spot: pencils, paper clips, a notepad. She put everything inside and zipped the bag. Just as she got up from the floor, she saw the edge of something sticking out from the other end of the couch. A thin plastic container with Lena's name and address on front. She turned it over in her hands, then snapped the lid open. Her stomach dropped. Birth control pills. Why in the world did Lena have birth control pills?

Feeling as if she'd just had the wind knocked from her, she sank back onto the floor. The container was full. A thousand thoughts ran through her head. Had she started taking them yet? *Why?*

The questions no more than formed in her mind when Lena sprang through the door. At the sight of Colby sitting on the floor with the packet in her hands, her face froze.

A hundred different emotions assailed Colby. Anger. Fear. Hurt. Denial.

Lena strolled into the living room and draped herself across the closest chair, defiance etched on her face.

"Millie called," Colby said in a stunned voice. "She wanted to know if you brought home your algebra book. I checked your bag for it, and these fell out."

Lena didn't say anything. She just sat with her arms folded across her chest, staring out the window.

Colby held up the packet. "What are these for?"

Lena met her gaze, her eyes narrowed. "What do you think, Mom? They're to keep me from ending up like you did! Pregnant and dumped."

Until that point, Colby had no idea that hurt could run so deep. It stabbed to the core of her and then spread outward in a white-hot spasm of pain. "Lena, you're not even dating yet."

"I will be soon. And if it weren't for your ridiculous rules, I already would be."

"Who are you taking these for, Lena?"

Lena turned around and looked her straight in the eye. "Luke McKinley. And don't worry, Mom. I know all about sex and what happens when you mess up. I don't intend to make your mistakes."

Colby stared at her daughter, feeling as if she were talking to a stranger. She didn't know this child. Only she wasn't a child, but a young woman who had decided that it was time for her to have sex. She'd seen a doctor on her own, without consulting Colby.

None of this would have happened if Ian McKinley and his son had never come to Keeling Creek. Colby dropped the pills on the couch and left the room.

43

It was the last place on earth she wanted to be. With her hands shoved in her coat pockets, Colby stood outside of Ian's newly painted door. Her breath made little puffs of smoke in the cold night air. Righteous indignation simmered inside her. The more she thought about it, the more convinced she became that she was right. Ian McKinley, with his city-wise ways, had wreaked havoc with her life. Now his son was doing the same to Lena's.

She'd started to call instead of coming over, but hadn't wanted to take a chance on Lena overhearing the conversation. She would only stay long enough to say what she had to say, and then she'd be on her way. Drawing in a deep breath, she knocked on the door and reminded herself that she could handle this situation with decorum even if she had acted like a sex-starved nymphet in the front seat of the man's car. Even if the Jefferson County Sheriff's Department was probably still chuckling about Colby Williams being caught parking with an unavailable man. She would just have to get past that. She—

The door opened, and suddenly she looked up at him. Despite the forty-degree temperature, she broke out in a sweat. "I need to talk to you, Ian. Do you have a few minutes?"

"Sure. Come in," he said, looking surprised to see her. He pointed toward the half-painted living room just down the hallway and followed her inside, closing the French doors behind them. "Sorry about the mess. I'm still under construction here."

Her anger did wonders for subduing the awkwardness she would have otherwise felt at seeing him again. "I won't stay long."

"Colby, you can look at me. I won't bite. Really."

She met his gaze and realized why she'd been avoiding doing so. His eyes. They got her every time. Focusing on her anger, she said, "I'm here about Lena and Luke. I accidentally discovered a packet of birth control pills in Lena's backpack today. Apparently, they're seeing one another."

"They are?" he asked, obviously surprised.

"I think she just started taking them. I don't know that they've . . . I think she was planning ahead."

"Oh," he said. "Oh. I'm sorry, Colby. I don't know what to say."

"Until your son came to town, Lena wasn't even interested in boys," she said, an edge to her voice.

Ian looked at her for a moment. "Are you saying Luke somehow coerced her into—"

"It's obvious that he's more worldly than she is."

"Worldly?"

"You know what I mean," she said quickly.

"You think he's corrupted her?" Ian asked, looking incredulous.

Ignoring the voice inside her that questioned her fairness, she said, "Sex was never an issue until she met him. Lena isn't supposed to date until she's sixteen, which is a couple of months from now. I'm going to stand by that. I'd appreciate it if you talked to Luke and asked him not to see Lena outside of school until then."

"You know that if it's what they really want to do, we're not going to stop them. It's the Romeo and Juliet thing."

"Please back me up on this," she said, her voice remarkably cool now for all the turmoil inside her.

"Colby, I don't think—"

"Just do it, okay?" And without looking at him again, she left.

44

Ian went after her, started to call her back, then stopped when another set of headlights arced across the driveway.

He let out a deep sigh and dropped down on the porch steps, watching Colby's taillights disappear around the bend as the cool fall air quickly seeped through his shirtsleeves. He stared up at the clear, star-sprinkled sky he had grown to appreciate so much since moving here. Colby's angry accusations had thrown him. He hadn't seen her since the night of the dance, and as often as he imagined what he would say to her when he did, he never envisioned this scenario.

Luke might be more experienced than Lena, but Ian knew the boy wouldn't try to talk her into doing anything she didn't want to do. He'd had the distinct feeling that Colby was thinking as much about the two of them as about their son and daughter.

The car stopped in the driveway and Luke got out of the passenger side. No time like the present to talk to him about the situation. He hadn't been surprised to hear that Luke might be having sex. He was like any other parent who hoped his child saw the wisdom in waiting until reason held some measure of control over hormones. Luke was seventeen, though, and reason had a few years to go. But the girl in question was Colby's fifteen-year-old daughter.

The car turned around and headed back down the drive. Luke strolled across the yard and stopped at the bottom of the stairs.

"How was the movie?" Ian asked.

"The special effects were good. What are you doing out here?"

"Thinking."

"Aren't you cold?"

"Not too bad. Can you sit down for a minute?"

Luke dropped his book bag onto the brick walkway and sat down on the step beside him. "Was that Dr. Williams leaving just now?"

"Yeah, it was. She found some birth control pills in Lena's backpack." So much for a lead-in.

Luke's eyes widened. A few seconds passed before he said, "And?"

"Lena said she started taking them for you."

When Luke didn't say anything, Ian felt compelled to fill the silence. "We've talked about this before, son.

Pregnancy isn't the worst thing that can happen to sexually active kids today."

Luke sighed. "Dad, you already gave me the lecture on safe sex."

"I'm not giving you one now. I just—"

"I don't know why she told her mom that," Luke interrupted, throwing up his hands. "We're not seeing each other anymore."

"But you were?"

Luke shrugged and nodded.

"What happened?"

Another silence followed the question, but Ian sensed Luke would answer him when he was ready. "I trusted her. I told her about what happened in New York, about me getting into trouble. She said she wouldn't tell anybody, and then, all of a sudden, I've got two jerks in my face wanting to know if I'm connected."

"And you think she told them?"

"It had to be her. Nobody else knew."

Ian put a hand on his son's shoulder and squeezed. He heard the pain in the boy's voice and wanted only to take it away. Even though Luke had resisted coming here initially, Ian somehow knew that he would like to put the past behind him, that something here had touched a chord inside him too. "Did you ask her about it?"

Luke shook his head. "What's the point? She lied. Apparently, she's pretty good at that."

"Lena's having a tough time."

"You mean because of her dad?"

Ian nodded. "Her mom doesn't want her to date until she's sixteen. Maybe what she needs most right now is a good friend."

Luke considered that for a moment, then reached for his book bag and got up. "I'll think about it." At the top of the steps, he turned. "Is that all you and Dr. Williams are? Good friends?"

The question caught Ian by surprise. "I'm not sure how to answer that, Luke."

"You know, I ought to be the one giving you the lecture."

Ian raised an eyebrow. "How do you figure?"

"I saw you with her at the homecoming dance. I've never seen you look at Rachel the way you were looking at her."

"Luke—"

"It's because of Mom, isn't it?"

"What do you mean?"

"I might be a kid, but I'm smart enough to know you've never let yourself love anybody since Mom. Loving somebody means you'll have to hurt if you lose them. You don't love Rachel like that, do you?"

Stunned, Ian said, "Luke, I don't know what to say. I—"

"What if we stayed here, Dad? What if we didn't go back to the city?"

Ian leaned against a post, the question more than surprising him. "You mean permanently?"

Luke shrugged, his posture and tone nonchalant. But something told Ian the boy had been thinking about this a lot.

"You know I've intended to go back all along."

Luke shoved his hands into his jacket pockets. "I know. But I just like the way things are here better. With us and everything."

A stunner of a statement. Ian had no idea how to respond to it. Before he could say anything, Luke said, "You're different since you met her, Dad. That ought to tell you something." He turned and went inside the house.

More than amazed, Ian sat on the steps, staring after him. Since the moment he'd dropped Colby off at the high school on Saturday night, he'd been miserable. For the past few days, he'd done little more than mope around the house. When Mabel finally asked him what on earth was bothering him, he'd waved away her concern, not wanting to talk about it. Apparently, Luke had been doing some observing of his own.

The truth? He couldn't stop thinking about the dance and what almost happened between Colby and him. Or the reasons behind it. He had always prided himself on being honorable. What was honorable about infidelity? Even if he hadn't been unfaithful to Rachel in the complete physical sense, the breech felt complete. At some point, he began to feel that the real relationship in his life was with Colby.

He'd never intended for it to happen. They'd started out as friends. He wasn't sure when that changed. But it had.

Colby had helped him rediscover a missing piece of himself. The part of him that finally remembered that life had more to offer than work. The part of him that had finally begun to build a bridge back to his son.

He felt good with her. Alive. Like a man living his life rather than just racing his way through it.

Sitting under the stars of a clear autumn night, he let himself admit that his son was right. For the first time in seventeen years, his heart ruled his head. His confusion over Colby had nothing to do with Rachel. As much as it should have, it didn't.

Colby terrified him. With her, he felt things he'd been determined never to feel again. Ashamed as he was to admit it, Rachel made things easy for him. With her, there had never been any threat of putting his soul on the line.

But Colby left him defenseless. She made him want to do exactly what his son suggested a few minutes ago. Through her, he rediscovered some vital and critical links to who he was and what he wanted his future to be. She made him yearn for things he never knew he wanted. Little things that had nothing to do with money or status. Quiet moments and days filled with laughter and silliness. She had shown him that some of life's best pleasures were found in the simple things. In watching a baby calf be brought into the world. In bathing a dog in tomato juice. In learning the two-step on a crowded dance floor.

He realized then that it would be wrong to marry Rachel. On some level, maybe he had known that for a long time.

He didn't know what the future held for Colby and him—or if it held anything at all. She wasn't even speaking to him now. But he wasn't the same person he'd been when he arrived in Keeling Creek. He'd come here to change his son and ended up changing himself. With inexplicable conviction, he knew there was no going back.

45

The next morning Colby waited at the breakfast table for Lena to come down. Her stomach jangled with nerves, and she debated the best way to handle this situation. She wasn't anywhere close to reaching a conclusion when Lena came in, went straight to the refrigerator, and poured herself some juice.

With her back to her, Lena said, "I wasn't completely honest with you last night, Mom."

Colby leaned forward in her chair. "About what?"

Lena turned around, clasping her glass in both hands and not quite meeting Colby's gaze. "I got the pills because of Luke, but we're not . . . we haven't. . . ."

"I see. Are you talking about it?"

Lena shrugged. "Not exactly."

"Then why did you say they were for him?"

"That's the only way a girl can get a guy!" Lena's

eyes filled with tears, and Colby had to force herself not to go to her.

"Why do you think that, Lena?"

"It's true. That's all guys care about."

"Did he say that?"

"No. But he took Melanie Cundiff to the homecoming dance, and everybody knows she puts out."

"Oh, Lena. I think you and Luke need to have a talk. I'd be willing to bet things aren't what you think they are."

"Why do you say that?"

"Because he seems like a nice boy," she said, meaning it. She'd flown off the handle last night. In the light of day, she would admit that she'd been lashing out at Ian in frustration over what was going on between them as much as she had been over Luke's part in Lena's sudden interest in sex. And that was grossly unfair.

Lena didn't say anything for a few moments. "I'm sorry for what I said last night. About not turning out like you. I didn't mean that," she said at last.

Some of the sadness inside her lifted with Lena's apology. "Thank you. I needed to hear that."

From the uncomfortable look on Lena's face, Colby knew she was aware of how deeply she hurt her.

"Since we're clearing the air, Mom, have you talked to my father?"

Colby blinked, surprised by the question. "Lena, I—"

"You got in touch with him, didn't you?"

"Lena—" Colby began again.

"Mom, just tell me the truth. Until now, I've been too scared to ask you. But I'm a big girl. I can take it."

For a moment, Colby considered not telling her daughter the truth, but she didn't want any more lies between them. "He wanted some time to think."

"He hasn't called back, has he?" The question held a mixture of pride and fear, giving Colby a glimpse of the little girl she had once been, and, in many ways, still was.

"No, honey, he hasn't," she said, aching for her. Above all else, this particular chapter of their lives would have to be closed before the two of them could really begin to mend their relationship. Colby wanted that so much. That meant Lena had to have some kind of resolution with her father, whether he wanted it or not.

Lena looked down at the floor. "He doesn't want anything to do with me, does he?"

Colby pressed her lips together, wishing to take the pain away from her, suffer through it herself. "It's not that. It's—"

"It *is* that, Mom. Just admit it. There's something wrong with me!"

Wheeling around, she tore out the back door before Colby could stop her.

That was it. Colby decided she wouldn't wait another minute for that asinine—

She grabbed the phone and punched in the number she had memorized so Lena wouldn't find it. Three rings, and the housekeeper picked up, telling her that the Jamisons were on vacation.

Colby slammed down the phone so hard her arm tingled. She stood at the sink and stared out the window, wishing only to get her hands around Doug's selfish, self-centered neck.

46

On Friday night, Colby and Lena headed for Blue Mountain Lake. Colby received a mysterious phone call from Frank on Monday, inviting Lena and her to a surprise party for Phoebe. She'd wanted to ask him if this was about guilt, but curbed her tongue. He made her promise not to breathe a word to Phoebe, and she could only hope that whatever problems the two of them had been having were no longer cause for concern.

"Whose house is this?" Lena asked as they pulled into the driveway of the address Frank gave them.

"I don't know," Colby admitted. It was the first thing Lena had said during the entire drive. She'd been quiet and withdrawn during the past few days, staying in her room when she wasn't in school. Colby wanted to ask her if she'd talked with Luke, but she'd refrained from doing so, hoping Lena would discuss it with her when she was ready.

Colby's own spirits had been pretty low, too, but she'd tried not to let it show. She didn't have a right to feel bad. Ian had never been available in the first place, so it wasn't as if she'd really lost anything.

But it sure felt that way.

She marveled at the house as she and Lena got out of the car. Sprawled across an enormous lot, it looked like a beach bungalow, bright and cheerful, with a white fence enclosing the perimeter. Obviously brand-new, the yard was still covered in straw, bits and pieces of building paraphernalia scattered here and there.

At the front door hung a sign that read:

Welcome Everyone!

Please go in and make yourselves at home. The bartender will be happy to get you something to drink. Food's set up in the kitchen and living room.

I'll be arriving with Phoebe around seven. Please take this sign down about ten minutes before. Knock her socks off with a big "Surprise!"

Frank

Inside, Colby smiled and said hello to the familiar faces. Parents and teenage children all but filled the living room and kitchen. Lena wound her way toward Millie, who stood in the kitchen next to a bowl of chips. Colby soon discovered that she and

Lena weren't the only ones in the dark about the party. No one seemed to know who owned the house.

The furnishings were incomplete, although most of the basics were in place—a sofa, some chairs, the kitchen table. The living room opened onto a deck, where several couples were talking, looking out at the lake beyond.

She had just asked for a glass of white wine from the bartender when she glanced up and spotted Ian in the kitchen. Standing next to him: Rachel. Colby's heart dropped somewhere within the vicinity of the floor.

The bartender handed her the wine with a smile. She took it, tried to smile back, and failed miserably. She couldn't pull her gaze off the two of them. How right they looked together. So right it hurt. It shouldn't have, but it did. Colby thought of the things she'd shared with this man in the past few months and realized that he had become a part of her life. There was no taking any of it back, pretending it never happened. And because of her own stupidity, she had to stand here and watch him with his fiancée.

Ian and Rachel left the kitchen, moving in her direction. Rather than turn and run, as she would have liked to, Colby stayed where she was, fixing a smile on her face when Rachel said, "Oh, hello. You're the pie lady, aren't you?"

Colby stuck out her hand. "You have a good memory. Hello, Miss Montgomery."

"Rachel, please. After all, it won't be Montgomery much longer."

The dart, intended or not, stabbed hard. She glanced at Ian. He looked every bit as uncomfortable as she felt. Optimist that she was, she might have even called it miserable had she not been aware of her own bias. "I don't suppose you have any idea why Frank's having a surprise party for Phoebe in a house no one's ever seen before?" she asked, desperate to fill the silence.

He shook his head, his gaze holding hers with pained intensity. "Not a clue."

"Shhh!" Mary Simmons, Phoebe's sister, stood by the window, peering around the edge of the curtain. "I think they're here," she said.

Everyone hustled for a place to stand where Phoebe wouldn't see them immediately. Colby stayed where she was. Unfortunately, so did Ian and Rachel. The guests were pin-drop quiet. The car engine outside cut off, then two doors slammed. Phoebe's voice rang out, "Frank Walker, what on earth is this all about?"

"Be patient, honey," he said.

The doorknob turned, and Phoebe stepped inside the hallway, Frank behind her.

"Surprise!!!" The room erupted in a roar. Phoebe let out a startled scream, one hand going to her chest. She looked at the roomful of people in front of her, then back at Frank, grinning ear to ear, and promptly burst into tears.

Frank put a hand on her shoulder. "Now, Phoebe, that's not exactly the reaction I was hoping for."

Laughter rippled through the crowd. Frank held up a hand, then leaned forward and kissed Phoebe on the mouth. "Happy fifteenth anniversary, honey," he said, one hand sweeping the expanse of the room. "You're standing in your present."

Phoebe looked down at the floor, then up again, realization dawning. "This house is my present?"

Frank nodded, looking so proud that Colby thought he might actually split at the seams. "You always wanted a summer house. I'm a little late for this year, but now you know where I was all those nights when you were wondering."

Phoebe stared at him for a moment before her tears started again. She took off down the hall to their right, leaving Frank at a loss. Knowing what lay behind the tears, Colby went after her. The bathroom door off the master bedroom was closed, and she heard Phoebe's sobs interspersed with hiccups. She knocked. "May I come in, Phoebe?"

She turned the knob, and the door swung inward. Phoebe sat on the side of an enormous tub, a wad of tissue in her hand. She looked up. "How could I have been such an idiot, Colby? I thought he was having an affair, and he was building me a house."

Colby sat down on the tub and put a hand on her friend's shoulder. "You made an honest mistake."

"But I should have trusted him."

"I guess that's the lesson to be learned here."

"How am I ever going to go out there?" she wailed.

"How can you not? Your husband, who happens to adore you, has just gone to an awful lot of trouble to throw you a surprise anniversary party. I think the least you can do is go back out and give him a big kiss."

Phoebe got up and turned on the water faucet. She rinsed her hands and dabbed at the mascara smudges beneath her eyes. "What will I say to him? To everyone out there? I can't believe I thought he was having an affair!"

"Just go back and tell them you were overwhelmed by what he did. It's certainly understandable. No one has to know the other part. Not even Frank."

"I've been so awful to him."

"Then I suggest you make it up to him here in your new house after everyone else goes home."

Phoebe caught Colby's gaze in the mirror and smiled. "That sounds like something Dr. Green would say."

"So maybe I should have been a radio psychiatrist." Colby managed to smile back at her.

"I take it that's Rachel with Ian," Phoebe said, her disappointment obvious.

"Yes. His fiancée. The one you didn't believe existed."

"Oh, her."

"Yes, her."

"I might have been blind to my own situation, Colby Williams, but I can see as plain as the nose on my face that you're crazy about that man. When are you going to admit it to yourself?"

Colby moved to the other mirror and feigned intense concentration as she finger-combed her hair. Frank had been unjustly accused. But Ian turned out to be just like Doug, after all. Nothing he'd ever said or done meant a thing. There was another woman in his life. Colby was the intruder, a role she had no desire to play. "Phoebe, think of how you've felt these past few months, thinking Frank had someone else. I don't want to be the other woman. If I ever find the right person, I want to be the only one for him. I want what you and Frank have, or I don't want anything at all."

Phoebe started to say something, then stopped. She put her arms around Colby and hugged her. "I'd like to argue with that, but I can't. I want that for you too. He could have been the one, though. I just know it."

"He could have been," Colby admitted. She tried for a bright smile.

Phoebe sighed. "Back into the fire?"

"Let's go."

For the next couple of hours, Colby stayed inside and mingled. Finally, she made her way out to the deck and breathed in the crisp night air, grateful to be alone to wilt for a moment without anyone noticing.

Maybe seeing Ian with Rachel was the cold dose of reality she needed. Facts were facts, and when they were staring you in the face, they were awfully hard to deny.

And the fact was, that as easy as it had been to pretend otherwise these past few months, Rachel Montgomery would soon become Mrs. Ian McKinley.

"Colby?"

She swung around, startled. "Ian! What are you doing out here?"

"Looking for you."

"I don't think that's wise."

"Colby, I wanted to explain—"

"There's nothing to explain."

"This isn't what you—"

"If you remember, I'm the one who told you I didn't want to see you anymore," she said, the two glasses of champagne she'd hastily swallowed earlier boosting her courage. "You really didn't need to draw me a picture tonight. I was quite clear on how things are."

She moved to step around him and go back inside.

He reached for her arm. Colby—"

"Ian?" Rachel stood at the patio doors, looking at them with a question in her eyes. "I think they're getting ready to cut the cake."

Colby pulled free of Ian's grasp, ignoring the look of frustration on his face. "I'd better go lend a hand," she said, and left them alone.

47

As soon as Lena had seen Luke come through the front door, she'd found a place in the back of the room where she hoped he couldn't see her. She stayed inside until Phoebe arrived, then slipped out to the backyard when no one was looking.

How would she ever face him? She'd been avoiding him in school for days now. If she had known he'd be here, she would have pretended to be sick and stayed home.

It was cold outside. Lena shivered and pulled her coat closer around her, shoving her bare hands in her pockets. Some fifty yards from the house sat a gazebo of sorts. She hurried across the yard and let herself inside. A shaft of light shone on the benches that circled the gazebo walls. Lena went to the back of the building and sat down in the shadows.

She'd been out there for no more than a minute

when she heard footsteps outside the door. Great. Who could that be? She tucked herself into the shadows and stayed quiet.

"Lena?"

Oh, no. Luke's voice. What was he doing out here?

The door opened, and he stuck his head inside. "Lena, I know you're in here. I saw you from the deck at the house."

"Go away, Luke."

He closed the door behind him, cutting off the only light. "I'm not going away. Why have you been avoiding me?"

She made a sound of half laughter, half disbelief. "I haven't been avoiding you."

Even in the dimness she saw that he didn't believe her. "My dad said your mom found birth control pills in your backpack. Since I was accused of being the reason why you had them, I'd say I'm not out of line in asking about it."

Lena's whole body went warm with embarrassment. She was thankful for the darkness. How had she ever gotten herself into this? "I decided it was time for me to have sex. Everybody else does. And obviously, you aren't interested in girls who don't."

"Why do you say that?"

She tilted her head to the side and gave him a look.

"You mean because of Melanie?"

Again, she said nothing.

"I never would have taken her to the dance if you hadn't broken your word to me."

She looked up in astonishment. "Broken my word? About what?"

"I trusted you not to tell anybody about my past. Then all of a sudden I'm getting tracked down by the school dope heads looking for a connection."

Lena had no idea what he was talking about. She hadn't told anyone. "But I didn't. . . ." And then she remembered. "Oh, Luke. I'm sorry. I did tell Millie. She's my best friend. And she swore on her life that she wouldn't . . . I'm sorry."

He studied her for several long seconds, a torn expression on his face. He'd trusted her, and she had let him down. She felt about two inches tall. She deserved his anger and more.

"I wanted to ask you to the homecoming dance," he finally said, "but I was mad at you when I thought you'd told everybody."

"I don't blame you. I'd be mad at me too."

"Why'd you tell your mom we were having sex?"

"I didn't exactly. She just assumed it."

"You must have said something to make her think—"

She dropped her gaze to the floor. To her horror, tears welled up in her eyes and trickled down her cheeks. She wiped them away with her hand, hating herself for not being able to hold them back. "I figured that's why you took Melanie to the dance."

He looked at her in astonishment. "Well, it wasn't. We didn't."

Immense relief flooded through her. She glanced up. "You didn't?"

He shook his head. "And if you're honest with yourself, you'll admit that part of your reason for getting those pills had something to do with your mom."

Lena didn't say anything for a few moments. He was right. "I guess I wanted her to know I would never let what happened to her happen to me."

Still holding on to her arm, he pulled her against his chest and hugged her. He smoothed his hand across the back of her hair and held her while tears slid down her cheeks. "Your mom's a nice woman. My dad sure is different since he met her."

"What do you mean?"

Luke shrugged, rubbing the center of her back. "He makes time for stuff. He didn't used to do that. And things are a lot better between us."

"I'm glad, Luke. I wish things with my mom were the way they used to be."

"Can't they be if you want them to be?"

"I don't know."

"My dad wasn't around as much as I would have liked when I was growing up. He worked a lot. Rather than talk to him about it, I just bottled up all my anger. When I got into trouble, I guess I figured that was one way to get him to notice me. I know now that it wasn't the right way."

Lena pressed her face to his chest. She knew what he was trying to say to her. That it was up to her to fix things with her mom. She wanted to. She really did. She just didn't know where to begin.

48

During the drive to Oak Hill, Ian and Luke said very little. Rachel did all the talking.

"I bet you two will be glad to get back to the city. The people here are as nice as they can be, but things are certainly different. You can't tell me you haven't been getting bored," she said, looking over her shoulder at Luke in the back seat.

When Luke didn't respond, Ian said, "Actually, we haven't. There's plenty to do around here."

"Like what?" she asked with a laugh. "Once you've rented every movie at the local video store, I'd imagine you're in trouble."

Logically, Ian knew Rachel was half joking, but her comments irritated him. She'd written Keeling Creek off as a backward hick town. Maybe a few months ago, he would have too. But he had changed. The realization made him more sure than ever that what he was about to do tonight was the right thing.

He'd been on edge all week, having decided not to see Colby until he talked to Rachel. He'd tried to get in touch with her earlier in the week with no success. Her secretary had said she would be in California with a client for a few days. He'd left numerous messages at her hotel, and the two times she returned his call, he had been out. This afternoon, she had shown up at Oak Hill to surprise him. And she had.

At the house, Luke went straight upstairs, leaving them alone. They walked into the kitchen, where Ian put on some coffee. "Would you like a cup?" he asked.

"You know I don't have caffeine after six."

"Sorry. I forgot."

She studied him for a moment. "You've been forgetting a lot of things lately. Like remembering to call me."

He met her gaze. "We have to talk, Rachel."

"So you said in your email. That's why I came straight here when I got it. Something *is* wrong, isn't it?"

"Rachel, I don't think there's any easy way to say this—"

"You didn't want to take me with you tonight," she interrupted. "I have the distinct feeling you wouldn't have if you hadn't promised to be there early and open the house for your friend. After I showed up at the last minute, you could hardly leave me here."

"Rachel—"

"It's that woman, isn't it?" she said. "Your little country vet."

"Her name is Colby," he said in a quiet voice. "And in every way that counts, this has nothing to do with her."

"Then what does it have to do with?"

"Me. Changes."

"If you're talking about your life here, that's not going to be forever. You'll come back to New York and things will be like they always were."

"No, they won't. *I'm* different. In ways I never imagined. I arrived here a workaholic, Rachel. For too many years, I haven't spent ten seconds thinking about anyone but myself and my work. And for that, I almost ruined my relationship with my son. Since I've been here, I've realized how much I missed out on. With Luke . . . and, well, just living."

"Then we'll change things when you get back," she said quickly. "You won't work as much. We'll go away more."

"But that's just it. I don't want to keep leading a life I have to escape from."

Rachel drew in a deep breath, then let it out slowly. "And I'm part of that life."

"You deserve someone who wants the same life that you want. I'm not that man anymore."

"Stop," she said, looking away and pressing the back of her hand to her lips. "You can deny it all you want, Ian McKinley, but you're in love with that woman. And, unfortunately, I can't fight her, because I don't know what her weapons are. Apparently, she has something I don't."

"Rachel—"

She held up a hand. "I guess I knew this was coming when I flew down here this afternoon. I just didn't want to let myself admit it. I'll sleep in the guest room."

Ian stood in the dimly lit kitchen, listening to the sound of her footsteps on the stairs. He heard the bedroom door open, then click closed. He felt a wave of sadness for the hurt he'd caused her. He waited for a surge of regret to swamp him, but it never came.

49

Colby had just gotten out of the shower Saturday afternoon when the phone rang. Lena and Millie were at a track club meeting, so she grabbed a towel and ran for the bedroom.

It was Phoebe. "You sound winded," she said.

"I just got in from the clinic a little while ago. I was in the shower. So how was your anniversary?"

"Wonderful. Better than wonderful. Oh, Colby, I'm such an idiot. All those things Frank did, the new suits, the working out, they were all for me. He thought he'd started to let himself go, and he didn't want me to lose interest in him."

"So much for Dr. Green's theories, huh?"

"Yeah. Things aren't always what they seem. Sometimes people do things for one another just because they love them, right?"

"Right," Colby said, truly happy for her friend despite her own misery.

"I have a big favor to ask of you," Phoebe said.

"What's that?"

"Frank had to run to town for something at work. He'd planned to come back out to the lake, but he's stuck there and I don't have a ride. Could you come get me?"

Colby had spent the morning working on a Golden Retriever who had eaten rat poison and was near death when brought in. Luckily a dose of vitamin K and a transfusion saved the dog's life. It had been a stressful case, and Colby had planned to spend the afternoon relaxing. But she couldn't very well leave Phoebe stranded. "Sure. Lena's at Millie's for the night, so I don't have anything to do for the rest of the day."

"Great. Can you be here around five so I can finish cleaning up?"

"No problem. See you then."

The drive out to the lake was a pretty one, but it gave Colby too much time to think. Too much time to wonder what Ian and Rachel were doing. Too much time to remember how painful it had been to see them together last night.

After she'd left Ian on the deck, she'd been miserable for the rest of the party. As soon as she could do so, she'd said good night to Frank and Phoebe, all too conscious of the knowing look in her friend's eyes. She knew she had no right to feel as she did, but the feelings were there, nonetheless.

She almost passed the turnoff to the lake house and swung in quickly. She parked in the driveway and got out. She knocked twice, and when no one answered, rang the doorbell. "Phoebe?" she called out.

She knocked again. Still no answer.

A car engine sounded from the end of the driveway. Colby turned around. Maybe that was Frank. But a second later, Ian's car appeared in the bend. Her stomach dropped.

He parked behind her truck and got out, looking as startled as she felt. "I didn't expect to see you here," he said, a note of uncertainty in his voice.

She did her best to mask her feelings, even though the wound still felt raw. "Phoebe called and asked me to pick her up, but she's not answering the door."

"That's strange. Frank called a little while ago and asked if *I* could pick her up."

"Oh. Well, maybe we had some kind of misunderstanding, but no one seems to be here."

Ian jogged up the steps and pushed the bell again. Still no answer. He turned the knob and opened the door. "Phoebe?" he called out.

They stepped inside the house. The lamps were on, and music played, soft and alluring. A wonderful aroma drifted toward them. Someone was cooking.

"What's going on?" Colby asked. They went into the kitchen, where a bucket of icy champagne sat on the island in the center of the room, an envelope propped beside it.

With a sinking feeling, Colby pulled out the card and read it in silence.

Just so you know, Frank refused to participate in this. So if it works, he gets none of the credit. If it fails, I guess I'll take all the blame. I'm hanging up my matchmaking hat after this, Colby. Really. I promise.

The Jacuzzi is off the master bedroom. Dinner is in the oven. The champagne is right in front of you.

No need to worry about Lena, since you said she's spending the night at Millie's. And Ian, I'll make sure Luke knows where you are.

Phoebe

Colby closed her eyes and sighed. "This time I really will have to kill her."

"What is it?" Ian asked.

She handed the note to him. He read it, then looked up and said, "Frank must have told her."

"Told her what?"

He paused and then, "Rachel and I aren't getting married. I told him when he called to see if I could pick up Phoebe."

Surprise ricocheted through her. "You're not?"

He shook his head. "No."

"Why?" she asked, taken aback.

Ian put the card on the counter and looked at her for several long moments before answering. "When I asked her to marry me, it wasn't for any of the right reasons. After Sherry died, I guess I stopped believing in fairy-tale love. What Rachel and I had always seemed like more of a merger than anything else."

"Oh." She felt hot and cold at once. This was the last thing she'd expected to hear.

"But then I met someone who made me believe again."

"You did?" she asked, her voice little more than a whisper.

"Yeah, I did. She's incredible, this woman. She's smart and funny and warm, and man, does she know how to kiss. . . ."

"She does?" Colby managed to whisper.

He nodded, a smile touching his lips. "And as much as I tried, I couldn't stop thinking about her. She's the kind of woman a man waits his whole life for, and when he finds her, he just knows it's right, no matter how much he tries to deny it."

She wanted to believe him. But the old wariness still warred inside her, questioning her, torturing her with what-ifs. What if this was just temporary? What if his feelings changed, the way Doug's had changed? What if—

"I can read your doubts," he said softly. "I know how much he hurt you. And I know how hard it's been for you to put that behind you. But I think that's one of the things that drew us together. My hurt was different from yours, but it had the same effect. We've both refused to really let ourselves feel anything all these years. Somehow, someway, I was waiting for you."

Tears welled up in her eyes. "Ian. . . ." she began,

unable to go on. She couldn't believe they were really here. That he'd said these things to her. But he had. The armor with which she'd shielded herself from him these past months fell away, and she stood before him now, fully aware of how desperately she needed to hear those words. How very much she wanted him. She could no longer pretend otherwise. To herself or to him.

She slipped into his embrace, her arms locking around his neck, her cheek to his chest. His arms secured her to him. In that moment, she felt as if she'd been headed here all her life. She knew, without doubt, that all these years, she had been waiting for this one good man to come along. This man who found such satisfaction in simple things, in laughing just for the sheer joy of it, in kissing. Ah, in kissing. This man with whom and from whom she wanted so much more.

"I wanted to call you this morning," he said, his voice low and uneven. "But I didn't think I should so soon—"

"Phoebe's never been known for her patience."

Ian smiled. "Right now, I'm glad about that."

"I won't admit it to her, but so am I."

Darkness had descended outside, and the lamps in the living room shadowed the kitchen with light.

Ian nodded toward the champagne. "It would be a shame to waste that now that we're here. Would you like a glass?"

"I'd love one," Colby said, welcoming the diversion.

He found a dishcloth in one of the drawers, pulled

the bottle out of the ice and wrapped the towel around it. He loosened the foil, then the wire and pointed the cork toward the ceiling. "Heads up." The cork zinged out of the bottle, slammed off the ceiling and whizzed back past them. They both ducked, shoulders colliding, champagne sloshing from the bottle and onto their clothes as their surprised laughter filled the room.

"You could take a girl out with a power shot like that," she said.

Ian grinned. "Packed a little more punch than I expected." He reached for the glasses that Phoebe had thoughtfully placed next to the ice bucket. He filled them both, then handed one to Colby and raised his own in a toast. "To meddling, good-intentioned best friends."

Colby smiled. "Here, here."

The champagne tasted crisp and cold and glorious. She stood inches from this man she had fallen for without even wanting to, and this was the only place on earth she wanted to be.

Another song started on the CD player. This one too slow and easy, and it flowed over Colby's skin like the finest silk. Goose bumps danced down her arms.

"Rumor has it you're a pretty incredible dancer," he said.

"Well, I'd hate to let Phoebe's efforts go to waste."

He put his glass on the counter, reached for hers and set it down. And then he reached for her. She moved into his arms, and there, in the middle of the kitchen floor, they swayed and flowed to the beat of the music, their steps in perfect unison. Torture of the sweetest, most painful kind. He held her loosely, but with every turn, their knees would brush or his thigh would graze her hip.

At some point, he stopped moving, and from the look in his eyes, she knew he'd found the dancing as intoxicating as she had.

"I think I might die if you don't let me kiss you," he said.

"Good. Because if you don't stop talking about it and just do it, I think I might die."

A smile on his lips, he pulled her to him, his hands splaying across her waist, his palms wide and encompassing and urgent. Her own hands sought the back of his neck and wound through his thick, soft hair.

His head dipped toward her, and his lips grazed the curve of her jawline. Gentle, butterfly kisses at first, soft and easy. Her eyes closed and her breathing quickened as his hands skimmed the length of her arms and cradled her neck while his thumbs brushed the hollow of her throat. He cupped the back of her head and kissed the tip of her chin. She turned her mouth toward his, needing his kiss. But still he evaded her and tortured the soft spot beneath her right ear. His tongue tested and tasted the lobe, and a thousand shivers danced up her spine.

"Ian." His name slid past her lips, softly pleading.

The kiss, when it came, was worth the wait. Their mouths met and melded, preliminaries ignored in a frantic attempt to know each other completely.

She tightened her arms around his neck, and he gathered her closer against him. This kiss that made up for all the years when she had thought she would never again know this kind of physical chemistry. Dates endured only because it didn't seem normal for someone her age not to go out once in a while. Kissing should be this, an act of intimacy that signals rightness, that prompts an instant internal awareness that says, *This is where I belong.*

In his arms, the message felt as impossible to deny as the stars in the sky.

The kisses became more urgent, their body language communicating more clearly than words that it wasn't enough. He drew back and looked into her eyes. "Are you sure this is what you want, Colby?"

"Yes," she said. "I'm sure."

To her surprise, he picked her up and continued kissing her while he carried her though the living room and down the hallway. Cradled against his chest, she kept her arms around his neck, one hand laced through his hair.

He stopped at the first door on the left, and they reluctantly pulled apart long enough to give their surroundings a cursory glance. Shadows draped the room, but the enormous bed in the center of the floor was impossible to ignore.

"Candles," Ian said.

Colby shook her head. "Phoebe thinks of everything."

He smiled and set her down at the side of the bed. He kissed her again, long and slow, one hand at the base of her spine, massaging, enticing, the other winding through the back of her hair. "Don't go anywhere," he said, his voice uneven.

Smiling, she said, "Phoebe probably has a booby trap rigged to go off if I step back out that door."

He laughed.

Maybe she loved that most about him. The sound of his laughter, a sound she would like to know for the rest of her life. Over the breakfast table. In crowded movie theaters. At night just before she fell asleep.

The enormity of the admission hit her then. She loved him. Loved him as she had never loved any other man. She loved him for his generosity. For changing his life for his son. For passing those grits around at the church breakfast when he'd never even heard of them before. For loving his dogs. He was a genuinely good man, and regardless of what happened here tonight, or how things ended up, she loved him. How simple that was. How profound.

Ian had found a match and lit the oversize candle on the nightstand. The scent of honeysuckle drifted toward her.

Candlelight danced across their skin, and she grew warm with longing. Ian reached for the hem of her sweater and pulled it over her head. Beneath it, she wore a white cotton blouse. He undid the buttons and brushed it open with the back of his hand.

His fingers trailed the length of her jaw, hesitated at the tip of her chin, then made a line down her throat.

A sigh of pleasure escaped Colby's parted lips. He

kissed the column of her throat, his mouth following the same trail his fingers had just taken. She began unbuttoning his shirt, the backs of her fingers grazing the hair-roughened skin of his chest. Halfway down, she yanked the shirttail from his pants, then undid the last few buttons and pushed it off him.

She let her eyes have their fill of him. He was a beautiful man. No other word for it. Fit and finely built. With wide shoulders and narrow hips, the kind made for blue jeans. His skin was still brown from the work he'd been doing outdoors in the fall.

They kissed again, and a wave of sudden self-consciousness assaulted her. It had been a long, long time since she'd been with a man. What if he didn't find her attractive? What if. . . .

"Colby, you're so beautiful."

Under his appreciative gaze, she *felt* beautiful. Powerful in the way a woman feels when a man looks at her with desire in his eyes.

She kissed him then. Wrapped her arms around his waist, while an orchestra of emotion struck up inside her. Need of the most overwhelming kind lent urgency to their movements and sent them toppling back onto the bed behind them.

The mattress dipped, their clumsiness lightening the intensity between them. They both laughed, breathless. When their laughter faded, they watched each other, assessing, appreciating.

"You scare me, Colby," he said. "You're everything I didn't know I wanted. I'd like to believe that means we were meant to be."

She pressed her lips to his temple and closed her eyes, tears seeping through her lashes.

He pushed a strand of hair back from her forehead, his fingers lingering in a gentle caress. He walked to the door and turned the lock, and when he returned to the king-size bed, she opened her arms to him.

50

Bummed. Lena had no other word for it.

Millie got sick at the movie, a virus or something. Mrs. Mitchell had driven Lena home, since there wasn't much point in her staying the night if Millie spent most of it in the bathroom. Ever since Lena confronted her with spreading gossip about Luke, Millie had been working overtime to make up for it. She'd felt terrible about ruining their afternoon. Lena agreed not to hold it against her as long as she kept her word from now on.

Lena arrived home to find a note from her mom on the kitchen counter saying that she'd gone out to the lake to pick up Phoebe. That was just like her. Lena wasn't even supposed to be home tonight, and she'd still left a note just in case she came by and wondered where she was. How many kids had moms like that? A yearning for things to be like they used to be swept over her. She thought about what Luke said at the party last night. Maybe he was right. Maybe she hadn't handled things like she should have. Was knowing her father worth ruining the relationship she'd had with her mom?

The question nagged at her as she went into the den and looked for the TV section of the newspaper, not finding it in any of the usual places. She peered out the window and saw the paper sticking out of the box. She put on her shoes and sprinted outside to get it. While she was there, she checked the mailbox and found several letters inside.

Just as she turned to head back up the driveway, she spotted the corner of an envelope sticking up from the edge of the brick flowerbed that served as the base of the mail box. She bent down and picked it up, then threw it on top of the other mail. In the house, she tossed it all on the kitchen table and leafed through the paper until she found the TV section. Nothing on worth watching.

She put down the paper, the letter on top of the pile of mail catching her eye. A plain white envelope, addressed to her mom and marked Personal and Confidential. She held it up to the light. No return address.

It was wrong to open it. The last time she'd read something that didn't belong to her, she'd wished she'd left the letter where she found it. A strong voice told her to leave the letter alone. But like Pandora, she couldn't help herself. It was from her father. She knew it.

She got a pot out of the bottom of the stove and put some water on to boil. The minutes ticked by like molasses from a cold jar until finally enough steam rose from the pot to loosen the seal on the envelope. She slid the letter out and unfolded it, her heart thumping too hard, her hands clammy.

Colby,

I know I'm a coward for getting back to you this way. But, as you know, confrontations were never my strength. I've gone over and over this during the past weeks, and I keep coming to the same conclusion. Lena is your daughter. I have a family of my own, and I can't bring myself to jeopardize what I have by telling them that I have a daughter they never knew existed.

I think it's best if we just leave things as they've been. Since Lena has never met me, she can't be hurt by my decision. I trust you to explain this to her in the best way you can.

Doug

Lena flung the letter away from her as if it had scorched her fingers. It fluttered to the floor like a fallen angel, and she stood staring at it, unable to believe what she'd just read.

He didn't want anything more to do with her now than he had sixteen years ago. Her stomach heaved. She ran to the bathroom and threw up until dry retching sounds echoed the emptiness inside her. She sat on the cool tile floor, her left arm and forehead resting on the side of the bathtub.

What was wrong with her? What had she ever done to make him hate her so much?

She sat there, miserable and crushed. When she finally got up from the floor, she wiped her face with a cool washcloth and then went into the kitchen and stood staring out the window at the backyard where she'd played and done much of the growing up that her father hadn't wanted to witness.

The pain inside her loomed so great that she had to find a way to make it go away. If not forever, then just for a little while.

She remembered the bottle of gin someone had given her mother for a Christmas present a year or two ago. She pulled a chair out from the kitchen table and scooted it over to the cabinet above the sink. She opened the door, and sure enough, there it was, in the back, unopened. Lena reached for it, then got down and poured herself a glass.

The first sip tasted awful. She nearly gagged, and when it hit her throat, still sore from being sick, it felt like fire blazing a trail to her stomach.

She went to the refrigerator and grabbed the orange juice container, watering down the gin with it. Still awful, but not quite so bad.

Taking the bottle and the glass with her, she went into the living room, sat on the couch, and, for the first time in her life, proceeded to get drunk.

51

She was drunk.

Luke knew it as soon as he answered the phone.

"H-he doesn't want me," Lena said.

The words were slurred and hard to understand. "Lena, who are you talking about?"

"He s-said I wouldn't c-care 'cause I never met him. But that's not true."

Her father. She must be talking about her father. "Where are you, Lena? Are you at home?"

He barely heard her answer.

Luke knew her mom wasn't home, because Mrs. Walker called earlier to say his dad had gone out to the lake to meet Colby. "Lena?"

No answer. The receiver dropped to the floor, and he felt his heart fall with it. "Lena, I'll be right there!" he yelled, hoping she heard him. He grabbed his keys off the kitchen counter and bolted out the door.

52

Ian lay awake, looking down at this woman who had come to mean everything to him. She had simplified life for him, brought into focus everything important, screening out the things that were not. Her innate goodness became more clear to him with each moment he spent with her. His heart belonged to her, and he could not imagine a future without her.

She stirred and opened her eyes to stare up at him with the expression of a sated woman. The sight of it filled him with an almost primitive gladness that he had been the one to put that look in her eyes.

She stretched beside him, her legs entwined with his. "You can't expect to look at a man like that and get away with it," he said, trailing a finger across the flat plane of her belly.

She wrapped her arms around his neck and kissed

him with renewed heat before saying, "I don't intend to."

They were quiet for a bit, just holding each other, while Colby thought how incredible it was that there could be such pleasure in companionable silence. It felt almost too perfect to last. "What are we going to do about this?" she asked, and immediately wanted to take the question back. It was too soon. He'd just broken his engagement, and she didn't want him to think she expected something more from him.

"You mean what happens when the school year is up?"

She nodded.

"I think that's something we need to talk about."

The phone rang. She sat up, wrapping her arms around herself.

"Phoebe?" Ian asked.

"I can't imagine she would call," Colby said, frowning.

The ringing stopped. A couple of seconds later, it started again.

"We'd better get it in case something's wrong," he said.

"The phone's in the kitchen," she said. She watched him leave the room, wishing she hadn't said anything about the future. She'd gotten so caught up in what had happened between them that she'd let herself forget he had another life in another world. He might no longer be engaged, but that didn't change the fact that his stay in Keeling Creek would be temporary.

He'd said he loved her, but she'd long ago learned the lesson that love didn't mean forever.

His footsteps sounded in the hallway. She looked up to find him standing at the door, his face creased with worry.

"What is it?" she asked, knowing immediately that something was wrong.

"We have to go," he said, clearly shaken. "Luke and Lena have been in an accident. Frank heard about it on his police scanner, and he and Phoebe are on their way to the hospital."

All the way back to town, Colby prayed. Harder than she'd ever prayed in her life.

Ian held on to her hand as the Mercedes roared down the driveway, his grip firm enough that she knew he suffered the same agonies as she.

It seemed like hours before they finally reached the emergency room door. As soon as Ian stopped the car, Colby jumped out and ran. He was right behind her. Colby went to the first nurse she saw. "Our children, they were brought in a little while ago. Lena Williams and Luke McKinley. Can you tell us where they are?"

"Certainly. Just follow me."

Ian took Colby's hand, and they anxiously trailed the woman to an examining room, where both Lena and Luke lay in separate beds. The blood drained from Colby's face. Lena looked as white as the sheet covering her. Her eyes were closed, and a nasty-looking gash arced across her temple. A doctor was stitching it up.

Luke lay on the other side of the divider curtain. Bandages encircled his hands, and white gauze covered the center of his forehead. A nurse adjusted the IV tube taped to his hand.

"Oh, thank goodness, you're here."

Colby swung around to find Phoebe and Frank hovering in the doorway. Phoebe had a stricken look on her face.

"They're going to be all right, aren't they?" Colby asked, hearing the fear in her own voice.

Phoebe nodded and waved them outside the door, where she said, "Oh, Colby, I'm sorry. I feel as if this is all my fault. If I hadn't sent you two off to the lake, maybe this wouldn't have—"

"Phoebe, what happened?" Ian interrupted gently but with a distinct note of urgency. ˙

Frank squeezed Phoebe's shoulder and said, "They were hit by another car, and . . . apparently, they had been drinking."

"Who had been drinking?" Colby asked, incredulous.

"Lena and Luke."

Ian leaned against the wall behind him and dropped his forehead onto the heel of one hand.

Colby knew what he was thinking. If Luke had been drinking when the accident happened, he would be in violation of his probation. She prayed that there had been some kind of mistake.

"They've both been out of it since they got them in here, so nobody knows anything for sure," Phoebe said. "And the blood work's not back from the lab yet."

"Did you call my mom and dad?" Colby asked, her voice raspy with shock.

"No. I thought you'd want to do that after we knew more."

"Good." Colby and Ian went back inside and talked to the doctor who just finished with Lena. He assured them that the kids were bruised and bumped up but should be fine. He'd given them something for pain, and they would both probably sleep for a while.

As soon as the doctor left the room, Colby slid back the curtain that divided the two beds. She and Ian stood between them, she holding Lena's hand, he holding Luke's, their own joined in the middle.

Luke woke up first. His eyes opened, and he made a visible effort to focus.

Relief flooded through Ian, making him weak with gratitude. "Luke?" He sat down on the edge of the bed and pressed his hand to his son's face. "I'm right here. You're going to be all right."

"Where am I?" Luke asked, still groggy. Before Ian could answer, the boy sat bolt upright and said, "Lena! Where's Lena?"

"She's right here next to you," Ian assured him. "She's going to be fine. Everything's okay. Just relax, all right?"

Luke sank back on the pillow, one hand pressed to his temple.

Colby moved to the other side of the bed. "How are you feeling?"

"Not too great right now."

"What happened, son?" Ian asked, his voice heavy.

"We . . . the car . . . it came out of nowhere. I was trying to get Lena to the hospital."

"Lena. Why?" Colby asked, her hands clasped together.

"She called me. She sounded upset about her dad, and I could tell she'd been drinking. I rushed over to your house, and she was passed out. She wouldn't wake up, so I was taking her to the hospital when—"

"You weren't drinking, son?" Ian interrupted, relief flooding through him.

Luke looked up at him and shook his head with a half-smile. "After all the trouble you've gone through to reform me, I'm not gonna blow it that easily."

Ian smiled down at him. "I should've known that."

"Old Pokey won't ever be the same though," Luke said.

"Don't worry about that old truck. It's probably had its nine lives anyway. You just rest now. Everything's going to be all right."

Lena awoke a half hour or so later. Colby was sitting by her side when she opened her eyes and realized where she was. Tears rolled down her cheeks, and she said, "Oh, Mom, I'm sorry."

"Baby." Colby leaned down and took her into her arms, holding her as tightly as she could with the tubes attached to her.

Ian closed the curtain between the two beds, while mother and daughter held each other for several long minutes, reestablishing the precious bond that had been threatened in the past few months.

Colby finally pulled away and smoothed a hand across Lena's hair. "What happened, sweetie?"

"I should have left it alone." Tears welled up in her eyes again, and she bit back a sob.

Colby waited for her to go on, knowing she needed to get it all out.

"A letter came for you today. It said Personal, but I opened it. I shouldn't have. It was from—" her voice broke, and fresh tears made their way down her cheeks.

"Oh, Lena." Colby's heart fell as she realized who the letter had been from and what it must have said. She held her daughter close again, wanting to absorb her child's pain. But she couldn't. For so long, she'd tried to protect her from this, and she had failed.

"He didn't want to know me, Mom. What did I do to—"

"You did nothing, honey," Colby interrupted with force. "Nothing. He's the loser in all this. Not you. You've got to believe that."

"I've been so awful to you, Mom. I just couldn't believe that he wouldn't want to see me if he knew about me. I wanted to blame you for it, to believe that you were the reason he didn't care about me."

"Oh, Lena." Colby held her tight, rubbing her back, her own voice wavering when she said, "You don't know how I wanted to spare you this."

"I know you did, but I asked for it."

Colby drew back and looked down into her

daughter's eyes. "You didn't ask for any of this. You've done nothing wrong, my precious girl. From the moment I felt you move inside me, you've been the joy of my life. And you always will be."

Lena buried her face in Colby's shoulder, crying silently and clinging to her. Colby held her close and sent up a silent, grateful prayer of thanks for her safety.

Colby decided to wait until morning to call her parents. Since the kids were all right, there was no point in getting them out of bed at two a.m. The doctor wanted to keep both Lena and Luke overnight for observation.

Colby and Ian stayed with them. Phoebe went home around three o'clock and surprised them by never even asking how their evening had gone.

Lena and Luke were both awake off and on, so conversation between Colby and Ian was limited. In fact, they had no chance to talk alone at all.

Colby called her parents at seven, and they arrived within half an hour, hovering over Lena to make sure she was all right. Even though her parents had met Ian and Luke once at the church breakfast, Colby introduced them again, and she saw that both her mom and dad were more than a little impressed.

The doctor released both Lena and Luke when he came to check on them around eight. It was after nine when they got the paperwork taken care of and checked the two of them out.

At the hospital exit, Colby's father insisted on driving Lena and her home.

Ian shook hands with her parents. "I hope to see you again soon," he said, before turning to Colby. "I'll call you later."

She nodded and watched him help Luke into the car, then pull away with a wave.

At the house, they got Lena settled into her bed, where she fell asleep within minutes. After assuring herself that her daughter was all right, Colby went back downstairs and saw the letter from Doug lying on the coffee table in the living room. She picked it up and read it, aching for the pain it had caused Lena. How could anyone be so cruel and callous? Even though she knew Doug never intended for Lena to see the letter, anger propelled her toward the kitchen. She grabbed the phone and began punching in his number, the letter still in her hand.

"He's not worth it, you know."

Colby swung around to find her mother standing in the kitchen doorway. She hung up and pressed her forehead to the receiver. "She might have been killed, Mom. And Luke too."

"I know." Emma stepped forward and put her hands on Colby's shoulders, pressing her cheek against her back. "I know. But you have to let this go. Whatever happens between Lena and her father will be between them. You tried to protect her and nearly lost her. Focus on what you can control—your relationship with her—and leave the rest alone."

Colby turned around and hugged her mother. "How'd you get so wise?"

"It comes with the crow's feet," she said, her eyes

shining with love. "I'm so proud of you, Colby. You're a wonderful mother. Don't ever forget that."

"I had a wonderful role model," she said. "And you're right." She opened the drawer beside her and pulled out a book of matches. Moving to the sink, she lit one and held it to the edge of the letter. The paper went up in a quick blue flame, crumpled, and turned to ash.

Emma squeezed her arm. "She'll be fine, you know. She's strong like you."

"I hope so."

They were silent for a while and then Emma said, "He's awfully nice."

"You mean Ian?"

Emma nodded. "Is it serious?"

Colby hesitated, not sure what to say. In the hours since she and Ian separated, she'd been bombarded by doubts, wondering if the things they'd said to each other last night would last through the light of day. "After all these years of thinking I'd never find someone who—"

"—was worth risking your heart for?" her mother interrupted softly.

"It's terrifying."

"There's always risk in loving someone, honey. And if he's the man I know he must be for you to care for him, then he's worth it."

Colby's mother and father stayed until after lunch, just to make sure Lena was all right.

While Lena took a nap, Colby put together a batch of her favorite cookies. She'd just slipped the first pan into the oven when the doorbell rang. Wiping her hands on a dish towel, she made her way to the front of the house, Petey and Lulu at her heels. She opened the door to find Ian standing on the porch, dressed in gray wool pants and a blue-green wool sweater. Good heavens, he looked good. Memories of last night flashed through her mind, and she met his gaze with difficulty.

"You have flour on your nose," he said, reaching out to rub it off.

His touch sent a thousand shock waves through her. "I was baking Lena some cookies. I was going to send some to Luke. How is he?"

"Mabel's with him. She may mother him to death, but, other than that, he's fine."

Realizing he was still standing outside in the cold, she stepped back. "Come in, please."

Petey and Lulu greeted him by nearly knocking him down. "Whoa there, guys," he said, smiling and then bending down to pat their heads.

"Okay, you two, scoot now," Colby said.

Looking disappointed, the two dogs slunk into the den and plopped down on the rug.

"I have to finish the cookies," Colby said, heading toward the kitchen. She picked up a spoon and stirred the remaining batter just so she wouldn't have to look at him.

"Mmm. They smell good. What kind?" he asked.

"Chocolate chip."

"My favorite."

"Lena's too."

"Good. That's one more thing we'll have in common."

Colby looked up, afraid to wonder what he meant by that.

"Want to know what the other is?" He moved closer and tilted her chin toward him.

"What?" she asked, her voice little more than a whisper.

"Loving you."

Colby's chest tightened. She couldn't breathe normally. "When you didn't call today, I thought maybe—"

"Hey," he said, shushing her with a finger on her lips. "You're messing up my plan here."

She looked up at him, shaking her head. "What plan?"

"The one where I ask you to marry me."

It took a couple of seconds for the words to register. She folded her arms across her chest and smiled up at him. "Oh, that plan."

He grinned, then reached into his pants pocket and pulled out a little black box. He opened the lid.

"Ian," she whispered.

"You'd be surprised what it took to get Gentry Saunders to open his jewelry store today. His wife had a baby in the middle of the night. I had to promise him free vet services for his potbelly pig."

Laughing, Colby looked down at the ring. Every bit of two carats, it might not have been the most practical piece of jewelry for a small-town veterinarian to wear, but she wasn't immune to feminine vanity, and she marveled at the size and sparkle of it. "It would be hard to get you out of a verbal contract like that," she said, emotion making her voice hoarse.

"Yeah, and I hear he's in pretty tight with the Better Business Bureau."

She smiled up at him, tears of happiness in her eyes. "Is that right?"

He nodded and pulled her to him. They held each other, renewing the bond they'd formed last night. He removed the ring from the box, took her hand and slid it on her finger. The stone sparkled in the light from the kitchen window. "Will you marry me, Colby Williams?"

Hope for a future she'd thought she would never have blossomed inside her. "Ian, are we kidding ourselves about this? You have a life in New York."

"I want my life to be with you. It might not be easy at first, but I'll find a way to make it work." He tilted her chin upward. "I called my partners this afternoon and told them I want to sell my interest in the firm. I still have some thinking to do, but I can work out of my office at Oak Hill. I have a few clients I think would be willing to stay on with me. Enough to keep me busy and still allow time for you and Lena and Luke. I might even try my hand at putting away some hay for Matilda."

"With the tractor?" she asked, a tearful smile in her voice.

"Only if you agree to give me driving lessons."

"I can do that. For the safety of the community."

"Think a city slicker like me could ever get the hang of it?"

"With a little practice."

His eyes grew serious again. "So how about it, Dr. Williams?"

"Yes," she said, a smile on her lips. "Yes."

They kissed with a hunger last night had only begun to satisfy. Colby again felt that sense of utter completeness she found only in his arms. It still amazed her that she knew with such certainty that this was the man she had been meant to find. The right one. The only one. And she realized then she hadn't feared marriage all these years. She had feared ending up with the wrong person: someone like Doug who would decide that he didn't love her as soon as the going got rough. Certainly there would be bumps along the way. Like the not-so-smooth road she and Ian had traveled as parents. Life would deal them a wild card now and then, but with Ian, she knew that he would be right there beside her, handling the bad right along with the good.

"Hey, Mom, who was that at the—"

Still wrapped in each other's arms, Colby and Ian looked up just as Lena stopped in the kitchen doorway and said, "Oh."

Remaining in the loose circle of Ian's embrace, Colby said, "Come here, honey."

Lena crossed the room, and Colby took her hand in hers. "Ian just asked me to marry him. What do you think about that?"

A smile broke across Lena's face. "Really? Well,

yeah, that's great! But, gee, Mom, you really know how to kill a girl's love life."

Both Colby and Ian broke into laughter. Ian put a hand on Lena's shoulder and said, "I hope you and I can work on being friends. You and Luke knew each other before we ever decided to get married, so I don't see why you have to start acting like brother and sister. The four of us will have to sit down and have a serious talk about things. Deal?"

"That's cool. But I sure don't want to think of him as my brother."

Colby pulled her daughter close and hugged her, with Ian's arm still around her. Lena still had pain to deal with. Colby would be there for her in every way she could. This new family they were creating wouldn't be a family in the traditional sense of the word, but it would be a family, nonetheless, and that filled Colby with a joyful satisfaction.

"Don't you think we should go see what Luke thinks about all this?" Colby asked, smiling up at her husband-to-be.

"I think we'd better. Phoebe might get wind of it, and the rest of the town would find out before he does," Ian said, chuckling.

"Let me get dressed first," Lena said, trotting off for the stairs.

"Are you sure you feel up to it, honey?" Colby called out.

Lena popped back around the corner. "My head still hurts, which I deserve. But I'm not about to miss this." She was off again, only to add from the bottom of the stairs, "Don't forget the cookies, Mom. Luke likes chocolate chip."

"I won't, honey," Colby said, smiling. "I won't."

EPILOGUE

"Wake up, sleepyhead. Today's the day."

Colby rolled over and stretched alongside her husband, naked beneath the sheet. The bedroom felt cool with the onset of January. Oak Hill was Colby's dream house, but they still had a lot of work to do, including installing a new furnace. She didn't mind the cool room with Ian here to keep her warm. She didn't think she would ever quite get used to waking up next to him. Or to having him wake her in the middle of the night with kisses and loving. Now that she had him, she couldn't remember how she ever lived without him.

"What's today?" she asked, her voice still husky with sleep.

"The day you get your wedding present."

They'd been married three weeks before at the First Baptist Church of Keeling Creek with Luke as best man, Lena as maid of honor and the front pews filled with her parents, Phoebe and Frank, and Mabel, none of whom managed to get through the ceremony with dry eyes. They'd decided to put off their real honeymoon and had gone to Manhattan for a short one right before Christmas, spending a few days at Ian's apartment—if something that elaborate could be called an apartment—in blissful solitude. He had decided to hang on to the place for a while, since he would occasionally need to stay in the city. When they returned to Keeling Creek, Phoebe planned a party one Saturday afternoon to help move Colby and Lena out to Oak Hill.

Christmas had been like a fairy tale. They'd gone in search of their own tree and decorated the house with white pine wreaths and candles in the windows. Colby couldn't have imagined a more fulfilling holiday. They had a full house—Luke and Lena, along with Critter, Petey and Lulu, Smidge and Rebel. Ian even insisted they bring Don Juan home from the clinic. What was one more dog when they already had four, he had asked her on Christmas Eve.

If possible, Colby's love for him had taken on new dimensions at that moment.

After the holidays, she and Ian took on the project of renovating the old place together. And she was enjoying every minute of it.

She slipped her arms around her husband's waist now and pressed her cheek to his chest. "So, how much longer do I have to wait?"

"Just how anxious are you to see it?" he asked, slipping his leg between hers and running his hand up her thigh.

"Well," she said, pretending intense concentration while the now-familiar hum began inside her and love for him played through her like the sweetest of songs. "I think we could put it off a bit longer."

He grinned. "As much as I would like to take you up on that, I'm going to be in serious trouble if I don't get you out of this house within the next twenty minutes."

Thoroughly intrigued now, Colby gave him a protesting kiss before getting out of bed and heading for the shower. A little while later, she followed him out to the car, begging for at least a hint. He remained stubbornly close-mouthed for the duration of the drive. A mile or so down the road from the house, Ian made a right-hand turn at the edge of a cornfield that was part of Oak Hill property. Since it was on the backside of the farm, Colby rarely drove past it, but she noticed now that a road had been cut through the field and covered with gravel.

"Did you do this?" she asked, more curious than ever.

"Maybe," he said, looking at her with a smile.

"But what on earth for?"

"Patience," he said.

The road wound on for several hundred yards and then curved to the right. Just around the bend, she saw Lena and Luke. They were both wearing face-splitting smiles, one on each side of a sign that read:

The Oak Hill Home for Animals
A Sanctuary for Pets
Waiting to Be Adopted

Colby stared at it, unable to believe what she had just read. Behind the sign sat a bulldozer with Davis Construction emblazoned on the side.

Colby's eyes filled with tears. She turned to look at Ian. "This is. . .you did this for me?"

He got out and came around to the other side of the car, took her hands and pulled her out. He put his arms around her waist and kissed her forehead. "Just for you," he said.

"Oh, Ian." She hugged him, unable to think of any words eloquent enough to express her feelings.

But he understood. She saw it in his eyes when she looked up at him. "Did I tell you I love you?"

Ian glanced at his watch. "Not in the past hour or so."

"I do," she said. "I do."

He kissed her, the gesture assuring her of his love more than words could. A few moments later, he said, "I wanted to tell you about this sooner, but I had to make sure I could get the building permits and that sort of thing first. It's been a real challenge making sure those two didn't spill the beans."

She sent a teary glance toward Luke and Lena, still standing by the sign, thoughtfully giving them a moment of privacy.

"When you two get finished with that," Luke called out, "we've got a building site to show you."

Colby looked up at her husband and smiled. "Teenagers. They don't know a thing about patience, do they?"

Ian shook his head. "That comes with age."

"And a lot of other good things."

"And a lot of other good things," he repeated, a not-so-innocent look in his eyes.

With their arms around each other, they made their way toward the son and daughter waiting to tell Colby all about her very special wedding gift.

***

THANK YOU!

Dear Reader,

I would like to thank you for taking the time to read my story. There are so many wonderful books to choose from these days, and I am hugely appreciative that you chose mine.

If you'd like to try another of my books for FREE, please click here.

Come check out my Facebook page for postings on books, dogs and things that make life good!

Wishing you many, many happy afternoons of reading pleasure.

All best,

Inglath

BOOKS BY
INGLATH
COOPER

Nashville – Book Four – Pleasure in the Rain
Nashville – Book Three – What We Feel
Nashville – Book Two – Hammer and a Song
Nashville – Book One – Ready to Reach
On Angel's Wings
A Gift of Grace
RITA® Award Winner John Riley's Girl
A Woman With Secrets
Unfinished Business
A Woman Like Annie
The Lost Daughter of Pigeon Hollow
A Year and a Day

REVIEWS

"Truths and Roses . . . so sweet and adorable, I didn't want to stop reading it. I could have put it down and picked it up again in the morning, but I didn't want to." – **Kirkusreviews.com**

On Truths and Roses: "I adored this book...what romance should be, entwined with real feelings, real life and roses blooming. Hats off to the author, best book I have read in a while."– **Rachel Dove, http://frustratedyukkymummy.blog.co.uk**

"I am a sucker for sweet love stories! This is definitely one of those! It was a very easy, well written, book. It was easy to follow, detailed, and didn't leave me hanging without answers." – **www.layfieldbaby.blogspot.com**

"I don't give it often, but I am giving it here – the sacred 10. Why? Inglath Cooper's A GIFT OF GRACE mesmerized me; I consumed it in one sitting. When I turned the last page, it was three in the morning." — **MaryGrace Meloche, Contemporary Romance Writers**

5 Blue Ribbon Rating! "...more a work of art than a story...Tragedies affect entire families as well as close

loved ones, and this story portrays that beautifully as well as giving the reader hope that somewhere out there is A GIFT OF GRACE for all of us." — **Chrissy Dionne, Romance Junkies 5 Stars.**

"A warm contemporary family drama, starring likable people coping with tragedy and triumph." 4 1/2 Stars. — **Harriet Klausner**

"A GIFT OF GRACE is a beautiful, intense, and superbly written novel about grief and letting go, second chances and coming alive again after devastating adversity. Warning!! A GIFT OF GRACE is a three-hanky read...better make that a BIG box of tissues read! Wowsers, I haven't cried so much while reading a book in a long long time...Ms. Cooper's skill makes A GIFT OF GRACE totally believable, totally absorbing...and makes Laney Tucker vibrantly alive. This book will get into your heart and it will NOT let go. A GIFT OF GRACE is simply stunning in every way—brava, Ms. Cooper! Highly, highly recommended!" – 4 1/2 Hearts — **Romance Readers Connection**

"...A WOMAN WITH SECRETS...a powerful love story laced with treachery, deceit and old wounds that will not heal...enchanting tale...weaved with passion, humor, broken hearts and a commanding love that will have your heart soaring and cheering for a happily-ever-after love. Kate is strong-willed, passionate and suffers a bruised heart. Cole is sexy, stubborn and also suffers a bruised heart...gripping plot. I look forward to reading more of Ms. Cooper's work!" – **www.freshfiction.com**

ABOUT INGLATH COOPER

RITA® Award-winning author Inglath Cooper was born in Virginia. She is a graduate of Virginia Tech with a degree in English. She fell in love with books as soon as she learned how to read. "My mom read to us before bed, and I think that's how I started to love stories. It was like a little mini-vacation we looked forward to every night before going to sleep. I think I eventually read most of the books in my elementary school library."

That love for books translated into a natural love for writing and a desire to create stories that other readers could get lost in, just as she had gotten lost in her favorite books. Her stories focus on the dynamics of relationships, those between a man and a woman, mother and daughter, sisters, friends. They most often take place in small Virginia towns very much like the one where she grew up and are peopled with characters who reflect those values and traditions.

"There's something about small-town life that's just part of who I am. I've had the desire to live in other places, wondered what it would be like to be a true Manhattanite, but the thing I know I would miss is the familiarity of faces everywhere I go. There's a lot to be said for going in the grocery store and seeing ten people you know!"

Inglath Cooper is an avid supporter of companion animal rescue and is a volunteer and donor for the Franklin County Humane Society. She and her family have fostered many dogs and cats that have gone on to be adopted by other families. "The rewards are endless. It's an eye-opening moment to realize that what one person throws away can fill another person's life with love and joy."

Follow Inglath on Facebook
at www.facebook.com/inglathcooperbooks

Join her mailing list for news of new releases and giveaways at www.inglathcooper.com